It's Always Mango Season

It's Always Mango Season

BY: MARISSA GERMAIN
PUBLISHED BY KEEPING IT GERMAIN, LLC.

ISBN-13: 979-8-9948933-0-2

For my family.

One. Un. Youn.

Paul gripped the soft leather of the steering wheel and slowed the car to better navigate the crowds that should have thinned after the holidays. He scowled as he stopped for a large group of market women dragging their tarp-covered wares across the road. From his climate-controlled seat, he peeked between the bodies into *Le Marché des Frères* or The Brother's Market. There, he could see the aged wooden tables threatening to collapse from the piles of cooking oil and canned foods. Chickens and goats harnessed by fraying sisal ropes relaxed under the darkness of the tattered canvas roof of the market. Women walked through the crowds with towering bags of rice on their heads, while men carried backpacks of charcoal from one row to the next. Halted by the chaos, Paul could only look at the digital radio and sigh.

7:15 a.m.

"So, tell me again why we need to go to this warehouse three hours before my plane is supposed to take off?" Paul said, trying and failing to keep the irritation out of his tone.

"You watch that tone, Paul."

Paul shivered as the ice in Reginald's voice froze the already machine-chilled air.

Reginald continued, "Didier told me we have some… pests that I need to clear out today. Not tomorrow, not this evening, today. Besides, if you miss this flight, you can just take my plane. It's not like you are that important to the conference, anyway."

Paul nodded slowly, keeping his thoughts to himself. Already, he felt exposed in his dad's bulletproof car, fresh off the lot. Flying around in his dad's private plane just felt like asking for trouble, especially when the people around them only had a week's worth of rice in their sacks. While grateful for the luxurious lifestyle, Paul always worried that the more he and his father flaunted their wealth, the more they would become targets. At least that was how it worked a couple of years ago. People whose cars were a little too shiny ended up on some kidnapping list, and they'd be hustled out of every dollar they had saved at the local bank. Paul was so worried about this that every time his father went too far, his side would cramp like he'd run a mile without water. His father's plane was truly a last resort.

The crowd opened up, and he relaxed his grip on the wheel. When the people created a space large enough, Paul carved through the masses until *Frères* faded in the rearview mirror. Silently, they descended the hills. With each curve and corner, they followed walled-off properties and passed people on their morning commutes. Purses and briefcases walked down weathered sidewalks or rode in overstuffed *tap-taps*. These colorfully painted pickup trucks, turned public transit, were the lifeblood of Haiti's capital city. Backpacks and uniforms walked in clusters on their way to school. If Paul paid attention, he'd notice the rich tapestry of life in Port-au-Prince. A life maintained by a delicate balance.

Once they passed through the last traffic light on the airport road, he picked up speed and tightened his hold on the wheel again as they drove past the entrance to *Cité Soleil*. As one of the most dangerous slums in the Caribbean, he wanted to avoid an accidental conflict at all costs. After darting between former American dump trucks that found a second life as city to city transit, Paul looked up and watched as the tumbling mountains spotted with green tufts of trees kissed the edge of the crystal blue waters of the Caribbean. Haiti truly was dangerously beautiful.

"Paul!" Reginald yelled, pointing his finger toward the other side of the road.

Paul followed the direction of his father's finger. One of the dump trucks had lost control and narrowly missed oncoming traffic, before crashing into the only tree on that side of the road. The explosion of the gas tank rocked their car as a handful of people escaped the flames.

Reginald lifted his sunglasses to inspect the site in case he knew any of the crash victims. Satisfied they were strangers, he lowered his sunglasses and waved his hand for Paul to continue driving.

Paul obliged and picked up speed before anyone waved them down to get involved or take the blame.

"If the police continue to let these trucks drive like this, I am going to have to start taking the helicopter," Reginald said, fiddling with the radio settings.

Paul seethed at the seemingly harmless suggestion. Why was his father like this? How much longer would he keep pretending that these stupid comments didn't bother him? The questions fueled the slow-burning resentment that started the day they got back from Colombia four months ago. He could taste the venom from the words he knew would ignite the fight, each one burning to be released.

I will never be like you.

Why are you so committed to flaunting what we have when there is so little around us?

Why on earth did you bring those women back from Colombia?

Instead, he swallowed each word one by one, ignoring the acidic trail each one left behind. As much as he wanted to, as much as he needed to, now was not the time. He had to keep his dad on track or risk missing the conference altogether. It had taken Paul four years to complete his research on turning mango sap into a sugar. It took just as long for anyone in the scientific community to believe it was possible. When the *Food Science of Tomorrow Conference* accepted his proposal, Paul just sat in his office staring at the wall for an hour. He finally received the validation that his idea could work and possibly make them a lot of money. But when he told his father, Reginald just lifted his sunglasses, stared at Paul, sniffed, and then returned the glasses to their perch. Mortified, Paul didn't speak of the conference again until his dad saw the suitcase in the car.

"Why are you making that face?" Reginald barked making Paul scowl at his father's tone.

Paul sat for a moment and finally said, "Acid reflux."

"Ah, be serious, Paul. You still can't be mad about Didier and Colombia. It has been four months!"

Paul gripped the steering wheel in response. The venomous words crawled back up, anxious to escape like a growing inferno about to jump the fire line.

"Seriously? Also, turn at the next break in the wall."

And that was all it took. Reginald's tone. It was the same tone he'd use to humiliate Paul in front of friends. The same tone that cut him down until he felt five years old again. Normally, he'd just take it. Normally, he'd ignore the comment and move the conversation elsewhere. Today wasn't a normal day. He had to meet his destiny in Orlando.

"Yes, Dad," Paul clipped. "We could have been arrested for human trafficking. It was irresponsible. If that's the kind of business you want to build, then maybe you should build it with the son you wish you had: Didier."

Paul swerved off the highway, and the smooth rush of tires on cement turned into the crunch and ping of a gravel road.

Reginald stared ahead at the cinder-block walls. The patterns of gray cement and white dust-covered gravel created a sort of tunnel. A symphony of small rocks thudded off the car, making conversation impossible.

The pair remained silent, and Paul remembered seeing this view on almost every news outlet in the troubled years. Ever since, he regularly met foreigners who believed there wasn't an inch of greenery on the island. Like everything else in Haiti, only those who looked past the surface knew what hid behind the walls. In this part of the country, the walls hid the view of the not-so-distant ocean on the left and the very distant mountains on the right.

Once the tires transitioned from gravel to packed dirt, Reginald fought back and said, "Ah, you're just being dramatic and jealous. Like a woman. It's not a good look, Paul."

As if trying to prove his point, Reginald waved his hand as if fanning the flames of Paul's jealousy. Bored with the conversation, he fished around in his briefcase until he found the cigarettes and lighter. He cracked open the window, instantly warming the car, and took a long drag.

Paul's left eye twitched as he could hear past arguments about why it was or wasn't rude to smoke in the car.

"But if Didier can turn this business around before you can, then he might just be a better fit for the company. It's nothing personal. Perform, or get out of the way of others who can. Stop at the field at the end of the walls," Reginald stated bluntly.

Paul slammed on the brakes. Reginald's hands flew out to protect his body from hitting the dashboard, bending his cigarette as ash sprayed across the new plastic. Some, still embers, left polka-dotted burns.

"Are you kidding me?" Paul's anger now roared to a five-alarm forest fire, threatening everything in its path and impossible to extinguish. Throwing the car into park, Paul twisted toward his father's smug face, determined to win this fight.

"You were just saying you want to fly your helicopter out here, and not a minute later, you're wanting to save the thing that pays for that helicopter. Which one is it? Are we thriving or in trouble? And if we're in trouble, why do we have a helicopter?" Sweat beaded across his forehead, and dots of spit escaped his mouth as he yelled. For only twenty-nine years old, Paul was convinced that this stress would be why he would have a heart attack by thirty.

"Paul, that's enough!" Reginald's voice boomed so loudly that the coins in the cup holder rattled. Catching himself, he took a moment and decided on a more casual approach. "What we do and don't have is not for you to decide. It is my money, and I spend it as I think it needs to be spent. We have always put business before family, you know that. So, make us some money so we can buy more planes or move on. Got it?"

"Got it," Paul said, sounding more like a scolded child than a business partner. Stiffening his body, Paul got the car moving again. As they moved, he could feel the tires crush the cinders of his rage, storing them away in an all too familiar practice. His father didn't take him seriously. Why would he? Paul's brainy nature kept him focused on daydreams and possibilities, not tangible business opportunities. Every idea Paul offered Reginald had a five-year timeline at least. Since the death of Paul's mother, Reginald had slowly lost his patience until it didn't exist at all. He'd never wait long enough for any of Paul's ideas to bear fruit.

The cinder block walls ended, giving way to a light green field of tall grasses. Each blade danced its way to meet the early morning glitter of the Bay of Port-au-Prince. Through his father's window, Paul could smell hints of lemongrass and rich clay. Up ahead, a worn walking path cut its way through the grasses to a rusting silo and barn. In the distance, he could see the darkened island of *La Gonâve*, veiled by sea mist. From it, gentle waves rippled, beckoning toward him while also warning him to keep his distance. The scene was like a landscape painting that could have been in a museum, idyllic and emotive.

Paul looked away to focus on the road ahead and said, "This is kinda far to store our sugar. What was it used for?"

"It used to be for rice production, some of the best in the region, until the Clintons." Reginald snarled at that. He then raised his left arm, signaling Paul to stop.

Paul obliged and parked the car right in front of a walking path.

"We'll use this for storing extra for the years we aren't producing enough sugar."

Paul pulled a face, then quickly returned to neutral to not catch his father's attention. He couldn't remember a time when they had produced so much sugar that it impacted its pricing. When Reginald opened the glove box to remove his handgun, check the chamber, and slide out of the car with ease, Paul decided not to press him. He'd never seen his father use his gun, but he'd heard rumors.

"Stay right here, I won't be long." Reginald glared at Paul so fiercely that he steeled his body so he wouldn't wince or jump when Reginald slammed the car door.

Paul watched as his father sauntered down the path. Reginald lifted the back of his crisp white linen shirt and slid the gun into the waistband of his jeans. If Paul wasn't managing the remnants of his extinguished rage, he'd think his dad looked like a rogue Ralph Lauren model who actually used his gun. Moments later, his father's tall frame and billowing blond hair disappeared among a set of bushes right in front of the warehouse. With his father gone from sight, Paul came back to what a strange place this was to store rice, and even stranger to store sugar. Over the years, these trips went from once a month to almost weekly. While he did get to see parts of the country most never saw, their frequency was getting annoying.

Paul picked up his phone and thumbed through his contacts until he found *her* name, then sent a quick text. After hitting send, he returned his phone to the cupholder and looked out to the seemingly empty silo.

What if he's up to something?

Paul immediately ignored the thought. His father was many things, and if any of them were remotely criminal, he had to pretend they didn't exist. Paul's survival depended on it.

Two. Deux. De.

Jiggling the gearshift in time with the rattling engine, Saskia prayed it would shut off without the regular drama. Eyes locked on the temperature gauge she whispered, "come on, come on" as if the mantra could keep the arrow firmly between the H and the C. And for the first time since she returned to Orlando, the '97 Honda Civic obeyed.

"Heck, yes!" she hollered and slapped the heat-cracked steering wheel.

"Maybe this won't be so bad after all," Saskia said out loud, cranking the window up and up until the damp, cool Florida breeze stopped. Sealed within her ruby rider, she looked around at the crumbling tan interior. All the joy from the cooperative engine dissolved into the familiar, murky feelings haunting her for the past six months.

When she boarded her flight at JFK, bound for her hometown of Orlando, Florida, dark, complicated feelings sprouted. When the plane lifted from the tarmac, the relief of leaving New York City didn't take off with her. Instead, like a cloth yanked from a well-set table, the mind-numbing despair of forced change had been lying in wait for its moment. It suspended her for months in a dark, guilt-ridden cloud of emotion. Decisions became impossible. Joy, non-existent. Even when she finally landed a spot at her old high school job, a teller at Walnut Bank, it felt like some cruel plot twist in some elaborate nightmare, not the life raft she needed from driving around Central Florida without air conditioning. Memories of passing out from the heat this summer while waiting at a red light made her shiver.

Saskia certainly didn't miss playing "guess the mystery liquid I just stepped in," or wrapping her face twice over in her scarf to protect from the cold. But the missing door handles and heat-damaged dashboard of this commute hammered the painful point home: she had failed. Miserably.

The day after graduating from college in 2007, Saskia ran to meet her hard-won destiny on Wall Street. Landing her dream role allowed her to skip the standard shoebox apartment and move straight into a decent one-bedroom in Gramercy Park. Complete with a doorman, a walk-in closet, and a view of a tree without breaking her rent budget.

In the New York version of her life, she always arrived first at the office. She'd turn on the lights, set up a box of pastries in the kitchen, and caffeinate using a white cup with a fancy logo instead of the office instant coffee. When her neighbor arrived at his cubicle, she'd grab another coffee to celebrate achieving inbox zero. Under her leadership, every branch of Walnut Bank across the U.S. delivered positive returns. After work, she'd join co-workers at a happy hour or two at the next *it* spot in the city. Her New York life was full and dynamic, and she felt like she was always one step away from greatness. She had loved every minute of it. Ok, even the smelly parts.

Now? Sipping on a homemade mocha from her dad's travel mug, she waited for someone else to open the office. The packet of hot chocolate dust mixed with espresso barely filled the chasm of shame between a life she'd loved for three years and her life today. As if the last six months hadn't been embarrassing enough, she now had to "gleefully" walk into a job she never thought she'd have to take. Maybe she should just save herself and go home.

A quick peek in the rear-view mirror killed that idea on the spot. Like the early shoots of dollar weeds, tiny hairs around her face began to pull away from the rest and stick out. Panicked, she ran her unpolished hand down the back of her head and stopped when she could feel it—the start of a rebellion.

Saskia dove for her Birkin-style purse and fished around for anything she could use to reclaim control of what was supposed to be a sleek blowout. Instead, her nervous sweat joined the battle with her rebellious frizz to liberate her natural curls. If she still had her New York job, she could afford the products that could keep things under control and kept her feeling human. She'd already given up on the manicures, the name-brand lattes, and the regular-priced outfits. To lose control over her hair?

This could not stand. Taking this job had already made a serious dent on her ego, but without it she'd continue to be a shell of her former self. She needed this job, and she was going to thrive at it. She had no other choice.

Before the rebellion turned into a full-blown war, Saskia swept up her hair with a well-practiced twist and pull. Then jabbed a couple of bobby pins into the gathered mass until it felt secure. She checked her reflection again in the rear-view mirror to inspect her deep mahogany strands wrapped into the perfect ballet bun. Satisfied with the durable, professional style and smudge-free makeup, she sighed and relaxed into the driver's seat. Glancing at the dashboard, she slumped a little bit further when she read the teal digital numbers next to the volume dial. It was only 8:15 a.m., and she didn't need to be inside until fifteen minutes before the branch opened at 9 a.m.

Thirty more minutes?

Saskia felt a familiar flutter in the muscle under her right eye. It only showed up when her concerns morphed into unending stress. Since accepting the offer, the flutters grew into tremors that sometimes blurred her vision. But that was a problem for another day. She would be fine. She had to be fine.

Exasperated, she returned to her purse for her BlackBerry, her fingers seeking the ridges of the phone and pulled it out. A couple of days ago, her mother had sent her a link to some stress-relieving mantras she found on some corner of the internet that she wanted to try. On the screen were texts from Annaliese in Haiti, Johanna, her sister, and Liam, her best friend from college. She replied to each one with exclamation marks and every ounce of positivity she could find. For a moment, she could feel the heavy cloud of despair lift, and her eye muscles relax a bit. Maybe this job could work.

Then came another message.

Hey! I know we kind of left things in a weird place
when you were here for Christmas, but
Annaliese told me you are starting a new job today.
Congrats and good luck!
x Paul.

Paul.

The eye muscles twitched until her right eye got so blurry she had to close both eyes.

Not today, stupid, stupid Paul.

Saskia leaned back in her seat and scrolled on her phone until she found her mom's text with the link. Saskia pulled up the list, memorized it, and then set her phone down in the cupholder. She closed her eyes, took a deep breath, and tried the first one.

"There are no small roles, only small people," she repeated, but the flutter continued, so she started the next one.

"I can do anything." The tension eased a bit with that one, but her right eye was still blurry.

"I am resourceful. I am successful."

At that, giggles turned into full belly laughs until tears threatened her makeup. How could she take that one seriously, given the circumstances?

Plastic rattled against plastic, beckoning her to answer a call from her

BlackBerry. Keeping her eyes closed, she indulged in the privacy of a car and answered with the speakerphone.

"Hello?"

"Saskia! Did you get there okay? How is your hair? I saw you left the windows down when you left."

Saskia's eyes came to slits. Of course, her mother was concerned about her hair and not about how she felt about this job.

"Yes, Mom, the drive was fine, and my hair is perfect, as expected, because it is January in Florida and there's low humidity." Saskia waited for a reaction from her mother—a scoff, a sigh, anything that signaled her mother was actually listening. Hearing nothing, she continued, "Obviously, I'm nervous, and this isn't exactly what I wanted, but—"

"*Ti fi*," her mother interrupted. Whenever Jacqueline called her "*ti fi*" or "little girl," Saskia crumpled in on herself and braced for the incoming lecture.

"It has been six months, and you still haven't told me what you did to lose your big job in New York. All through Christmas, you were in such a bad mood. You were like a dark cloud on what should have been a fun family time *en Haïti*! Do you understand how expensive it was to get all of you there? I've tried the American way. I let you *boude*, like an injured child, for months, and now you want to quit the only job you have before you even start your first day?"

Her mother's voice got louder and louder until her Haitian inflection rattled the windows. While everything she said was a fact, Jacqueline's tone wrapped every word in barbed wire. It cut Saskia down until she could fit into the palm of her mother's invisible hand.

"You lost everything, and are living back in *my* house and now you want to give up your only option because you are being picky? Or it doesn't feel right? Come on, Saskia! You can't be serious."

Unsure of what to say and afraid to bite back, she stayed silent. Anyone with a Haitian mother knew that winning an argument with her was impossible. She had a better chance of sprouting wings.

"*Ti fi*, are you still there?"

What could she say? Her mother was right. How could she even consider quitting this job before it even started? Saskia was living with her parents while driving to her only work option in a Civic she bought off Craigslist that should have been sent to a junkyard years ago. Glancing at her bun in the mirror settled it. She couldn't quit this job for anything.

In New York, she was an example of how the world opens to diligent workers. But it all came crashing down because she tried to do the right thing. For weeks, she took minutes at executive-level meetings, driven by panic about how to avoid getting caught overvaluing their assets. Saskia had no idea that talking to the press would lead to the greatest financial collapse of her generation. But how could she tell her mother that?

Every night, she could hear her parents praying to every god they knew to spare them from a layoff or some unknown issue with their mortgage. On the days when news came in of a neighbor losing their home, the prayers would shift from standard church fare to the pleading Saskia had only seen in documentaries. Bearing witness to their anxiety, she committed to never tell her parents. She could never live with the looks on their faces that their daughter was, yet again, the root of their problems. So, Saskia chose silence. Heavy, resounding silence.

"*Bon*, fine, Saskia. Do whatever you want, but do not come back here unless you have a job." Her mother's words dropped like weights on her shoulders.

Under their pressure, she only responded with, "*Oui, maman*, yes, mom. Talk to you later."

Her mother harrumphed into the phone and responded, "Good luck, and we'll talk later. I'm making lasagna."

Saskia grumbled at the dead phone, then threw the BlackBerry toward her purse. Petulantly crossing her arms across her chest, she stared out at a yellow wall with white trim behind some recently pruned hedges. Among the branches, she saw a dew-covered spiderweb. The drops of moisture laced the branches in natural diamond strands. Its beauty relaxed her, as nature always did. Then the web began shaking violently as the spider took care of unsuspecting prey. When the web went still, she couldn't help but feel like she, too, had been caught.

Settling into the harsh reality that no matter how hard she tried to ignore what happened in New York, it would keep finding her. Every time it did, it would unsettle her until ultimately rupturing the veneer she was trying so hard to maintain. One wrong step and everything could fall apart—again.

Somewhere in the small parking lot, a car door closed, followed by a beep and the sound of high heels scraping against the parking lot cement. Through the side-view mirror, Saskia spotted Sherri, the middle-aged woman from her interview. Everything about her felt cold and severe. Even the handshake at the end made Saskia queasy. Or maybe it was the desperate hope that Sherri wouldn't recognize her from the scandal. In her application, she had ditched her easier-to-pronounce New York name, Sarah, just in case someone recognized her. Either way, her new branch manager made her want to run. Watching Sherri unlock the doors and rub at an invisible smudge by the handle brought back the nervous sweat at the nape of her neck. She let out a restricted breath as Sherri disappeared inside.

"Well. I guess I'll give this a try," she said in a hush to her side mirror's reflection.

She turned toward the rear-view mirror for one last look when her wooden bracelet caught her eye. Pulling it out from her crisp white sleeve, she could hear her mother's familiar song, "Are you sure you want to attract *that* kind of attention? You don't want to come off as too exotic. Not all attention is good attention."

Her fingers lingered and danced across the familiar beads linked together by wax-covered twine. The beads met at a rectangular piece of wood the size of her thumb. On the front, a carving of a flower made Saskia smile. It reminded her of the tall hibiscus bushes at her aunt's house in the mountains surrounding Port-au-Prince. She could hear the melodic voice of her favorite aunt, Tatie Alice.

...

"Saskia, your mom tells me you're going through a rough time?"

Saskia sighed at the Caribbean breeze of her aunt's voice as it soothed her hidden wounds. The whole week, she had performed the role of thriving city slicker only to choke out her tears when everyone was asleep. Drained and afraid that if she said a word, everything would become real, she sat on her aunt's front step, speechless.

Tatie Alice's hands wrapped around hers, and when they pulled away, the bracelet was there.

"I'm giving this bracelet to you, and you need to wear it all the time," she said, waiting to see if Saskia heard her.

Saskia nodded, and Tatie Alice continued, "If you ever get nervous, afraid, or begin to doubt, just remember the inscription on the back."

Saskia studied the bracelet, then said, "But what is a—" when the crash of a soccer ball into one of Tatie Alice's terracotta pots pulled the women from the moment. and kept Saskia from the answer.

...

Flipping over the bracelet, she now read the hand-carved words: *Tend to the Guardian Within.* Smiling at the memory, Saskia steeled herself and dropped the bracelet into the empty cupholder, trusting that Tatie Alice would forgive her this once. She pulled her heavy purse from the front seat and got out of the car. Pushing the lock button on her remote, she gave a slight nod to the worries locked inside. Saskia walked toward the red-brick building and used every step to commit to making this job work. It just had to.

Three. Trois. Twa.

Without his dad's loud breathing or constant button pushing, Paul could finally relax into his seat and listen to the gentle waves kissing the distant pebbled beach. He watched the tall grasses lean into the ocean-born breeze, capturing whatever golds and yellows they could from the early morning sun. This spot was isolated, quiet, and breathtaking in its rural beauty. Under other circumstances, he might have sketched the waves of grass or the vibrant emerald mountains, but his tools were packed away in his suitcase.

Lacking his sketchpad, Paul let the more acidic thoughts and words he'd avoided all morning gently bubble to the surface.

Why did I move back here if it was going to be like this?

Should I be this worried about Didier?

It is only the two of us, so why is my dad such a jerk to me?

Paul closed his eyes and thought back to the week after graduating from the University of Central Florida. Their sugar business had been squeaking by, surviving the little losses year over year. The toll on Reginald was clear. Each year his body grew more rigid, his tone sharper until Paul couldn't take it anymore. To find the root of the problem, Paul went through every part of the business and tightened things up. He also added mangoes to their product list, and within two years, they saw even healthier profits. Almost enough to justify the helicopter.

And yet, despite all the money they had, Paul, not the driver, took his father around for his errands. Paul hated it. Instead of reviewing the financials or negotiating better pricing, he'd sit in the car, windows cracked, and wait for him. In the summer months, he'd sit in the heat because gas was too expensive to waste on such a thing like air conditioning when Reginald could be gone for hours. At that thought, Paul brought down the windows and let the chilled Caribbean breeze into the cab before turning off the car. He could now hear the distant bleating of a goatherd, and a belled-up cow releasing a low, guttural moan. The cool air brushed Paul's face, still tender from Reginald Lancelin's molten glare.

Thinking through the hundreds of fights, this one felt unjust. Throughout his childhood, Reginald reserved that glare for major offenses like breaking a chair, or finishing off a special bottle of whisky when Paul didn't even have his first hairs. To Paul, those were fair. He got what he deserved. But this time? This time, all he had asked was if this errand was truly necessary, especially ahead of Paul's flight. Impatiently, Paul flipped his wrist around to check his watch: eight a.m., Tuesday, January 12.

He now had less than two hours to get to the airport. Every ding of the cowbell, every screech of a goat, was a reminder that he should have, could have, gone to the airport without Reginald. Why, at twenty-nine, was he still bending to every one of his father's whims? If he had just asked their driver, Stanley, to give him a ride instead, he wouldn't have the backwoods, off-brand version of the Sound of Music going off around him. Instead, he'd be drinking a coffee and eating a flaky *pâté* to the sounds of a small, yet busy airport. But here he was, getting bullied by the cows and the goats of the Haitian countryside. The drive from here alone would take at least thirty minutes without traffic.

Please God, please don't let there be traffic, Paul said to himself as he could feel the pressure building on his temples. Squeezing his eyes closed, his mind went through every transgression at warp speed until Paul couldn't think, couldn't breathe. He had to do something.

Paul opened his eyes and looked around. Not a single human in sight. He was alone. Satisfied with his isolation, he prepared to use his favorite coping strategy. He closed his eyes again, moved his jaw around, and filled his lungs with air until they were near bursting. Then, he let out a yell so fierce, so embarrassingly pitchy and pained that he'd never survive if someone heard him.

"Excuse me, are you okay?" A frail woman's voice startled Paul so badly that he shot up into the car's ceiling and came away with a sizable bump. He let out another series of screams.

"Oh! I'm so sorry. Here!" the frail voice continued.

Paul cracked his eyes open to see where it came from. Standing next to him was an elderly woman in a royal blue nun's habit holding out a cold bottle of water. The classic white band encircled an oaky face with eyes so green they were almost unnatural.

"Um, thanks?" Confused, Paul took the water bottle and inspected it, trying to figure out what to do with it.

"Put it on the bump to help with the swelling," she said with a click of her tongue.

Paul obliged, and soon it went from a raging volcano on the brink of explosion to a tame, gentle bump.

"There, that's better. Now, what is wrong with you?" The nun swatted at Paul's arm hanging out the window. "Why are you alone and yelling out here?"

Paul didn't know where to start. Was it his frigid dad or the fact that he was now late for an important flight? He didn't know this woman, even if she was a nun, he didn't have to tell her anything. He said, "Ah, I am just waiting for someone."

The nun stared at him and said, "Boss, no one comes out here to wait for someone unless it's something illegal. The girls around here have been through enough. Get out of here before I call for *le maire*."

"Whoa, whoa, wait—no. No. I'm not here for *that*. You don't need to call them. I'm just here *with mon père,* who just bought the silo and warehouse down the path." Paul waved in the general direction of the barn as evidence. "I brought him out here to check on it," Paul said quickly, hoping the truth would keep him out of trouble. Calling *le maire,* or the mayor's office, only ever made a problem worse. Without a local police office in this area, they were all too eager to make a show of handling any problem that could win them the next election.

"Wait, and who are you?" Paul asked, suddenly irritated that he needed to deal with this nun in the first place. What right did she have to question him?

Instead of answering him, the nun stared at Paul until he shrank down like a mischievous child in need of correcting. She brought her face so close to him that he could smell the minty fresh toothpaste from this morning.

Then, she inhaled, taking in every molecule of Paul's scent. Once satisfied, she pulled away, and a click of disapproval emerged from deep in her throat.

"My name is Sœur Nicole of the Convent of St. Rose de Lima. Once a week, I come out here to tutor the area's children." She paused for a moment, appraising Paul. "I also work with adults who lost their way into a bottle of the locally made *clairin.* And you look a little lost," she said, with the gentleness of a mean aunt who finally decided to offer a compliment.

Mortified, Paul shrank further into his seat and scrambled for the words to get out of this situation.

"Oh, I can see why you would think that, but no. Like I said, I am waiting on my dad." Paul pointed to the rusting warehouse in the distance.

Both looked in the direction of the silo and saw a couple of shadowy figures move around the outside of the barn carrying large sugar sacks.

"Ah, Reginald Lancelin is your father?" Sœur Nicole asked without expecting an answer.

Paul nodded suspiciously. How could she know his father from this distance? They were at least forty-five minutes away from Port-au-Prince, and even then, there is no world where their paths could have crossed.

Sœur Nicole nodded and sucked in a big breath before she said, "Then you definitely need one of these." Her arms disappeared into the layers of her habit, creating ripples of cloth over her body.

Each wave fanned the almost forgotten embers of his rage. Who did she think she was? And what was his dad up to that a woman, a nun, this far away from the city knew all about him. The air around him felt like it was closing in.

"Wait, what? What are you talking about? Also, who do you think you are? You have no right!"

Sœur Nicole found what she was looking for and shoved a plastic-covered business card at him. Bordered with pink roses threaded by a gold vine, the designs were strange and resembled a medieval storybook. The front of the card held the usual information:

Chapel de Dieu, St. Pierre, Rue Lamothe, Port-au-Prince, Haïti.

But the back? That was what confused him. Although the border continued the same pattern as the front, there was a strange phrase written in English.

Paul read out loud, "Tend to the Guardian Within?"

He looked up at the nun.

"It's our little saying when we find ourselves in trouble. Especially if you ever find yourself alone in a field like this again." Sœur Nicole swept her arm toward the sprawling lemongrass.

Paul looked down at the card again and ran his fingers over the detailing, finding new images within the vines.

Hesitant, Paul said, "Thanks? I guess I'll keep this for next time?"

Hearing no response, Paul looked up, and the nun was gone. Bewildered, Paul looked around but couldn't find a trace of her. How strange to come all this way, and then some random nun shows up with a business card, knowing his father. Then, like magic, she disappears? Paul worked through the logistics, and nothing made sense.

In the distance, a collection of small houses, long abandoned, peeked up from the fields. Covered by the towering banyan tree above, light and shade added to the mystery of those cinder block homes. Maybe she disappeared into one of those buildings? Looking closer, he swore he saw a shred of blue disappear further into one of them. Satisfied that it wasn't some strange country magic, Paul relaxed into his seat, closed his eyes, and let the cold-water bottle ease the bump on his head.

The passenger door opened with a deep metallic creak. Paul jumped only to see his father easing back into his seat.

Sliding the gun from his jeans and into the glove compartment, Reginald barked, "Are we just going to sit out here for the rest of the day? Let's go." Waving his son along, Reginald reclined the seat, ready to take a morning nap.

Paul simply nodded and cranked the engine to life. After checking the area to make sure it was clear, he turned the car around. Dust lifted into the air, creating a billowing trail behind them as they crunched their way back to the highway. With each passing house, Paul turned over every detail of his strange morning and the embellished card hiding in his shirt pocket. He opened his mouth once or twice to ask about what happened at the silo, but every time thought better of it. Better to pretend that this whole thing wasn't weird at all.

Once they were back on the highway, Reginald pushed the buttons on the radio until the news from *Radio Métropole* filled the car with updates from the capital.

With his father distracted, Paul gripped the steering wheel, thinking through what came next. If he could find the right investors at the conference in Orlando, he could finally prove that he had something to offer. That he could grow his father's company and beat out Didier. That he could do it in an innovative and legal way.

Tapping his fingers against the rough threads of the steering wheel, Paul focused on keeping the growing anxiety in check. No use getting into an accident when he was this close to getting on the plane. Letting his mind wander to anything other than the current scenario, he realized something had gone unfinished. Saskia hadn't texted back.

The sounds from the radio shifted from the news to a dramatic ballad from Julio Iglesias. Yearning dripped from every note as the melody poked at the holes she had left in his heart. She'd be the first person he'd text when he landed; he had to fix what he had broken.

Four. Quatre. Kat.

Nope, nope, nope, I can't do it.

Saskia made it halfway across the parking lot before she couldn't take another step. Turning around, she walked back to her red car, flicking her fingers every step of the way. Leaning against her car, Saskia sized up the building. Two stories of red brick appeared to have been recently cleaned. Tidy hedges bordered a sidewalk that led directly to a set of glass doors. Not a brick had changed since her six-year-old self opened her first checking account. But she had.

Back then, she'd fatigue her parents with her never-ending supply of joy. Now? She couldn't find a single thread of it. All she had was resentment. Her jaw tightly set, Saskia needed the low boiling discontent to go somewhere. Normally, she'd go into the Facebook comments of some low-stakes post and start a war with a stranger or completely empty a bag of M&M's. She couldn't do any of those, so instead she went for an old habit that started back then.

...

Saskia stood before her Hello Kitty calendar uncharacteristically frozen. Today was a big day, but all she could move were her little fingers. Flicking her thumb and pointer fingers, she let out the nerves one little spark at a time. For the whole year leading up to her sixth birthday, she consistently asked for one thing: her very own bank account. Saskia wanted to write checks from her sparkly pink plastic wallet, just like her mom.

Her mom, Jacqueline, would sigh and say, "When you turn six, we can take you to open your own account."

That day, she ran to the calendar and circled the day with a glitter-infused purple crayon. Every day thereafter, she'd take that glitter-infused crayon and draw a line through the square. Excitement grew with every stroke until the big day: April 16, 1992. When she slashed through the date square, the day felt even more special, more important.

Her mother had spent all morning shining shoes and carefully assembling their outfits so they would look presentable.

Once Jacqueline could pin down her wiggly daughter, she brought Saskia into the bedroom she shared with her husband, Emile. Plopping the six-year-old down on her bed, Jacqueline finally had the right angles to slather oil before cream before gel to keep every last hair in place, no matter how much humidity tried to undo it.

While he starched and ironed their dresses, Emile attempted to keep Saskia still by asking her for every detail about their upcoming trip to the bank.

"*Papa*! This is the most exciting day of my life! *Maman*! Can you believe it?" she screamed.

"More than your birthday at Disney?" Emile playfully responded.

Saskia squealed out a 'yes' while rolling off the bed onto the carpet.

Jacqueline hissed at Emile and pulled her daughter back up to the bed.

"Right. Saskia, sit still and tell me what you are most excited about?" Emile patiently said, spraying at a persistent wrinkle in Jacqueline's butter-yellow sheath dress.

"Oo, oo, oo, the lollipops, and then once I have my account, I can buy *more* lollipops. Oo oo, and the dragons that are protecting the gold." Saskia almost jumped out of her mother's lap, earning another scowl and a tighter pull on her ponytail. She howled at the pain and flailed to prove her point.

"Saskia," her mother said, letting her warning drip on every syllable, "Stop moving, we're almost done." Jacqueline shot Emile a glare, which he received with a smirk.

"Listen to *maman*, Saskia. Today is a special day with a big responsibility, so you have to be your very best self, otherwise the dragons will eat you all up!" he said as he raised Jacqueline's wrinkle-free dress from the ironing board.

Though impressed, she glared at him for encouraging such a wild imagination.

"Mmm. Starched to perfection, just how they taught me in the Marines," Emile said with satisfaction. He examined the yellow sheath just in case he missed a spot.

Jacqueline had picked it out on a recent trip to Miami. She loved how the gold buttons added a touch of class.

"You were a Marine!" Saskia gushed with curiosity, and Jacqueline shot another warning look because she knew this pattern well.

If she didn't stop this conversation, Emile would start sharing all his stories, and they would be late to their appointment.

"Saskia, we can ask Papa about that later. Your hair is done, so go put on your dress."

"Okay!" Saskia shouted. She hopped off the bed onto the very old shag carpet her parents didn't have the time to remove, but had all the time to complain about. She started to skip down the tiled hallway but stopped mid-skip when she heard her mother say, "I'm worried."

Silently, she tiptoed back to her parents' doorway and pressed herself against the wall.

Emile chuckled as he helped Jacqueline up off the bed to pull her in close.

"Try not to worry so much," he said. "They can't deny you a bank account. We're citizens now, remember? They have to treat us like normal everyday people *ti cœur*."

"You know as well as I do that is not how this works." Jacqueline huffed into his chest. "Look what happened to Fritz and Mariel, and then to Ronald and Linda. They weren't bothering anyone, hadn't been to Haiti in years by that point, but then they lost everything. Just like that? What if that happens to us?"

Saskia knitted her brows in confusion from her side of the wall.

"*Bon, ti cœur*, that's why she is getting her bank account today, right? If something happens to us, she'll have a way to make it through. She was born here, so she'll be okay." Emile tightened his hold on Jacqueline.

"Just relax, and everything will be fine as long as you don't mention Haiti, okay? I'll keep the other two alive while you're gone, and you'll be back here in no time. *Pas de quoi*, nothing to worry about," her father said.

Saskia heard her mother sigh, and shivered. This big day was much bigger than she thought.

"Okay," Jacqueline resigned, "but I swear, if there is a mess when I get back, I am going to Macy's for the afternoon."

"Don't worry," Emile said while swaying Jacqueline, his go-to move to help her relax, a move that Saskia could watch her parents do for hours. "I'll keep them from making too big a mess."

"Wait, why is it so quiet? Saskia! Are you ready yet?" she yelled, and Saskia's little feet pattered down the hall.

...

With their crisp dresses, shiny flat hair, and spotless shoes, Saskia and Jacqueline pulled their blue Volkswagen Beetle into the small bank parking lot. A white wall surrounded the lot and supported a well-pruned hedge that circled the lot. It was easy to find a spot under the youngest oak tree.

"You ready *ti cœur*?" Jacqueline calmly asked after shutting off the car, hoping that a calm exterior would lead to a calm interior.

Forgetting everything that happened at the house, Saskia beamed and screamed, "Yup! I'm ready!"

"Saskia, how many times do I have to tell you, no screaming inside?"

"But we're not inside."

"We are inside the car; it's a small space."

"But—"

"Saskia." Jacqueline's tone snapped her mouth shut. She let out a sigh that filled the car with her frustration, pushing Saskia into the worn leather seat. And then she saw it: a flash of doubt across her mother's face. She didn't think Saskia could do it. What if she couldn't handle this errand? She sank even deeper into the seat.

"Are you ready to be on your best behavior?" Jacqueline asked a subdued and nodding Saskia.

"Ok, grab your purse and let's go."

She obeyed and fetched her pink and red Hello Kitty purse from the floor of the car. Sliding the pink plastic cross-body strap over her white cotton dress, Saskia was armed and ready.

Stepping out of the car, careful to smooth the creases from the ride, Jacqueline took a firm grasp of her daughter's hand as she nervously walked up to the heavy glass doors. She couldn't even think about all the what-ifs.

Once inside, the frigid air almost took Saskia's breath away as much as the grandeur of the bank's lobby. Large, white marble tiles made the small lobby feel expansive, restrained only by dark wood paneling on the walls and the cashier's counter. Four green leather chairs faced each other, separated by a glass coffee table with a large bowl of lollipops.

Eyeing the varying colors under the lobby lights, Saskia whispered loudly, "Wow, this is amazing!"

Jacqueline's mouth came to a thin line. Unwilling to give her daughter the same lecture in less than ten minutes, she said, "Yes, it is, now let's go to that desk over there." She pointed her red manicured finger to one by the far window.

Saskia nodded and let her mother guide her across the marble floor to a large banker's desk that matched the wood paneling behind it. Proudly perched behind it and clacking away at his keyboard was a young man fresh out of college, attempting the Lethal Weapon mullet. The front part of his head looked trimmed and clean, while the wild back made her wonder if a dead animal had been glued there.

Seeing the question form on Saskia's face, Jacqueline jumped in before she could speak.

"Hello!" she said a little too loudly, prompting her little six-year-old to get lost in a fit of giggles.

Leveling her volume to match the polite indoors, Jacqueline continued, "My daughter and I are looking to open a bank account. Is this the right place?"

Saskia's eyes widened as the hair moved before the man's head did.

He cheerfully replied, "Hello! How are you all doing today? My name is Robert Friedman."

Robert dramatically waved his hand over his bronze and wood nameplate.

"But you can call me Bob." Bob extended his hand stiffly to Jacqueline, as if he were practicing how to be a professional.

She shook his hand, eager to finish this transaction as quickly as possible.

Then Bob turned to Saskia and asked in the grating sweetness adults who don't understand a thing about kids use, "And who might you be?"

Ignoring his awkwardness, she practically popped out of her black, patent Mary Janes and frilly socks as she responded, "I'm Saskia, but you can call me Sarah."

Her eyes sparkled, hoping to get a chuckle out of Bob, but he didn't laugh.

Instead, he gave a funny look and let out a big sigh of relief. "Oh, good! Sarah is *much* easier. Thanks, kid. Now, what are we here for again?"

She looked to her mom and saw the familiar lines of frustration emerge.

Jacqueline straightened her posture, smiled widely, and stared directly at Bob as she said, "Like I said. We are here to open an account for my daughter."

Offended, Bob's cheery cheeks melted into a bit of a frown as the rest of his body collapsed like an under-baked cake.

Jacqueline had struck a nerve.

His eyes came to slits as he surveyed the pair, looking for a way to even the score.

Saskia's grin faltered under his scrutiny, so she grabbed Jacqueline's hand for comfort.

Finding nothing, he finally said, "Well, there's no need to take that tone. Take a seat and let's get started."

After the mother and daughter settled into their pleather seats, Bob pulled a stack of papers from his desk drawer with a performative assertiveness.

Jacqueline assumed this was meant to intimidate and help him reclaim the power in this dynamic. It did not. His arrogance only made Jacqueline seethe and flare her nostrils with impatience.

Seeing no meaningful change in her demeanor, Bob slid the application packet across the polished desktop as if he were in a movie.

The pages fluttered on their way to her, and just as they were set to take flight from the desk, Jacqueline squashed the packet with her hand. Having stopped the flying packet, she slowly turned it until the top of the page faced her: Walnut Bank Account Application.

Unamused and slightly appalled that a man in such a position of power would behave this way, Jacqueline fought every desire to just get up and walk out. She had overcome too much to protect her daughter to give in to a man who wanted her to feel small. Her daughter was watching. Jacqueline twitched with annoyance and took her time inspecting each page of the packet as if something sinister hid between the perfectly pressed black letters.

Bob shifted in his leather swivel chair, impatient with how long this exchange was taking. "Are you having trouble reading the application? I would be more than happy to read it to you and walk you through it," he said with a sweetness so artificial, its aftertaste would linger with Saskia and Jacqueline for years.

Jacqueline's hands shook with a rage so fierce that it threatened to explode from her and burn Bob down to the most useless of ashes.

Worried that her mother's throbbing blood vessel was about to burst all over the desk, Saskia moved into Jacqueline's lap and, like a fire blanket, suffocated her mother's rage.

She knew fighting back would be useless. If she went anywhere else, there'd be another Bob, or Karen, or Stephen, and she'd have to endure this humiliation again, and again, and again until she finally started believing what went unsaid. She was not worthy of a bank account, not in this country.

Regaining her composure, Jacqueline simply said, "No, I'm fine. Just making sure I understood what we were signing." She flashed a quick smile and glanced at Bob as she began scratching and scrawling across the pages.

Saskia watched her mother's pen-laden hand fill in boxes with familiar letters and words. "*Maman*, is that my name?"

"Yes, *ti amour*, that is your name."

"And is that our address?"

"Yes, that is our address. Now, can you sit over here while I finish this up?" Jacqueline asked.

"Yeah," Saskia sighed as she slid from the warmth of her mother's lap and back into the cold metal guest chair.

"Alright, there you are. Anything missing?" Jacqueline flipped the packet around and carefully pushed it toward Bob, the way it should have been done.

Bob pulled the application toward him and gave a curt nod.

"Looks good to me. Let me get this in the computer and we'll be ready to go. Oh, and can I please have your licenses?"

Jacqueline nodded and reached for her wallet, relieved that the exchange returned to some normal.

Without the view from her mother's lap, Saskia was bored and needed something to do. How could something so important be so incredibly boring? Looking around for any distraction, she noticed a variety of posters hanging between the windows. Some were colorful and fun, others dark and sinister. She wasn't interested in what they said, but she liked the pictures. Bob's fingers clacked the plastic buttons on his keyboard, pulling her attention to the glass ball that looked like the Earth and a little tray for cards that matched the nameplate. Curious, Saskia reached for the little cards when she heard a *thump*. Then another. She looked down and saw that every time the front of her shoe hit the wooden desk, it would make a delightful sound: a *thump*.

She hit the desk again, and neither adult reacted. She kicked again, a little stronger this time, and still no one reacted. Finally, she gave a mighty swing and kicked the desk so hard that the now familiar *thump* came with a faint crack. Both Bob and Jacqueline paused to glare at Saskia until her feet stopped mid-swing.

"Saskia, *ça suffit*, that's enough!" Jacqueline hissed, and it was now Saskia's turn to crumple in shame. She returned her feet to parallel with the floor.

"Oh, is that Spanish you all are speaking?" Bob asked, sliding the IDs from Jacqueline for scanning.

"No, it's French! Because my mom is from Haiti!" Saskia shouted, oozing with pride.

This was her favorite fact about her parents. At school, all the other kids talked about their parents' jobs or hobbies, but no one had parents like hers. Every day, they taught her a little bit more about their special language, their special food, music, and movies, and Saskia devoured every detail ravenous for more. In this way, Saskia grew increasingly connected to her parents' very own island —Haiti. It was her secret wish to one day call that island hers, too.

Her mother's face froze, hoping Bob hadn't heard her.

"Did I say something wrong?" Saskia asked Jacqueline in a voice so small she wasn't sure her mother heard her.

"Haiti?" Bob's fingers stopped, silencing the keyboard. His voice went up a key, terrified of the answer. "Y—you all are Haitian?" Bob stuttered out the question. Hanging in the air between them, he could feel a deeply held fear gurgle up through him.

Jacqueline froze. From the politely crossed hands in her lap to the tiny muscles around her mouth, everything froze. She knew they weren't sick, and this whole exchange was the irrational fear of an ill-informed man in an ill-informed country, hell-bent on pushing aside ugly truths to maintain appearances. Everything from microwaves to Aqua Net, the States would sacrifice anything to keep the economy going.

One by one, minuscule beads of sweat sprouted across Bob's forehead as images from the nightly news came to mind. Bob's eyes grew wider and wider still as nameless emaciated bodies in hospital beds emerged through his fear. No longer seeing Saskia and Jacqueline, he only saw a poster by the entrance and blanched.

Following his gaze, Jacqueline turned around to see a black poster of a white skeleton holding a yellow sign that said,

AIDS!
The Death Warrant!
Avoid the 4H's!
Heroin Addicts!
Homosexuals!
Hemophiliacs!
Haitians!

Resignation at what was to happen, Jacqueline gently reached for Saskia's small hand, took a deep breath, and quietly said, "Yes."

Bob sucked in half the air around him and puffed out his cheeks until they became two shiny red apples of concern. He sat like that as if holding in the panic would somehow make this situation disappear.

"*Maman*, is Mr. Bob okay? He's changing colors like my cup at home," Saskia asked.

Watching Bob's face turn from apple red to bruise purple, Jacqueline silently rehearsed how she would handle whatever came next. Embarrassment? Heartbreak of letting her daughter down? Certainly not shame, there was nothing to be ashamed of. They just needed to survive this man's prejudice.

Before Jacqueline could reclaim her voice, Bob slowly deflated back to his original pale complexion and said, "Ah. Well. Let's proceed then, but…" He paused, looked at her daughter, then at Jacqueline with an expression that made her think he might throw them out, given this new information.

"I insist that you two wear these gloves and keep your distance as we finish up your application. And then you will need to leave," said Bob. A sharp-edged smile cut across his face. He would finish this task, but they couldn't dare ask for more.

"I hope you understand and that you find this more than fair, given your *condition*. The CDC says to be wary of the four H's and Haitians are one of them. Wouldn't want to catch AIDs you know?" He pointed to the skeleton sign.

Of course, her mother understood. Ever since the Centers for Disease Control announced that AIDS was only contracted by the 4H's, everyone Saskia's parents knew changed overnight. Promising friendships and casual acquaintances that used to set aside a little extra for her mother vanished. With three kids and their precarious jobs, it wasn't like they could pick up and move. They had to make Orlando work.

Saskia watched as Jacqueline spent weeks carefully recalibrating her family's identity so they could continue living their lives without causing panic among strangers and risking losing everything over imagined fears of contagion. She noticed how Jacqueline had stopped mentioning she was from Haiti and instead replied to the "Oh, you're so exotic, where are you from?" with the vague "Oh, the islands, my family is from a little bit of everywhere."

She noticed, even as a child, that the weight of keeping up this charade left her mother more exhausted than managing the three of them on a sugar high. Little by little, she watched her mother let go of parts of her Haitian identity in the hopes she could be more accepted. Those sacrifices must have felt worth it when she heard the stories from their family and friends from back home. Someone would call her with *zen* about "so and so" in New York having job offers revoked, and "so and so" very successful business in Miami having to shut down because their customers were too scared to come in. How had Saskia forgotten how important it was to forget about Haiti, too? The stakes were too high for their family.

"Of course," Jacqueline quietly said and went about letting the sickly yellow rubber gloves first devour Saskia's little hands and then eventually her entire arm.

"*Maman*, I'm a scary monster, *rawr*!!" Saskia wiggled the palms of the gloves, sending the empty fingers flittering.

Jacqueline smiled, leaned over, and said into her plastered hair, "Oh, you have no idea." And kissed her lacquered head.

"Saskia, don't take those off until we leave," Jacqueline said, sliding on her pair and using an accent Saskia had never heard, possibly to mask the embarrassment. From the corner of her eye, she could see Bob putting on a pair of gloves for himself as well as a face mask.

Once Saskia's account was set up, Bob used his gloved hands to slide the folder toward Jacqueline. With a tight smile, she tucked the heavy folder under her daughter's arm, thanked the man, and ushered little Saskia to the door.

As they walked away from Bob's desk, Jacqueline's eyes went glassy at the smell of bleach. It chased them out of the bank, sanitizing everything in their wake. In the car, Jacqueline couldn't hold them back a moment longer. Tears quietly streamed down her face while she got busy with the details of starting the car.

"*Maman*, why are you crying?"

"I'm allergic to bleach. It makes my eyes water," Jacqueline said.

Saskia sensed this wasn't entirely true but decided to stay quiet for the rest of the ride. As they passed the familiar streetscapes, the folder with her new bank account information felt heavy and dirty. Their weight made her wonder, was the account really worth it?

...

Thinking back on that moment now, Saskia realized she hadn't seen her mother use bleach ever since. She suspected neither of them really shook off the shame from that moment. New York mixed with that shame kept her from enthusiastically walking up to the glass doors and embracing whatever came next. A rattling from her purse pulled her out of her thoughts. She reached in and answered her phone without looking at the screen.

"Hello?" Saskia answered, voice hollow.

"*Ti fi*," her mother's voice jolted her back to reality. To this parking lot. In her hometown. With a desperate need to earn some money.

"Do you want to lose this job, too?" Her mother continued, "I drove by on my way to the office, and I would have stopped if your brother hadn't parked behind me. I can't have two of my children doing this to me today when I am already running late. I swear, Saskia, if you don't go inside, I am going to send you to your grandmother in Haiti. You are an adult. Do your job and then go home. This is nothing more than that. Do you hear me?"

The familiar threat of going to Haiti had lost its power over the years, but Saskia gave in all the same.

"Yes, Mom, thanks for the encouragement."

Her mother harrumphed in reply and simply said, "Good luck and have a good day."

The silence on the other end was enough for Saskia to shake her gel-crisped head and walk across the parking lot. Anxiously flicking her fingers every step of the way.

Five. Cinq. Cenk.

Walking through the glass and white metal atrium of the Orlando airport, Paul checked his phone for the tenth time. He bristled against the perfect climate, annoyed that she didn't even bother to send a "k" or a "thx." Without her response, he fixated on his phone and didn't notice the renovations to one of his favorite airports in the world. The new wall-sized screens with ads for SeaWorld and Universal didn't pull his gaze. The new escalators and little coffee shops went largely unnoticed. It wasn't until a stuffed mouse fell in front of him that he stopped. Picking up the toy from the brand-new carpet, he returned it to the free-standing shelf holding more of Mickey's friends. Paul smirked as he, too, was returning to his friends.

Marcello Giraldo, Paul's best friend and roommate, was also an international student who took on the world like he already owned it. His constantly rotating luxury cars and the never-ending social plans, ranging from wholesome to depraved, opened up a whole new world to Paul. A lot of these things existed in Port-au-Prince, but not nearly at the same scale. He was familiar with beach houses where helipads were unique, and boat parties happened two or three times a year. In the States? Paul remembered the first time he woke up in a bedroom he thought was a hotel. It was only when he padded over to open the curtains that he remembered he was actually on a celebrity's yacht docked in Fort Lauderdale. Their college life was madness.

Paul passed his classes due to the unending investment from his favorite professor and advisor, Dr. Oakley. For reasons Paul still didn't understand, Dr. Oakley quickly befriended him. He saw this potential in Paul and pushed him to study Biology instead of International Business. In his junior year, Dr. Oakley intervened with another professor to ensure Paul received a passing grade. It was always his aspiration that Paul would pursue a Ph.D. That same year, Marcello must have felt that he was losing his best friend, so he took Paul out to even more audacious parties and trips. Everything came to a head when Dr. Oakley kept Paul after class one day to go over a research paper. By the time Paul left Dr. Oakley, Marcello had already left for a weekend trip to Tampa. Furious that Paul never showed, Marcello stayed out of the house for a week and stopped inviting him out until Paul apologized. After that, their friendship took an interesting turn. Communication was strained, and their outings felt forced rather than heady and limitless.

While it had been at least five years since all of that, Paul was a little nervous about juggling these two characters again. Dr. Oakley had one of the thickest stacks of business cards from agricultural and scientific research investors. He also still counted Marcello as one of his best friends, who conveniently had a lot of money. Paul needed both of them to get mango sugar off the pages of his notebook and onto the shelves of grocery stores around the world. But how would he manage both when they very clearly didn't like each other?

Breezing past the baggage claim, Paul walked through the two sets of glass doors separating the perfect airport climate and the unpredictable Florida climate. When they opened, the air felt heavy and humid compared to the light, breezy version in Port-au-Prince. He walked toward a cement bench and rolled his carry-on to the side of it. Paul sat down as his clothes absorbed the last dewy bits of morning.

Marcello said he'd be there in fifteen minutes, so he decided to pass the time by pulling the plasticized business card out of his jeans pocket. His earth-worn fingers examined the delicate pink roses, their golden stems intertwining with the next. It reminded him of his grandmother's leather-bound book of fairytales. He half expected a dragon to be hiding among the vines. Looking at the address, he ran through his memory of the Cathedral and couldn't remember there ever being a chapel. Curious, Paul fired off a text to his driver, Stanley, asking him to investigate the location.

Tend to the Guardian Within.

The statement played over and over in his head, as if the next time it would make more sense. It never did. On top of all that, it wasn't even a statement that had anything to do with Catholicism—so why was a nun passing out these cards?

Stumped, he decided to leave it alone and opened Facebook to see who might be around. He flipped through the list of old classmates, lab mates, and the occasional person he wished to forget. Then he paused the scrolling when he saw it. A picture of Saskia drinking coffee at a sidewalk café brought back memories of Didier's Christmas party.

A couple of years ago, Didier built a small house in the mountains and, over the holidays, had a bonfire for his friends and family. Among the fragrant pines, the fire dissolved the cold, steeped humidity and created tricky corners of light and shadow. Saskia stood there among the crowd, vacantly staring into the flames when he arrived. The way her long, curly hair framed her light, brown eyes, reflecting the flames. She brought the red plastic cup to her full lips robotically. Paul had heard something had happened, but what he saw now worried him. Every time she visited, it felt like she was dancing among the clouds and might bring him up there with her. The woman who stood before him felt weighed down, anchored to the land without a hope of ever soaring again. Curious, he approached her until he finally caught her attention. Seeing him, she lit up, and every hint of whatever haunted her disappeared with the smoke.

He heard the car before he saw it. A deep mechanical roar echoed off the arrival terminal's cement walls, amplifying each rev of the engine. Paul rolled his eyes. Marcello always preferred a dramatic entrance. He stood up and rolled his suitcase to the curb just as a bright yellow Lamborghini Aventador with the windows down pulled up in front of him.

"*Marica*! Dude! Welcome back!" Marcello had stayed a trim, debonair man who dripped of sex and privilege. Since college, it looked like he had shortened his hair from long enough for a man bun to a leading man's style where bits would fall into his eyes.

Rubbing his bald head, Paul missed how his hair used to do the same thing.

"Thanks!" Paul leaned into the car from the window to initiate their handshake. Cuffing their fists together, then bumping them, the men went through five different moves until they couldn't remember what came next. Paul remembered, then led them to the last move where they stuck out their tongues and wagged them.

"Ha, nice bro! I almost forgot the new part from your last Colombia trip," Marcello said, leaning back in his seat.

"Yeah, it was an easy one to forget." Paul laughed and pointed to his carry-on. "Where should I put this?"

Marcello nodded and said, "You can hold on to it. Remember, these babies don't have a trunk big enough for that. I'll take it easy on you, so you don't lose it." He winked as he pushed the gas pedal to rev the engine.

Paul slowly nodded and pushed the button under a ridge on the door until it started to swing upward. Once the door was all the way up, he crawled under it to reach the passenger seat. Crouched and a little annoyed at being so close to the ground, he pulled his suitcase onto his lap. Then, he pulled the strap of the door down to close it.

"How was the flight?" Marcello asked Paul, still settling himself into the car.

"It was good, there was this old lady—"

"Whoa, bro, we aren't wasting any more time on what sounds like a lame story. Old ladies never lead to fun," Marcello howled and then turned up the volume when the opening beats of "Danza Kuduro."

As Paul remembered it, Marcello always had a party in the pipeline and danced on life's razor edge. It thrilled him and terrified him at the same time. He'd joke with friends in Haiti that Marcello was likely involved in something very criminal and very shady, but he'd never really know.

Forgetting the weight of his suitcase, Paul relaxed as the engine gently vibrated his seat. In that moment, he finally understood why people would spend so much money on cars like this. His usual vice was buying cigars and whiskey; he rarely indulged in motor luxuries. As he got more comfortable, Paul wondered if exotic cars might be his next obsession.

The Lamborghini purred softly as he admired the interior details. After figuring out the seatbelt, Paul asked Marcello, "When did you get this one?"

"Not important. Did your dad send anything for me?" Marcello barked, almost impatient that Paul hadn't already produced it.

Taken aback, Paul looked at Marcello, confused. This sudden tone shift made him feel unbalanced. Paul replied, "Why would my dad send anything to you?"

Marcello raised his eyebrows above his sunglasses and frowned. Quickly recovering from his disappointment, he said, "Well, that changes things. I have to run an errand before going to the conference. Down for the ride?"

"Yeah, that's fine. I want to get there before the dinner at six," Paul replied.

"Perfect! Well, hold on, *wajon*, because this is going to be the ride of your life."

Paul rolled his eyes at the familiar dramatics of doing anything with Marcello. Pumping the clutch and gas pedal, Marcello woke up the Lamborghini. The Aventador's roar reverberated off the cement airport walls as the car leaped from the curb and back into traffic. Marcello pushed and swerved around cars like they were insignificant fish, and he was a shark, not drivers moving toward their loved ones. The slower the car, the more audacious the swerve.

Paul gripped the door strap and dug his other fingers into the seat as if holding on tightly could slow the terror of this very uncontrollable situation.

The car bellowed as they broke free from the terminal's concrete encasement, letting its power and pressure evaporate into Florida's humid atmosphere. Marcello punched the gas, the Lamborghini crouched in reply and launched into a speed Paul could not remember feeling. Barreling down the straightaway, the engine screamed so powerfully that Paul could only close his eyes and clench the strap harder. Marcello's wild laughter danced over the deafening speed.

Clearing the airport and joining the local highway, a red light glared half a mile away. Marcello let off the gas, coasting down the smooth roadway as if testing his timing in the hope he wouldn't have to tap the brakes.

Paul opened his eyes as he felt the car slow, just in time to see the light switch green.

"Marcello, really, do we need—"

The Lamborghini roared again to cut through the stopped cars, sending Paul's hand back into a vice grip on the door strap. In that moment, he surrendered to the fact that this situation was completely out of his control. Whatever Marcello wanted to do in town, he wanted to get there fast. Paul closed his eyes again and let the rushing winds drown out every thought from his mind. Because if he was going to die in this car with Marcello, he might as well make it peaceful.

Six. Six. Six.

A couple of hours after lunch, Saskia successfully made it through all her orientation work. She had shadowed a more senior teller, a demeaning task because she had designed the very system he was using. She had rearranged the stacks of banking forms just like her interns used to do for her. She had even started a list of things that would have driven her old office on a firing rampage. Every task she completed hammered in the reminder that she had gone in the wrong direction. She should have been here as a trainer or an auditor. Instead, she had to pretend that all of this was new to her because she couldn't risk losing this job. She couldn't go another month without a paycheck.

Running her hands over the highly glossed wood of her desk, she remembered the choices she had to make last week, applications for personal loans, draining savings accounts from healthy numbers down to zero. The humiliation alone wired her mouth shut in an attempt to make this job work. She glanced at the wall across from her to read the large white-and-black clock that likely came from an office supply catalogue.

2:45 p.m.

How could it only be 2:45 p.m.?

Saskia furtively looked around the branch, hoping to find someone to give her a task. Everyone was either with a customer or busy at their desks. Worried they'd call her out for counting the seconds between the minutes, Saskia thought, *Well, if I've got everything done and no one needs me, I guess I might as well check what is happening on Facebook...*

And in three clicks, the familiar white and blue webpage opened on her computer. Pictures of family and friends doing mundane things like drinking coffee, or beautifully plated dinners filled her newsfeed. She scrolled down a bit further until a post from a friend of her parents caught her eye. It had over fifty comments under a pixelated Jesus pointing to a map of Haiti. In bold white Comic Sans, **REPENT** spewed from his finger. Curious, Saskia peeked at the comments.

That's right! The country's obsession
with vodou is going to be the end of us.

Nah, it's the Americans.
They are testing something off our coasts;
that's what will be the end of us.

Well, if Duvalier was still around,
none of this would be an issue.

Are you serious?
That assassin is the reason we are in this mess.
Anyone who voted for him or Aristide should repent,
not the entire country that's just trying to live their lives.

That "assassin" was the only time the country ever knew true peace.

It was always like this among the Haitian diaspora: a never-ending debate about the root causes of Haiti's troubles that served as a replacement for therapy. Because in the end, they all knew that everyone was a little bit right. And they also knew everyone was a little bit traumatized from the cycle of chaos that stubbornly kept Haiti in its place as the "poorest country" in the Western Hemisphere. But if they ever gave up the fight, who would they be then? How would they cope with the reality that they might have had the solution all along if only they were brave enough to claim it?

Nostradamus predicted that in 2010, Haiti would suffer a great tragedy. Now is the time to repent, to avoid our possible suffering!! Si ou paka wè kisa bon dye ap eksplike ou, wáp mouri dan filmlan. We have to return to our Lord, and he will bring us peace.

Saskia rolled her eyes at that one and scrolled back to the top of the page. She came to Facebook to distract herself from how she was feeling. Isn't that what it was for? A break from the weight of reality? Not group therapy or gossip disguised as Haitian "politics."

Grazing the plastic keys with her finger pads, Saskia slowly typed out the name of her very guilty pleasure: Paul Lancelin. When his profile loaded, memories of their time together played in fast forward. The moonlit walk along the beach. The furtive glances all weekend long. How her arm hairs would rise when his arm bumped into hers. His amber-flecked eyes were always ready to launch into a joke. Even in the recycled air of the bank lobby, she could taste the sea air.

And then came the memories of Didier's bonfire party a couple of days before they came back to the States. She didn't want to go. Everything in her wanted to hide under a quilt and let her mind spiral down the disappointing corridor of falling so far down the corporate ladder. Her cousins, Annaliese and Alex, with her siblings, Johanna and Robert, refused to leave her and practically carried her into the car. From the moment they left the house, music blared, and loud voices made it impossible for Saskia to dwell on what waited for her at the end of this trip. When they pulled up to Didier's, the red metal gate was open, and they drove through the darkened yard toward the fire in the back. Once they passed the cabin, at least twenty cars covered the space between the house and the bonfire. Squeezing between the cabin and a car, Alex parked the car and had everyone get out through the trunk of his SUV. After each one rolled out of the car's trunk, they rushed toward the plastic table covered with drinks and plastic cups, except for Saskia.

Struggling to shake off her heavy coat of disappointment, she moved a bit slower and pretended to be flying on the same high as everyone else. She filled her cup with some beer and smiled or laughed when she was supposed to. But it drained her, taking up more energy than socializing should. After a while, she just peeled away from the conversations to stare into the roaring flames of the bonfire. Then she saw him. Paul was staring at her in the same way he did that night on the beach. A hunger for his fingertips gently pressed against her lower back returned. She nodded, and he stumbled toward her, clearly drunk. His lips grazed her ear, and his breath warmed the nape of her neck as he said, "I liked you more when you weren't so, whatever this is."

Saskia shivered to shake off the memory. Running her hands over her arms, she could feel the weight of obligation to respond to his text. How dare he have an opinion on what she was like. They weren't even in a relationship—at least that was what he said.

"Oh, Bob! Good to see you! Oh, it's been ages, simply ages!" A hollow, breathy voice broke through Saskia's reverie, bringing her back to her cold, lacquered desk and away from the salt-dusted warmth of the Caribbean.

She spotted an older female client dripping with plastic costume jewelry glide across the floor. The client and Bob air-kissed as if they were in a scene from a 1940s film, where the monochromatic characters were lovers who had known each other for decades. Saskia half expected a velvet fainting couch to appear for the breathless woman.

"Now, Ms. Beckwith, I do believe you were here just last week. Is it already time to order a new checkbook?" Bob let a wisp of his Southern drawl escape as he guided Ms. Beckwith to his desk. It was in the same spot and had the same nameplate from all those years ago. He even pulled the chair out for her, something Saskia hadn't seen him do for anyone else. While a clean crew cut replaced the mullet and he had grown soft around the middle, Bob had kept the same habit of being inconsistently kind.

"Oh, you," the woman breathed with such force that her plastic jewelry clicked in time with her. "Am I really that predictable?" she replied, gasping between each word, like she was about to cry.

Bob smirked in reply as he typed her name into his computer.

Saskia silently gagged behind her monitor.

"Well, I certainly wouldn't accuse you of being predictable. I'd only accuse you of being my favorite client."

At that, Ms. Beckwith flushed into various shades of crimson and leaned toward the desk to carry on their conversation in a hushed voice.

Saskia just stared at the exchange. Is this what living in Orlando would be like? With life operating at a slower pace, would the only excitement she'd ever find be as an accidental witness to weird client meetings? At least in New York, there were so many distractions that she never had the time to notice the lives of anyone else. Everyone moved like little blood cells, ceaselessly keeping the organism of New York City alive. But here, she felt like she was one wrong step away from entering someone else's soap opera.

Desperate for something else, anything but *this*, she went back to Paul's Facebook profile. Pictures of Paul at the beach with friends. Pictures of sunsets and sunrises in the mountains. Pictures at his farm among the mango trees. He seemed to be so happy. Everyone in those pictures seemed to be so happy. And yet, here she was, broke, humiliated, and an extra in the lives of everyone around her. Is this all her future held for her? Locked in her hometown, always looking back at her almost life? If she had fought harder and kept better notes, she'd still be in New York. If she had been brave enough to tell Paul how she felt instead of running away, they could have built a life together.

If. If. If. If…

The ifs linked together like a chain, leading her down, down, down to an all-too-familiar place. A place that used to hold a brocade-framed mirror—a worldview where anything was possible. Where love always won, and trusting everyone was the right thing to do. She didn't know that place existed until, little by little, rocks chipped the mirror. The delicate fissures turned into cracks until it was so weak that, when she finally boarded her flight from New York to Orlando, the whole thing shattered on takeoff. This corner of her mind now held the scattered shards of what was left. And this all could have been avoided, maybe, if she had just made a different decision.

"*Sass Kia*, can you please come here for a moment?" Sherri's cigarette rasped voice clipped the chain of ifs, bringing Saskia back to the lobby, back to the mundane clicking and clacking of her colleagues.

Saskia pushed away from her desk and grabbed a pen and notebook. In three earnest strides, she rounded the glass partition into Sherri's office and offered a perky, "Yes?"

Sherri leaned back in her leather chair behind a bigger, shinier wooden desk burdened with stacks of manila folders and a computer that desperately needed replacing. On the wall behind her hung a college diploma, a Walnut Bank award for fifteen years of service, and a picture of her and a man in a suit wearing a cowboy hat. All were encased in expensive wooden frames with glass panes.

Impatiently drumming her manicured fingers behind a placard that read, *Sherri M. Lovestone—Regional Branch Manager*, she scrutinized Saskia from head to toe. "Saskia, come and take a seat."

Saskia moved into the office and took one of the hard plastic guest seats.

"You know, I worked in New York for a couple of months, too, and I knew people like *you*. Poised, put together, and think they are truly brilliant. I imagine you think you've finished the orientation checklist. Correct?"

The artificially warm yet stern voice set Saskia on edge, as memories of bosses past flitted across her mind. What had worked in the past was to make herself smaller, and an indisputable delight.

Saskia nodded her head in affirmation and let out a "Yes, I did," hoping that would be enough to protect her from whatever came next. The smaller she was, the safer she would be.

Raising a perfectly tweezed eyebrow, Sherri appraised Saskia with her petal pink lidded eyes and continued.

"Look, people like *you*..." Sherri paused to weigh her words and then sniffed as if responding to a greater power that told her to take the high road, "...almost always find ways to get into trouble in trying to make things 'better.' So, toss out that recommendations list I know you have on your desk and focus on being a pleasant presence out on the floor. Our clients expect to only see pleasant things when they visit our branch. Not sad desperation. Got it?"

"Got it," Saskia replied with a tone cultivated from years of challenging bosses: demure and deferential with a hint of resistance. It had been a long time since she had been addressed this way, and it only added to the mounting shards of glass reminding her that she had failed miserably.

"Good," Sherri said with a finality that closed the short-lived conversation.

Saskia adjusted herself in the chair, unsure of what to do. Should she leave? Should she stay?

Sherri's pinched face scrutinized Saskia, assessing her to find all her hidden flaws and any hint that she was not a good fit.

Saskia sat still, focusing on keeping her face relaxed and demure. Whatever this weird test was, Saskia would pass it; she had no other choice.

Sherri opened her mouth, and before she could reveal her assessment, her black iPhone lit up with an incoming text message. Her eyes darted to the screen, and a slow, mischievous smirk emerged when she saw who sent it. Sherri grabbed the phone and disappeared into the text. Relaxing into her leather office chair, she creaked as she flicked her manicured nail down the phone. She stopped suddenly and removed her glasses.

"*Sass Kia*, you speak French and Spanish, right?" Sherri moved on to her computer and began typing frantically, searching for something.

"Yes, ma'am, I do," Saskia replied cautiously. Most Haitians she knew spoke these three to some degree but were always cautious of letting on. After decades of being portrayed as subhuman, being underestimated was the greatest asset. She didn't know Sherri well enough, but something had shifted. Sherri had gone from looking for ways to dismantle Saskia into a good little employee to now wanting to include her in whatever was happening on her phone.

"Good! Well, we have some very important clients on the way, and I'd like for you to be here to do some translating and anything else they need. Understood?"

Saskia nodded.

"Yes, I can do that." Saskia smiled as pleasantly as she could to push aside the growing feeling that something was not quite right. A little unnerved at how quickly she went from being a problem to a solution for Sherri. Someone who could shift so quickly usually caused trouble for Saskia, eventually.

"Good. Now, hurry off and check your makeup. You've got a smudge." Sherri's gaze shifted abruptly to the lobby as two sets of sneakers squeaked across the tile floor.

"Too late. We need your seat?" Sherri said with as much sweetness as a lemon.

"Um, yeah. Sure." Saskia scrambled out of the guest chair to find a spot next to a fake fern, attempting to get out of the way and wait.

Sherri furrowed her brow and said, "Really? That's the best you can do?"

Saskia stared at Sherri, nodded, and moved around the fern, looking for a new spot.

When the sound of sneakers on tile changed to sneakers on carpet, Sherri rose from her chair and said, "What perfect timing. We were just talking about you!"

Sherri moved around her desk to greet the clients, blocking Saskia from getting a closer look. From what she could see, one had golden curls and entered the room as if he owned it. When he hugged Sherri, it was as if they hadn't seen each other in years. The other was all too familiar, and Saskia froze. He was shorter than the blond one, and he awkwardly moved about the office as if he wanted to apologize for being there. That gait, that sloppy smile, and the way those slightly guarded light amber eyes locked in on hers set her heart ablaze. It was him, that stupid, stupid man.

"Saskia?" His voice rooted her in place.

"Paul? Wow, um, hi! How crazy to run into you here," Saskia responded, trying and failing to appear put together. How could he be here? Was the universe playing some sick joke?

"It's good to see you." His eyes danced in the fluorescent lighting. They were separated by the guest chairs, a coffee table, and a large fern.

They could have stumbled toward one another. Instead, both stayed in their spots, rooted by awkwardness.

"You, too. How long has it been?" Saskia said, squeezing her notebook to her chest and smiling so hard her cheeks hurt. She pushed her back against the wall, hoping she could be absorbed into the next room. Too bad real life wasn't more like a movie.

"What are you talking about? I'd say less than two weeks. Why didn't you tell me this was your new job? I thought you had a fancy banking job in New York. Why didn't you text me back?" Paul shifted his weight and couldn't seem to figure out where to put his hands.

The air was thick with a tension Sherri couldn't point out. She cleared her throat because she wanted no part of what was happening here.

"Well, she's here now, and today's her first day. She's still got a *lot* to learn, but I'm optimistic. I'm Sherri." She held out her hand to Paul, and he carefully shook it.

"And I'm Marcello. Nice to meet you," Marcello said while standing so close to Saskia that he could practically kiss her.

Paul wasn't sure how he got there, but the way Marcello's gaze raked over Saskia's body made him close his hands into fists while imagining different ways to punch him.

"Nice to meet you, too." Saskia extended her hand, hoping Marcello would take it so she could create distance from him. Marcello, instead, made small circles with his fingers on the back of her palm. She pulled her hand away and wiped it on her skirt.

Saskia looked at Paul. "My New York life is in the past, and I am here now looking forward to learning from Sherri," Saskia said, fearing a trap.

"Ain't she lucky?" Sherri's smile held no warmth as she walked toward the frosted glass office door and stood there. Then she said, "*Sass Kia,* how about you let us have a moment?"

Saskia nodded and quickly escaped just as Sherri firmly closed the glass door, which made a dull clang.

"What was that?" Bob stood in the middle of the lobby, briefcase in hand, ready to leave for the day.

Saskia opened and closed her mouth a couple of times before she replied, "I honestly don't know." Feeling the tears that threatened to emerge, she swallowed and focused on slowing her breathing.

"Wow. Well, newbie, you clearly found a way to piss her off," he chuckled as he loosened his necktie. "Good luck with that." Bob did a small salute and shook his head as he walked the rest of the way to the glass doors.

"Thanks," Saskia grumbled to the offbeat pang of the closing glass doors.

It was her first day. In a low-stakes job. How could Sherri already be her enemy? All day, she was polite, respectful, poised, and did everything she was asked and more. Nothing they had asked of her that day was difficult, so how could she have messed this up? This job was supposed to be easy, uncomplicated, and a simple way to earn some money until she knew what to do next, not a daily battle with a vindictive boss.

A dull rattle from the bottom of the desk drawer brought her back to the lobby. Saskia walked over and slid the drawer open. Inside, she could see her BlackBerry light up and rattle against her keys. With nothing else to lose, she lifted her phone from her bag and saw one unread text from Liam.

Sask! How is day 1?
Want to meet up for happy hour to celebrate?

Saskia quickly typed out,

You will not believe how messed up it was,
and my manager is an absolute monster so yes!

After hitting send, she let go of the phone, and it thudded into her purse.

As if Sherri saw the text, her door opened, and all three walked out, sharing a professional chuckle.

"That does sound like fun!" Sherri's voice stung like an accidental finger against a cheese grater. "Well, if you need anything while you are here, reach out to *Sass Kia*, and she'll organize it for you. Think of us as your personal concierge service," Sherri said with the kind of sultry bedroom voice that put Saskia on high alert.

After shaking Paul's hand, Sherri winked at Marcello while he fished in his pocket. Finding what he was looking for, he hugged Sherri, sliding his hand down her back until a small plastic bag holding a white powder landed in her back pocket.

Saskia's eyes widened and darted toward the computer screen. Her mind throttled into overdrive. Sweat pooled at the nape of her neck as memories of the flashbulbs and aggressive questions from the lawyers twisted her stomach.

"Are you sure you saw him in the office with the receptionist?"
"Yes."
"Aren't you also the one who spoke to the reporters about how TNC Bank's assets were being undervalued?"
"Yes."
"So, how can we trust you? This should have been handled internally."
"I'm sorry, I didn't know what to do."
"And that is why we have to fire you. Leave immediately. Do not stop at your desk,

do not talk to anyone else, or security will bring charges against you."

That last thought slowed the electricity coursing through her to a dull hum. After what she went through, she would pretend she didn't see anything. She would not risk her only income over something like this, no matter how low the income.

"Hey, Saskia. Uh, so, how, uh, how long have you been back in Orlando? And why didn't you tell me?" Paul's accent smoothed the blunt edges of the English language into something like a song. Its slow melody comforted her frayed nerves.

She looked up from the screen and met his eyes. "Oh, I have been back for a couple of months now. It was a big shift moving back here, and I took some time to figure out what I was going to do next, so I didn't want to get into it while I was supposed to be on vacation," Saskia said with a tone so falsely bright, she noticed it made Paul squirm.

"Ah, well, I'm glad I ran into you. I know we last left things on a sour note. I'm here for a conference. If you want to meet up while I am in town, let me know."

Paul searched her face, hoping she'd forgive him. For the last two weeks, he had tried to remember what exactly he had said at Didier's party. He could only remember Saskia's face collapsing, the beer in his face, and how she disappeared into the dark. The next day, he wanted to send her a bunch of texts, but between managing his dad and getting ready for this trip, all he could manage was the message he had sent earlier today.

"Let me think about it, and I'll get back to you. Does that work?" Saskia said.

Paul didn't believe her. "Sask, I am sorry for what I said, whatever it was."

"Not here. Not now. Paul."

How she clipped each phrase felt like she was snipping away at the connection between them. Paul didn't want her to cut away from him; he wanted to work this out. He wasn't going to lose her over a misunderstanding.

He grabbed a pen and the stack of pink Post-it notes from her desk. Pressing down with blue ink, Paul carved *The Royal Hotel, International Drive* into the pad. He pulled the top note and pasted it on her computer screen as Marcello clapped him on the back.

"Ready to go, bro? We gotta get to the conference before happy hour." Marcello didn't even wait for Paul to respond as he pushed Paul across the lobby to the front doors.

"Ciao, chicas, and thank you, Sherri," Marcello said.

"Call me!" Paul shouted just as the glass doors closed.

"Well. That was certainly something, wasn't it?" Sherri said as she sat on the edge of Saskia's desk.

The invasion of her space brought back the humming current, leaving her speechless and only able to nod slowly at Sherri's dumb question. Sherri looked over at the wall clock as the windows rattled from the roar of an engine in the parking lot.

"You know what, Saskia, go ahead and leave early. We can pick up where we left off tomorrow. Good work today." Sherri didn't even look at Saskia as she stood up from the desk and disappeared into her office.

When Sherri's door clicked shut, Saskia didn't hesitate. After sending an email to Sherri recounting the conversation and thanking her for the early dismissal, Saskia shut down her computer. She stared at the Post-it note for what felt like ages, pulled it from the screen and into her purse for later consideration. Then she texted Liam:

I'm on my way, and holy hell…
Have I got a story for you.

Seven. Sept. Sèt.

"What a rush, right, *wajon?*" Marcello draped his arm over Paul's shoulders as they walked through the expansive atrium of the conference center. The latticed glass and steel beams soared above them like a commercial-grade aquarium, only they were the fish, and the rocks were sound-absorbing, industrial red and green carpet.

"Sure, but we were always centimeters from dying," Paul replied, exasperated by this never-ending conversation. He twitched as two kids ran past them. His body was still humming with adrenaline from the close calls. How Marcello ignored every traffic law Florida had on offer only sharpened the humming.

They had been debating this throughout hotel check-in, dropping off his luggage, and the walk through the atrium.

"Bro, but we didn't, and that's what makes it fun. What's the big deal, *marica?*"

Paul sighed to avoid exploding at Marcello. Why were the people in his life so committed to dancing on the edge of death and then called him crazy? He liked the life he was living and wanted to keep investing in Haiti's future by finding a new product that could set the country apart. He loved beach days and mountain hikes. Life was good. Why risk it?

The recycled air of the atrium made Paul cough, and he took the moment to find his next words carefully. "Marcello, it's almost like you want to die in a fiery crash instead of just slowing down and letting life take you where it is going to take you."

The arms drooped over his shoulders, grew heavy, and no longer felt warm and brotherly.

A flash of deep sadness crossed Marcello's face, shocking Paul— maybe he was right about his longtime friend.

"Ha, *wajon,* no way!" Marcello recovered quickly and sucked his teeth as he tightened his grip. Releasing Paul from the friendly chokehold, he started flexing his arms like he was a bodybuilder. "But wouldn't that be an epic way to go? I'd be a total legend." He danced around like he scored a game-winning goal for an invisible stadium of fans.

Paul rolled his eyes and walked ahead of Marcello. He was there for something important: to bring Haiti onto the world stage for something other than its notorious poverty. After months of talking about this conference, why didn't Marcello understand why this was important? Between the random trip to the bank and the cutting through traffic, Paul started to wonder if this conference wasn't really important to Marcello.

And then there was Saskia. He could feel his shoulders relax at the memory of her at the bank. But something about the whole exchange just felt wrong. Whenever she came down to Haiti, she was a different person. Relaxed, fun, and carefree. Her hair was always loose, and her smiles came naturally. Her giggles danced in time with the rhythm of the constant island breezes. For the past month, she was all bound up, artificial. Her hair slicked back, pulled tight into a bun, and her eyes were all sharp edges. All his favorite parts of her were caged up, and for what? How did she end up there? Did she even want to be there?

His muffled footsteps transitioned to squeaky ones as Paul walked from the carpeted atrium to the tiled hallway. He picked up the pace, his footfalls thundering through the cavernous hallway. If he walked a little faster, he could ignore the need to push Marcello, to push aside the heavy thoughts in his head.

"Eh, what was the deal with that girl? What a tight ass, right, *marica?*" Marcello said, catching up to Paul.

"Oh, it's nothing. We met a long time ago and kind of lost touch. I was just surprised to see her there. She was doing big things in New York, but something obviously happened. She's smart, has her stuff together."

"OK? But did you tap that?" Marcello asked as he bumped into Paul.

"What?! No. We're just friends." Paul flushed and picked up the pace, almost to a light jog.

"Huh, interesting. Yeah, women like that, you gotta watch out. But… You don't mind if I tap that?"

Paul stopped and whipped around to face Marcello. The wolfish look on his face triggered college memories of Marcello's near-constant parade of women. Paul wouldn't allow her to be added to that parade.

"Bro, what? Marcello, you absolutely cannot do that to her."

"Do what, *marica?*" Marcello asked in a tone that brought Paul back to every moment when they were about to do something very, very stupid.

The pair stopped behind the other conference attendees at the check-in line, and Paul lowered his voice to continue, "Marcello, I've known you since college, and this is what you always do. You find a nice girl and all you want to do is make her believe she has a chance, then you sleep with her, and it destroys her. Saskia is too nice to do that, too. Stay away, ok?" Paul noticed Marcello was calculating something.

"You sure you don't like her? She's just a friend?" Marcello waited a moment and then continued, "Because if that's all it is, you don't really get to say what I can and can't do."

Paul grabbed Marcello by the shirt and lowered his voice, "I swear to you, I am willing to throw out seven years of friendship if you mess with her. Do. Not. Mess. With. Her."

Marcello raised his hands and said, "Ok, bro."

Paul let go of his shirt, but the men kept their eyes locked on each other.

"*Wajon*," Marcello whispered, "you gotta get that attitude checked. It's not healthy for you to go around grabbing guys' shirts over church mouse girls like…"

"Welcome, gentlemen, to the Food Science of Tomorrow Conference! Can I have your names?" A woman behind a blue-covered check-in table shouted, but neither man responded.

"Seriously? Can you please move? Some of us have places to be." A voice from the line shouted.

Paul broke, gave a throwaway apology to the line, stepped up to check in, and received his name tag with a blue ribbon attached, bearing the words *Rising Star* in gold.

Marcello followed and received his name tag as well. Cleared to enter the conference, they approached the ballroom in an uncomfortable silence. He said, "I think I am going to get a drink. I'll catch you later."

Before Paul could respond, Marcello abandoned him and disappeared into the crowd. Paul let the conference-goers stream past him to join the party as he shivered from the arctic air of the hall.

"You know, I always thought he was a tricky customer," said a familiar voice.

Paul turned, and behind him stood a short, round man wearing a canvas vest with khaki pants. Round eyeglasses proudly framed bushy gray eyebrows, and a white elastic held up his plasticized name tag.

"Professor Oakley!" Paul rushed toward the man for a handshake, and the professor hugged him instead.

"Oh, you know you just need to call me Tom. It's so good to see you, Paul." Tom held Paul at an arm's length, examining him. "You haven't changed a bit. Let's go take a sit over by the planter, and you can catch me up on what is going on."

Paul nodded in reply, and then followed his favorite professor to the bench. As they exchanged life updates, he looked back to see Marcello watching them, jealousy darkening his features.

...

"And so that is how we were able to make mango sugar. We're still testing to see if it can be the lower glucose option, but the early tests are promising."

Professor Oakley clapped Paul on the back in approval. It had been an hour. Both men had set aside their name tags and had tousled their hair as they wrestled with Paul's research approach. Cocktail napkins with blue scrawled calculations layered between conference agendas with notes in the margins.

"That is some really amazing work there. Next year, maybe you all could be the next major sponsors? You know we always need donors for the science scholarships," Tom said, poking Paul's shoulder like he did when Paul was a student.

"Ha, ha, let's see if we get a buyer first. You know things have been so good at home. Haiti is on the rise; we're getting traffic lights and reliable electricity. You can practically eat off the roads. Factories are going up, and the economy seems to flow."

"Wow! I'm glad to hear it. I know it was a bit touch and go there for a bit."

"Yeah, but I think we are finally out of the mess we had been in. I think it's finally safe enough to relax and really invest, you know? I'm actually thinking about asking Marcello to invest in the mango sugar processing factory since his family does some of that in Colombia."

Paul noticed Tom's face drop a bit and braced for what came next.

Then he said, "Paul, I think you should reconsider how close you keep Marcello. You know, I always thought he wasn't really deserving of your company. Frankly, I worried he would derail you and keep you from achieving what I thought you deserved. But there are some things I've learned since he chose to expand his father's *business* here." Tom slowly shook his head, unable to look Paul in the face.

Confused, Paul asked, "What do you mean? I've known him for years. He knows my dad very well. There's no way he could be doing anything bad."

Tom turned to Paul and looked him straight in the eye. "Paul, it's just rumors, but several people here think he's using his father's business as a front. I can't get into the details, but please promise me you will keep your distance from Marcello and maybe even your dad until I can get more information."

"More information? What is this, some CIA mission?"

"No, Paul, but word gets around. I want to verify it's true before telling you."

"Telling him what?" Marcello said as he walked up to the pair, his eyes glassy.

Tom blanched and stuttered as he struggled to find the right words. "I didn't want to ruin the surprise, but I think you might get considered to join the board, Paul," Tom said. "Especially if you are successful with the mango sugar, they'll absolutely want you to join the board."

Paul sat a moment to take in the information, knowing there was a chance it was just a story for Tom to have some cover. Unsure of what was going on, Paul decided it was safer to play along.

"Wow. Really, Tom?" Searching his favorite professor's face, he hoped that this wasn't a lie and that it really was something worth celebrating.

He'd positioned himself to join the board for a couple of years but couldn't quite figure out how to balance the rigors of being an academic with the demands of being a business owner. If he were honest, that was at the heart of the conflict with his dad. Reginald wanted mind-blowing profits yesterday. Paul wanted to make investments and conduct research that could pay off later.

"Obviously, there are several steps before it's official." The sincerity in Tom's voice meant that it had to be true, that his work would actually be recognized and celebrated.

"*Wajon*, there's an after-party we need to get to," Marcello said, swaying to stay upright.

Tom placed a protective hand on Paul's shoulder and said, "We weren't exactly finished here."

"Listen, old man," Marcello barked, "I came here with Paul, so I am leaving with Paul." Marcello looked over at him and said, "Let's go."

Paul sat back and quickly weighed his options. Going out with Marcello was like going out with a celebrity. He had all the connections at every club, and they never did anything less than VIP. Gorgeous women swirled around them, all ready to chase away the demons. Inevitably, there would be drugs. Inevitably, there would be moments he'd never remember. Nights out with Marcello were always a good time, but they always felt a bit forced, like Paul couldn't really leave.

A plastic edge dug into Paul's thigh from his pant pocket. He touched the card from earlier in the day. *Tend to the Guardian Within.* Paul sighed as he could almost hear the old lady's voice and knew what he needed to do.

He steadied his voice and said, "Honestly, I think I will stay. I have my session tomorrow and want to be rested."

Marcello stumbled back from the pair as if Paul had punched him. He stood for a moment, working through what to do next, because he always got his way. Finally, he said, "Fine. Do what you want, but there will be consequences."

Like a wounded animal, Marcello stumbled toward the exit of the building, kicking a nearby trash can in his way.

Once he was out of earshot, Paul said to Tom, "That was a little much, right?"

Tom sat quietly for a while. Finally, he decided to respond and said, "Yeah, but not surprising from what I heard. It sounds like he has become what you kids call 'cray cray.'"

Paul cringed and shook his head.

Tom chuckled before becoming serious and said, "He also knows some dangerous people, so be careful with him. Ok?"

Paul could hear the worry threaded between each word. It stitched itself to his slowly growing anxiety about the future. Since this morning, Paul had been jostled from one bizarre scenario to another. Each one unsettled him and made him crave a shower and a book in the hopes he could regain his grip on his life. Instead, here he was with a beloved professor who somehow kept up with his former students.

For a moment, Paul considered sharing his suspicions about his father and Marcello, but what could Tom do? Besides, these were just thoughts, feelings, not facts. Paul couldn't point to a single bit of hard evidence that either man was dangerous or untrustworthy. They were just a little aloof and a little closed off. That was likely due to them handling too many projects at once and not being fully present in their lives. No, it was better to keep these thoughts to himself until he could be sure that he had facts rooted in something concrete. Tom's worry challenged Paul's careful arguments that kept him believing in his connections.

"Yeah, yeah, I'll be careful," Paul said, "And I think I'm ready to head to the hotel. I didn't really have a chance to settle in before the conference."

Tom nodded, and after saying their goodbyes, Paul began his walk back to the hotel. He had picked the recommended hotel, which was supposed to be only a fifteen-minute walk through the convention center. However, ten steps in, the walk felt like an hours-long trek through a tube of recycled air. In Haiti, only extreme privilege and gallons of gas for the generator gave him access to this kind of air conditioning. But in the States? It was everywhere, and it was stifling. Since he arrived, he hadn't been exposed to the natural air for more than thirty minutes, and his breath grew so shallow he could barely breathe under the weight of the day. He walked toward the nearest exit like the last desperate strokes of a swimmer on the cusp of drowning.

When the automatic doors slid apart, the slightly humid air blasted Paul, and he gasped and took in deep breaths. Drinking in every molecule, as if he broke through the water's surface. The late afternoon sun softened the heat into a warm blanket instead of the soaked towel of high noon. Paul closed his eyes and could hear the persistent traffic and the passing conversations of other conference-goers. Another deep breath, and the tension of the day began evaporating into the air. He took in another deep breath, and the only smells he could identify were car exhaust and air conditioning. The U.S. always smelled like this: mechanic, sterile. The layers of development smoothing out the layers until it was only one note. It made Paul miss the vibrant smells of Haiti, of the ongoing cycle of death feeding life. Even sitting by the warehouse that morning, he could smell the trash fire down the way mixed with sea air and various crops from the field. Haiti was bursting with life, while the U.S. seemed to have paved over the life; they had to build yet another shopping mall.

A cement awning connected the convention center to the parking garage, which was later connected to his hotel. Paul crossed the street and walked along the garage. With each step, the chaos shuffled in his mind until it landed into neat little boxes. Regardless of what his father and Marcello are up to, he was connected to them and relied on them. What would he even do if he ended those relationships? He didn't have the contacts or the money to be okay on his own. He'd need something undeniable to reconsider those relationships.

Rapid footsteps broke Paul's train of thought, and before he could blink a fist landed on his left cheek. His flesh tore open under the pressure. The pain was so intense, so immediate, everything went dark.

Eight. Huit. Uit.

Drained from such a strange first day, Saskia decided to avoid the mind-numbingly straight highways for a more interesting drive through the neighborhoods to give her time to think. Her tires rolled over red brick, to smooth pavement, to roads dotted with holes, desperate for attention. She passed small bungalows with darling window boxes and sprawling mansions that looked like pages from a magazine.

Saskia turned down a quiet neighborhood road and slowed to watch the gray curls of Spanish moss sway in the breeze. There must have been hundreds of these parasitic chains carpeting the sky above her. Saskia rolled down her windows to let the outside air in.

After the confusing day at the bank, Saskia closed her eyes, just for a second, and wiggled her fingers on the wheel in an attempt to let go of everything that had happened. From here, she couldn't hear the cars from the neighboring highway or moments of conversation she'd catch on her commutes in New York. Now all she could hear, smell, and see was tranquility. In that stolen moment, Saskia finally understood why people around the country thought this place was heaven.

An earsplitting screech pierced her thoughts, and she jumped out of her seat. Her eyelids flew open to see a male peacock on display just five feet in front of her car. Saskia shifted her gear into park and sat mesmerized by the rippling of his feathers. The blues and greens speckled with yellows dazzled her, until he squawked again. Another squawk broke Saskia out of this spell entirely.

Annoyed with the earsplitting screeches, Saskia started honking at the peacock, hoping to scare him off. Instead, he just squawked right back and then jumped onto the hood of her car. Saskia didn't remember screaming until a voice yelled at her to stop. She paused and looked at an older gentleman looking out from a small yellow bungalow. He calmly beckoned the peacock back toward him. The peacock politely folded his feathers, jumped off the car, and tottered out of the road and toward the man.

"Sorry about that! He gets a little territorial," he shouted. With shaky hands, Saskia waved at the man, slowly released the brake, and drove the rest of the way, vigilant and not at all relaxed.

About ten minutes later, she found a street-side spot just down the street from the neon red sign for *Pounders*. Still shaking, she walked toward the club and spotted a man on the other side of the road with several protest posters leaning on wooden stakes. They said things like:

You will burn. Repent. Sodomy is a direct line to hell.
When the world ends, who will be your savior?

His voice rasped into his bullhorn variations of his signs. She rolled her eyes and stayed focused on the club entrance, ignoring the increasingly personal bullhorn harassment. In the city, she'd gotten used to men like him as they were all over the place yelling about all sorts of sins and the need to repent. There, she could disappear into a crowd and ignore him. But this protester made her nervous. The streets were empty, and his protest felt targeted, personal. She walked a bit faster until she was safely inside *Pounders*, hidden away from the outside world.

"Five bucks and ID, please," said a bouncer in drag, who looked like they'd rather be anywhere else.

After completing the exchange, Saskia entered the central room of her favorite club in all of Orlando. In front of her, slow pop jams beckoned her to another bar and stage for that night's drag show. To her right, quietly thumping dance music served as the soundtrack for the patio-facing bar. At night, the club's lighting and various rooms created a feeling of safety. It was here that Saskia felt like she could relax and have fun. Now, the bright afternoon sun mixed with overhead lighting put everything in the club into sharp focus. She could see the scuffs from shoes, cracked paint, and the layers upon layers of spilled drinks that had built a sticky layer of well-loved grime. Without the crowds, the music melded and wrapped her in the competing tracks. Finally, her shoulders relaxed.

Not a single one of her straight friends really understood why Saskia almost exclusively went to *Pounders*. It was a gay club after all, and the chance for a storybook romance was an absolute zero. But for Saskia, *Pounders* was safe. The other places in town made her feel like a dangling animal for starved alligators. So, she'd dance smaller, dress quieter, all to avoid being club prey. But at *Pounders*, she could just be. *Pounders* felt like a literal no-judgement zone. It didn't matter if she wore a daring plunge dress and let loose on the dance floor, or her office clothes to get a drink with a friend; it didn't matter. *Pounders* was her safe place.

For a few precious moments, Saskia closed her eyes and let herself be embraced by the music and dewy air. Her shoulders relaxed, her cheeks no longer throbbed from the hours of forced smiles. She felt at home. Taking in a deep breath, Saskia tried to quiet the mutinous tears that had been plotting their exit the moment Sherri called her into her office hours ago. Letting out a deep breath, she calmed and flitted her eyes open again.

Then she spotted him. Her bald-headed best friend, Liam, had claimed a spot at the bar with a perfect view of the patio and the dance floor. Wearing a neon pink t-shirt and Lucky jeans that clung to all the right places, he casually drained the liquid from the plastic cup. Everyone in the room stole glances at him, but Liam didn't even notice.

He seductively waved Saskia over in time to Lady Gaga's "Love Game," earning him a few more stolen glances.

Saskia briefly wondered what it must be like to have that kind of magnetism and not to worry about the watcher's underlying intentions. In her experience, that kind of spotlight inevitably attracted people who dedicated their lives to clinically assessing her like a specimen in a lab. Saskia's name made her stand out enough. Strangers used it as a reason to ask all sorts of personal questions.

"Where did your parents find that name? It sounds exotic."

"Oh, hey baby, that's hot. I'd love to get closer to you, Sask."

After years of figuring out how to deal with such invasions, she just wanted to blend in, to be normal.

And yet, on lonelier nights, she'd burn for the kind of attention made famous by books and movies. The kind of slow, seductive, undressing gaze leaving her unmoored to drift into the arms of someone who actually cared, unlike Paul, the king of mixed signals. But here at *Pounders*, she'd get exactly what she wanted: to disappear into the club's decor.

Saskia took stock of the people in the room. A happy hour for gay professionals electrified the air at *Pounders*. In the middle of the dance floor, a group of men mingled amongst themselves, dressed in their mid-class Miami club attire. Men in tiny red and blue shorts weaved among them with trays of little neon shots while colorful lights speckled their bodies. It all seemed a bizarrely perfect way to end her day: an afternoon party with shirtless men.

Saskia playfully sashayed her way to Liam and the melting vodka soda. Freeing her hair from the ponytail holder and removing her blazer, Saskia closed her eyes to sway to Nelly Furtado's "Promiscuous Girl." Suddenly, ice and unknown beverages rained down as she crashed into professionally dressed bodies.

"Hey! Watch where you're going!" said a now drink-soaked man. "This is *not* how I was trying to get wet, sweetie."

"Yeah, the straight bar is on the other end of the block," said his friend.

Mortified, Saskia offered replacements and scurried to a laughing Liam.

"Well, that's one way to make an entrance," Liam said between chuckles.

Saskia shot him her sharpest glare and returned to the dance floor to make amends. After setting everything right, Saskia shuffled back to Liam at the bar and struggled to get her shorter frame onto the stool. Wasting no time, the pair dove into the details of their respective holidays between gulps of their drinks.

"So… yes, my cousin's toddler stole Johanna's thong and was running around the house with it. Johanna was so embarrassed. To make things worse, all the aunties jumped into a whole debate on whether Johanna should be wearing thongs in the first place. All Johanna could do was just sit there and listen to the debate until the story moved on." Saskia laughed as she set down her drink.

"Well, that's better than what happened at our little Florida farm in Arcadia," Liam said carefully.

Saskia perked up. "What happened?"

"Well, Josh and I got into a fight. I accused him of being a homophobe, and he accused me of being a pedophile. When I brought up his underage girlfriend, and everyone in the living room took my side, he stomped off and drove off on his ATV. A couple of minutes later, we could hear gunshots in the forest."

"Oh my god, is he okay?"

"Oh yeah, before we had a chance to go look for him, Josh rolled up in the ATV all proud and covered in the boar's blood, and our dad just stood there, stared, and said, 'Josh, what in the hell? Were you trying to kill the thing or wear it?' Josh was so pissed, he threw the dead hog toward the house and drove off again into the woods. We didn't even hear him come back in later that night. We just saw the bloody footprints all the way up the stairs."

Saskia let the music from the speakers wrap around them and give space to Liam's story. Every time he went home, he came back with stories that would feed her nightmares for months. She couldn't share what she really thought, so instead she said, "Yikes, I mean, I am glad he's okay, but is he really okay?"

"I have no idea." Liam took a long swig from his vodka soda.

When he set the clear plastic cup down on the lacquered bar, Saskia could see his face harden a bit. For as long as she had known him, Liam's family danced on the delicate line between acceptable violence and criminal violence.

"I guess it reminded me of when I came out to them. Mom had to take me away for a couple of days while the rest destroyed what they needed to. Then she brought us back and cleaned up before the media could find out before Dad's next re-election campaign. But I'm just tired of all of this drama. I decided I'll only go back to Arcadia two times a year. I just don't want to be in all that anymore. It's just too much." Liam drained what was left of his vodka soda and signaled to the bartender for another one.

"It's a little funny how I have only met your mom. It still makes me sad for you that the rest of your family didn't come to our graduation." She swirled her plastic cup as if to stir up the memory.

"Exactly. Maybe we are just a transactional family," Liam said in a voice so hollow and brittle it made Saskia desperate to ease his pain.

Unsure of how to help Liam, Saskia offered, "Well, I guess that means you can do more of those fun side trips after your disaster recovery assignments?"

Liam gave her a sidelong look and took a hearty gulp from his fresh vodka soda.

"Yes," Liam finally said. "I just wish I were taking those trips for fun and not to avoid my unhinged family."

Squeezing his hand and giving a gentle rub on his shoulder, Saskia responded, "Yeah, that's fair. But things always change, so you might only have to do that for a couple of years? I don't know, families are weird."

Liam tapped his plastic cup against hers, and they sipped at their drinks in silence while Saskia looked for what to say next.

Finally, she set down her glass and said, "And… the upside is you get to avoid the tourists on I4."

Liam gave a small smile and a nod as Saskia watched his mind cycle through the never-ending debate: find a way to make this place a home or build a life somewhere else. Sensing that she was losing him, she switched the direction of the conversation.

"So, tell me what happened today at work, Saski. Your texts seemed a little cagey."

She rolled her eyes and made a face. "Well, I am bored to tears because this is so far from managing my team in New York. My boss hates me because I was in New York, and I ran into Paul."

Liam paused mid-sip, and his eyes grew wide. "Forget the boring work details. We're talking about Paul? Like Paul, moonlit dancing and sparks by the bonfire, Paul? Like the Paul you keep running into when you travel to Haiti, and you obsess over, but he never commits? *That* Paul?"

Saskia glared at Liam. "I don't obsess. I like spending time with him. It's not complicated, except now it is since I saw him over the Christmas holidays."

Liam rolled his eyes. "Riiiight, that whole thing. So, what happened now?"

"Well, he walked into the bank with some guy I've never seen, but gave me the creeps, and—" the rattling of her BlackBerry against the lacquered bar startled her. Looking at her phone, she saw a text from Mom.

Noticing the time, Saskia said, "Ah, I should get going. I promised my mom I would be home around five-thirty, and that's going to be impossible in five o'clock traffic." Saskia winced, waiting for Liam's response.

"Ugh, fine, go. But you owe me an update on what happened," Liam said to Saskia as she jumped off the stool while chugging her water.

She hugged Liam hard and scurried through the crowd until she was through *Pounders* front door.

Turning around on his barstool, Liam signaled to the bartender for another round. Above the wall of liquor, Liam noticed a T.V. in the corner flashing white and red *Breaking News*. As the text wiped away, a map of Haiti perched itself to the left of Wolf Blitzer. The ticker below announced that an earthquake had just rocked the capital. Liam immediately pulled out his iPhone and texted Saskia.

Hey, Haiti is in the news. I think there was an earthquake. Is your family okay?

Liam's phone started pinging as his work colleagues started planning the logistics of getting down to Haiti.

What do you think? Do we need to bring all the supplies, or do you think we could source them there?

Dude, the dust hasn't even settled yet, the counts haven't started, how can we even talk about logistics?

I'm just trying to be prepared. If the reports are right, this one is gonna be mega. Maybe we can tag along with CNN or something?

Yeah, from what I am hearing, everything is gone, so we might have to get creative. This really sucks. They were just starting to turn around.

I know! Tough break. But it will be a great assignment. Have you ever tried the food?

None of the texts was the one he wanted. Each second his phone stayed silent without a reply from Saskia, the harder he'd jab the red plastic stirrer into his drink. When the stirrer finally snapped, he remembered that when Saskia drove, she completely fell off the grid. Setting down his phone for the fifteenth time, Liam ordered another.

Nine. Neuf. Nèf.

Since the day she got her driver's license, she eliminated as many barriers as possible between her and the outside world. With the windows down, sunroof open, and a radio-sponsored sing-along on her hometown roads, Saskia always found peace. At the stoplights she'd throw her head back and sing to the Spanish moss swinging from the oaks; she'd sing to the long-legged herons and eagle-eyed osprey overhead; she'd sing to the kids staring at her from their car seats. These were the moments where she felt most alive and the most free. At home, she played the role of peacemaker. At work, she pretended to be whoever her boss needed in the hope of onward success. But in the car, she could play whatever role she wanted, and today she was a Pussycat Doll.

Saskia pulled into the driveway of her parents' home and let the engine run as her imaginary bandmates closed in on the chorus. She belted at the closing windows with all the angsty yearning the song demanded. Dramatically throwing her head back to her seat, she watched the sunroof lazily march to a close. Just as the hanging ceiling cloth stopped moving in response to the Florida breeze, her car doors flew open, and her mom and siblings climbed in.

"Saskia, there's been an earthquake *en Haïti*," Jacqueline shouted. Her normally tidy hair was wild, set free by worry.

"Wait, what? What do you mean?" Saskia didn't understand. She'd only ever heard of earthquakes on the Dominican Republic side of the island, never on their side.

"Yeah, Saski, it's very, very bad," said her younger sister, Johanna, with a voice ready to break apart in grief. "We were watching the news and—"

"Johanna, now is not the time," said Jacqueline. "Saskia, I'll tell you as you drive. We have to go. Now!"

"Ok, ok." With shaking hands, she moved the gearshift and backed out of the driveway. Pressing hard on the gas, she hugged the turns until they got to the traffic light to exit the neighborhood. She went to flip on her blinker but didn't know which way to turn.

"Wait, where are we going?" Saskia turned to her mother. Rage and fear had contorted her mother's beautiful face in a way that left Jacqueline's face completely vacant, her eyes staring somewhere far away.

Sensing their mother didn't hear Saskia, Robert, her younger brother, quietly said, "We have to go to Tatie Marcel's house. Everyone is gathering there and staying up to date on what is happening. We only heard from Tante Alice, but no news yet from anyone else."

Saskia turned to face her younger brother. Unsure of what to do after college, Robert chose to work at the local car repair shop. He sat in her back seat, nervously picking at the black grease crusting his nails.

"You don't think…" Saskia trailed off.

Robert and Johanna shook their heads and shrugged. Jacqueline shut off the radio, plunging the car into muffled silence.

"Saskia, if you cannot stop with the questions and just drive, then give me the keys," Jacqueline snarled.

Quivering with adrenaline, Saskia turned around, and when the light turned green, she turned left.

They drove in stifling silence, each digesting what all of this could mean.

Johanna and Robert each stared out of their respective windows and responded to the occasional text.

Jacqueline just stared straight ahead, occasionally looking at her phone as calls came in and ended.

Saskia bit her lip with every question she wanted to ask but put aside for later.

After twenty minutes, they approached and turned to face the familiar red-brick wall with the gold text for *Shadow Lakes*. Known as a highly sought-after neighborhood, the houses varied in shades of the same model, meant to create a sense of conformity and comfort. Saskia hated the nondescript parade of homes. Of course, her cousins loved it. They'd find creative ways to weave into every conversation how it was just "So American!" and "So nice!" Saskia suspected they loved it because it provided the predictability that had been lacking in their not-so-past lives in Haiti.

Normally, she struggled to pick out the house marked 817, but today it stuck out. The butter-yellow house with white accents and a porch swing would have looked like every other house on the block if it weren't for all the cars.

At least ten cars politely crammed together along the street, careful not to block a driveway or squish the curated lawns. Saskia slid in at the end of the line, parked, and cut off the engine. A few moments passed, and no one moved. They all sat there, staring out their windows, hardly noticing that the car had stopped moving.

Jacqueline broke the silence and said, "Tatie Marcel will have all the details, but I think everyone is okay. Before we left the news said the epicenter was downtown, and no one in the family was downtown at this time of day." Jacqueline turned toward her children, her face slack. "I already talked to your dad, and he will meet us here. Everyone inside will be scrambling to find their family and friends, so be respectful. No loud music, no asking to leave because you are bored, no bothering Tatie Marcel with anything. If you need something, ask me or Saskia. Got it?"

The siblings looked at each other and said nothing. Jacqueline asked again, but this time through gritted teeth, "I said, got it?" she clipped.

"Got it," they said in unison.

"But you know that we're not teenagers anymore, right, Mom?" Johanna said.

Robert and Saskia exchanged a scared glance through the rearview mirror as they braced for what came next.

Jacqueline slowly turned to face Johanna and stared straight into her eyes. "Do you really want to have *that* debate today? Because who is still eating my food? Who still needs me to remind them to do their chores and keep up with their homework?"

Johanna shrank down in her seat.

"Exactly," Jacqueline replied coolly. Then she exited the car and slammed the door shut.

"Good job, Jo. Now we get to deal with that when we get home," Robert said as he left the car.

Saskia let the two go inside before turning to Johanna, "I don't think you deserved that, but be gentle with them, okay? You know how our family is, and I can't imagine this is going to be easy."

Johanna just nodded in response and slammed the car door closed as she exited the car.

Saskia sighed, grabbed her purse, and followed her family into the house.

On any other day, walking into Tatie Marcel's house meant music, wax-infused smells from several candles, and a warm invitation from Tatie to sit in the kitchen for coffee. The house Saskia walked into now was nothing like that. Instead, this house felt like an anxious airport where all the flights had been canceled. The collection of adults who shaped Saskia's life became abandoned passengers, unsure of where to go or what to do next. The normally levelheaded, exuberant adults evaporated into tremoring elders hunched over their devices, praying to be spared from the worst.

It had been twenty years since the Roys had left Port-au-Prince, and while they kept close ties with their families in Haiti, they needed support in handling the day-to-day and the holidays when it was too dangerous to journey home. This community eased the loss of brothers, sisters, aunts, uncles, and parents. Navigating the oddities of "American Life" bound them together as closely as blood. To Saskia, this was her Orlando family. The people who had a joke at the ready for any ailment of the heart and made every graduation and every holiday memorable.

From her chosen family, Saskia only knew love, warmth, joy, and safety. Normally, from the minute the door opened, the Roys would completely transform. Hair would come out of scrunchies, and shoulders would relax. Voices would expand as they joined the vibrant tapestry that their community would weave with their individual mixtures of French, Haitian Creole or kreyól, and English. Some would go up an octave, and others down. Chuckles and giggles replaced breaths between words. Sentences never ended. Turns of phrase were never meant literally. Instead, they were the spice or *epice* that turned a trip to the grocery store into the spiciest, most hilarious story of the year. If two people went on the same trip to the grocery store, the story would be completely different depending on who was doing the telling.

Each person had their words that kept them connected to the lives they left behind. They would string into their own patterns, their verbal comfort blanket. Papa used Creole when he told a joke. English and French were for reasonable political discussions. An explosive combination of all three were used if anyone dared defend Duvalier, the father/son dictator duo, who left a bloody and controversial legacy. Someone *always* tried to defend Duvalier. And if anyone brought up Aristide? The house would shudder in the debate, the children hoping the walls survived.

Jacqueline expertly mixed French and English to demonstrate her years of grooming to be the cosmopolitan wife and mother of every man's dream. But give her enough *kremas*, her favorite rum and condensed milk cocktail, and the *kreyól* would start flowing like the *kremas*. And if the *zen* or gossip was *épicé* or spicy enough? The *kreyól* would dig in and be there *pi rèd ankò*.

These moments were the unique threads that reminded them of the people they used to be. Doctors, bankers, engineers, the elite of a country made famous by its bygone glory and legendary suffering. At the time, each of their weddings were featured in the newspaper, *Le Nouvelliste*, and celebrated on *Radio Métropole*. They were small country celebrities. But when friends began disappearing, and violence slowly crept from the poorer neighborhoods over their walls around their homes, all they could do was run and find safety. In finding safety, they discarded everything frivolous, anything too beautiful to lighten the load. They discarded everything they had until they could neatly fit into their new American boxes. They became convenience shop owners or permanently placed middle managers in a country with a tenuous relationship with skin color.

They learned quickly: keep your head down, and you might enjoy whatever you had built. As each family member released the people they used to be, the gathering habits changed, too. At first, Saturday nights at Tatie Marcel's brought the whole community together. The mothers would bring dishes that took days to make, creating a decadent feast that couldn't be found anywhere else in town. But as work hours went longer and kids' schedules grew busier, no one had days to prepare a dish, let alone an hour. These Haitians mixed spruced-up Costco appetizers with those prized dishes so the parties that went until sunrise could wrap up with a clean kitchen by 10:30 p.m. They adapted and did what they could to protect the slowly fraying connections to the country that had given so much, but had robbed them of almost everything else.

Coming to the U.S. in the 1980s and 1990s was critical to the survival of these families, and each carried a unique scar from the transformation. Some romanticized Haiti until they forgot why they left. Others religiously chose French fries over *diri kole* as evidence of their American loyalty in case anyone came asking. While the American grind was leaving its mark, returning to Haiti wasn't possible. Stories of chaos and mind-bending violence made twelve-hour shifts seem reasonable. The kidnappings, the deportations, each one weighed more heavily than the next. Every member of that Orlando family had a story, had a person who served as a reminder of why a life could not be built back home. A reminder of why no matter how bad things got in the States, their horror-laced gratitude kept them in Orlando.

Somewhere deep in the house, her aunt's familiar voice screamed for answers. "Where is he? Where is Jean-Bernard? Why isn't he answering?" Her children's voices could only respond with a hollow, "Mom, I don't know."

Around Saskia, others quietly shook their heads, afraid to voice a possibility that might come true. Then, Tatie Marcel emerged from the recesses of her home, stomping her way toward the living room. Like an ocean-fed storm about to release its fury, her gray bathrobe billowed with the movement and chased away the guests in her path.

Saskia had never met this version of her aunt before. Tatie Marcel was the family beacon. Never a stray hair, her makeup always perfect, she wondered if it was tattooed on. Tatie led the family through every crisis with a calm assuredness that made even the near-death experiences seem manageable. When Robert "accidentally" stole a car and was trapped in a warehouse near the airport, he called Tatie Marcel instead of their parents, and within two hours, everything was resolved as if nothing had happened. Tatie Marcel hadn't even chipped a nail. Saskia could only dream of being as flawless as her.

But this unceremoniously unraveled woman scared Saskia. Between the wild hair and bare feet, Tatie Marcel had devolved into a "Marie La Folle" or a crazy woman found in every Haitian folklore. A silent stream of tears flowed from her unseeing eyes, darting all over the house, not even registering Saskia and Johanna in the foyer.

As the pair passed, Saskia could hear Tatie Marcel mutter, over and over, "Where is he?"

In her wake floated the older women of the group, worry lining their faces. Once in the living room, Tatie Marcel roared at Wolf Blitzer, "Where is he? He was supposed to be home an hour ago."

Wolf ignored her and kept delivering the facts and details of how the town they all called home had crumbled to dust.

Saskia and Johanna cautiously approached the living room, just in time to see their mom place a comforting hand on Tatie Marcel's shoulder and another offering her a small white pill with a glass of water. Tatie Marcel took it, slowing the silent stream of tears, her breathing returning to an even pace. Around the living room, adults sat frozen in various positions, locked onto CNN's coverage, the contrast from the adults who sang and danced through anything. Watching Port-au-Prince crack open was the last blow to their armor. The moment almost made her cry.

"Why are they watching CNN?" Saskia asked Johanna, who stood next to her.

"Nowhere else was covering it. It's the only place where we could see what was happening," Johanna said quietly.

As Saskia settled against the couch, an eerie backtrack of voices wrapped around her, echoing off the tile flooring.

We have breaking news from Port-au-Prince.

They found Ti Charles! He's with Sassine, but their house is gone.

Rachelle is safe. She's with Tony at the store.

Thank God, you know it was built by Ti Henri?
Il construit des immeubles an Chili, so he knows what he is doing.

We have an update. The U.S. Military will be docking in Port-au-Prince within the next twenty-four hours.

Non, c'est pas possible, the Montana hotel is gone.
Pou kisa Preval ap kriye la? Doesn't he know no one cares that he has nowhere to sleep? His country is bleeding, and he is crying for his safety. God, this country will never change.

Breaking news, the Dominican Republic has over thirty doctors on the ground now.

Woy! Mwen bezwen yon Ativan.
Marc, where is the Ativan?
Bagay sa trop pou mwen.
Coming! M'la wi.

Marc came from the kitchen, shaking the pill bottle, the percussion section of this twisted track. Once he entered the living room, a flock of aunties and uncles swarmed around him, hoping for a little cut. Happy to oblige, the pills were handed out to each one.

The familiar melody of the safe and comforting voices of the group was now completely out of whack. Tones were too shrill, thoughts were too fragmented, and every spoken word dripped with fear. The quiet ones just sat on chairs and stairs, calling out status updates from Facebook.

The weight of this chaos had Saskia thinking about ways to get out of this situation and back to something normal.

But Johanna got there faster. Hearing the voices of their younger cousins upstairs, Johanna bolted up to the safety of the bedrooms.

Seeing Saskia alone, Jacqueline turned to her with wide, glassy eyes and said, "I am going outside to order some pizzas if anyone is looking for me. I will be right back." And her mother disappeared to the front of the house.

Stranded, Saskia awkwardly turns toward the living room and awkwardly inched toward the T.V. The 60-inch surround sound entertainment center, which normally added to the allure of Tatie Marcel's house, instead amplified the perpetually concerned Wolf Blitzer.

About an hour ago, a 6.5 earthquake struck the poverty-stricken capital of Haiti.

The utter devastation is shocking, and the footage we are about to show is disturbing.

Frantic shots of Haitians choking in the streets, completely covered in white dust, dominated the screen. The green mango trees, the colorful tap-taps, the vibrant people: everything was painted in the white ash of broken buildings. When coverage cut to a hospital, where dust-covered people with red blooms scattered across their bodies sat in various stages of shock. Still, Saskia didn't cry.

Saskia couldn't connect the scenes on the screen with the memories she had of the city. On her last trip to the capital, every person in the streets was dizzy from the hope in the air. A safer, vibrant Haiti was right around the corner. Crime dissipated, the markets bustled, and everyone from the fat wallets to the light coin purse found a way to enjoy life. Dreams crept into reality, becoming something tangible instead of being secreted away in the depths of the heart.

Saskia remembered when she returned from that trip, the adults started dreaming of retiring on the island. Haiti already had everything. A slower pace, food with flavors as nature intended, beaches to soak their aching bones, all the things they wanted in their sunset years. It was all within their reach. Looking around the living room now, hope fractured and pulverized into the gritty grief they knew all too well. Each adult could feel it wrap around them like a blanket with holes and pulled-up threads. For some, this would be enough to bury those dreams forever. Others would fuse with it and never let it go.

A voice worn down by a pack a day of cigarettes wondered, "How, how could they possibly start over now? There is nothing left. The cathedral downtown? Collapsed. The National Palace? Collapsed."

"Yes, this is dark, but *kenbe la, frè'm*. We always find a way out of these situations." A softer, older voice shakily cooed from the other side of the room.

A thick silence blanketed the room, as no one could pull away from the tragedy of their homeland unfolding on international T.V. Saskia's chest tightened, her breath fighting through the constricted space.

This is how it really ends on T.V. and a cloud of dust.

The front doors swung open to Jacqueline, and a couple of aunties came in carrying pizza and sodas. It was the public admission that this was going to be a long night. The door stayed open as those carrying in pizza forgot to shut it. Before she could reach it to close the door, a tall man with a thinning, buzzed head filled the doorway. Her father. Slowly, she approached him, afraid to make eye contact. When she met his eyes, the tears finally came.

Ten. Dix. Dis.

Quiet slapping followed by a hushed retreat reminded Paul of his beach house in Haiti. There, the Caribbean waves rushed through the pebbled beaches with a gentle urgency and slapped onto the land like a winning hand in a dominoes game. The subtle taste of salt in the air and the sunbaked warmth of each stone cradled him every time he visited. He'd sleep under the stars, the mist of the ocean his blanket. Nowhere else in the world did he feel as safe as on his beach in Haiti.

While the sound of moving water soothed him, something was very wrong. Where the gaps between stones galloped when the tide went out, these sounds quietly, gently, almost lazily etched themselves on the land as if they hoped to be doing anything else. Paul wiggled his nose, searching for the familiar smells. Expecting salt, he scrunched his face when he didn't find it. Just neutral water with a hint of rotting eggs. Sulphur.

Running his hands over the sand, it felt rougher and inconsistent. Every couple of inches, twigs and waterlogged wood poked and scraped at him. Wait, why was he lying in the sand? Where was the salt? What were these waterlogged… twigs? Why did his face hurt?

Paul carefully opened his eyes to find a world on its side. Oranges, reds, and pinks reflected off the unburdened waters of a… *lake?* The last bits of sunset slid behind a Spanish-style mansion.

Paul pushed himself up to sitting to take stock of his surroundings. Looking around, he realized he was in the middle of a lake. A very, very large lake. Never in his life had he been so close to so much calm, fresh water. He only knew smaller, pulsing rivers like Haiti's *l'Artibonite*. But here, the waves were gentle, hesitant. Like the people who surrounded this water, the lake never needed to be anything more than gentle. Protected on all sides and always celebrated, the vast lake quietly lapped the grains of sand between his toes. Paul couldn't think of a body of water in Haiti that didn't have a violent undercurrent, a fighting spirit to claim its spot in the world. Where in the world was he?

He tenderly explored his damaged cheek. Nothing had broken through, and he could still move his jaw. He ran his hands over his body and found his clothes were still on, and that his pockets only had a soaked leaf and a twig. No wallet. No phone. No hotel key. Nothing. Panic surged through him, lifting Paul off the ground so he could stand and assess the situation.

"Paul. Hide." A hushed woman's voice rang in his head. A voice he hadn't heard in over a decade. Closing his eyes, he could see her face from the window of the burning house as men carrying all kinds of guns watched with pride. Paul opened his eyes, swallowing down the scream that usually followed that memory. This was not the time.

Ignoring the echoes of the woman's screams, Paul stood up and walked around the island, trying to figure out what resources he could use to get back to the mainland. Avoiding the twigs that jutted out at odd angles, Paul navigated the rapidly cooling sand while looking for signs of life along the water's edge. Mansion after expansive mansion sat relatively empty. The only signs of life were large yellow squares of light that dwarfed the postage-stamp sized ones of Port-au-Prince.

These lakeside squares were powerful enough to haphazardly illuminate swimming pools he suspected nobody swam in because of some annoying inconvenience, like they were too pretty or expensive to enjoy. Where the parade of lights stopped, empty docks with boats suspended high above the waterline began. Paul wondered if having a boat was the price of admission to this lakeside neighborhood. The closer he analyzed the vacant houses, the more his hope for mainland help dwindled. No one was home.

Paul then looked across the water and noticed a black branch interrupting the smooth surface. Stepping into the cool water, he could see his toes sink into the mushy sand. Squatting into the water, Paul pushed off and began swimming toward a darkened red brick house. At first, he could see the swaying grasses below until about ten minutes later, the water became dark and murky. He looked back to see he had only made it a few meters away from the island. The subtle current was working against him. He would have to turn around.

Swimming away from the red brick home, he found a good pace. Focusing on his arms and legs, he positioned them for efficiency. It felt good to focus on something tangible, something with a clear beginning and a clear end. Ignoring the gentle brushes from the submerged tape grass, Paul swam harder until his feet could sink back into the soft, sinking sand of the island. He walked to a cement bench on the forest line to catch his breath and think.

A distant motor intertwined with voices whooping and screaming to go faster, but when he looked around, he didn't see a ripple. He was stuck, and the only way to get off would be by boat. Paul leaned his head against the trunk of a nearby tree.

"Well, if I'm going to spend the night here, might as well see what's available," he said to the trembling leaves above.

The island took less than five minutes to walk around, with the only interesting feature being a weather-worn dock just big enough for a kayak. Disappointed that no one on the other side could help him, he walked around the island again—this time assessing what was in the center of the island. Thicker sections where mangroves and sprawling vines collided in a tangled mess, making him nervous. Paul suspected an animal or two must live there. Other parts were thin enough for him to walk through to explore the center of the island. A brisk wind meandered through the trees, chilling Paul in his wet clothes. He needed to find a warm place to wait.

Paul found the only path leading into the woods and followed it. Along the tree and brush-lined path, toy cars, buried princess dolls, and the occasional Lego block broke the sandy surface. Paul hoped that meant he wouldn't be on the island long if kids were leaving toys behind. Judging the thickness of the sandy mud and how much the toys had degraded, Paul assumed they must have been there a long time. Maybe no one really came to this island after all.

He shuddered at the realization. Without any resources, but surrounded by homes, he wasn't sure how to work himself out of the situation. Unattainable abundance, a lot like the plight of his home country. That tension, that contrast, had plunged many Haitians into madness as they took increasing risks, building lives on thin wires of hope that things would change. Thinking back to the fear-filled nights watching distant gunfights from his father's living room. Better to stare directly at fear than to hide from it.

A bat swooped at him, forcing him to duck until his fingers sank into the soft sand. Certain he was safe, he noticed the various tracks marching alongside him. Most of the prints were shoe marks and toe marks in between the peaks and valleys of the sandy path. But then he looked to the sides of the walking path. Big claw marks bordered long, curving lines.

Birds.

Snakes.

No. Alligators.

He'd only ever seen them on the American and British nature shows on DirecTV. As a kid, Paul didn't even know what he would do if he ever saw a snake, let alone an alligator. He couldn't believe there was a way for alligators or snakes to be on this island. To him, the United States—especially Orlando—was the safest, happiest place on Earth, at least that was what the commercials said. Shaking off the nerves, Paul continued along the path as distant bushes would spontaneously rustle.

"It's just the breeze. There's nothing on this island that can hurt me," Paul said to himself as he forced his feet to continue down through the lake-fed sand.

After a couple of minutes, the tree-lined path opened up to a small clearing. Gathered in a corner was a wooden sign that proudly stated, "Dog Island, City of Winter Park." Beneath it was a graveyard of abandoned beer cans and boxes, as if a trash can wasn't just a couple of feet away in the middle of the clearing. Next to the trash can sat a stone bench and a grill—that was it.

Paul walked into the clearing, looked around, and growled. It felt so good. He growled again. On the fourth growl, he let out a howl so loud that a flock of cranes in the trees above took off into the darkening evening. Paul watched the outlines of their delicate bodies as he thought about how he had ended up in this situation. His life had been relatively peaceful until he met Marcello.

In college, Marcello could be a little inconsiderate and transactional. But man, did he have the sickest parties. Whenever Paul hung out with Marcello, the next morning, he had to go through the pictures on his digital camera just to make sure it all actually happened. Miss *that* college experience? No way.

Marcello was the only "cool" friend he had. His friends in Haiti were always up to the same old thing. Every. Single. Weekend. Hanging out with Marcello almost always woke him up to the world beyond the Caribbean. They'd meet in Miami, or Mexico City, or Bogota, and in every city, Paul would forget everything that chased him out of Port-au-Prince. To lose that life-saver, that tether to the outside world, scared him.

Losing that connection may have been why he reached out to him ahead of this conference. For the last couple of months, Marcello had grown distant. They hadn't spent dedicated time together in almost a year. Marcello had visited Haiti a couple of times and mostly focused on Paul's childhood best friend, Didier. Even though he'd swing by the office, Didier and Marcello would spend all afternoon on some adventure, and that never included him. Paul worried it had something to do with him becoming less interesting, more responsible, more worried about doing everything right to keep the family business going.

He felt like he had been losing his best friend, and he didn't know how to get him back, except for inviting him to the conference. Paul had hoped that getting the chance to sell him on mango sugar would bring them back together. It could have brought his dream to life. What a stupid thing to expect from his most unreliable friend.

Thinking through the day, every minute was normal. Nothing particularly out of place, except for the creepy nun. His father had always been a jerk. Marcello and Dr. Oakley had been at odds for years. He didn't have any enemies in Orlando, and Saskia wasn't the type to have shady connections. Then how did he end up on a desert island after getting punched in the face? How could he have avoided this?

Dr. Oakley's warning. It had to be Marcello. The fire from earlier in the day rose up with nothing to slow it. How could he have been so stupid as to trust him?

A flap of feathered wings grabbed his attention. Looking up, he watched the last crane disappear into the night. Paul yelled after them, "I am such an idiot!" He immediately winced and held his cheek while listening to his voice echo across the lake. Except for the quiet waves gliding up the sand, everything else around him became silent.

"Man, I really am an idiot for yelling at some stupid birds and now talking to myself?!? Gah! Ow!" Paul's cheek throbbed as he stood in the clearing, waiting for a response. "Why am I waiting for a response? AH! I need to get out of these woods. This clearing is creepy, and Marcello is a jerk."

Paul sucked his teeth, ignoring the pain in his cheek, and stomped his way back to the water's edge. Between the trees, he could see the inky black water of the lake dotted by the interrupted glare of the moon above. The homes on the other side had not moved closer. Once on the shore, Paul looked in all directions, hoping for a sign of anything or anyone who could help him. Coming up with nothing, he plopped down onto the sand and, in the privacy of that remote island, allowed the faintest trickle of tears to form.

"This is temporary. This is temporary," Paul said over and over to drown out the scream of the memory of the woman.

Not far to his left, a loud snap brought him back to his spot on the island. Paul darted his gaze to the source of the sound, and his stomach sank. In all of its natural glory, hissed a six-foot alligator.

Paul was a dead man.

Eleven. Onze. Onz.

Saskia closed the heavy front door behind her and paused on the stoop. Breathing in the slightly damp night air, the voices inside blended with the rush of the traffic nearby. She shivered a bit in the rapidly cooling air, regretting she had left her work cardigan in the car. Her short-sleeved blouse and pencil skirt suddenly felt very out of season.

For most of the year, she lived her Florida life in sundresses and jean shorts. She'd find comfort from the night-blooming jasmine in her aunt's backyard, or the magnolias from next door. Whenever her head ballooned from information overload, those smells always brought her head back to normal, back to believing anything was possible. But it wasn't the season for those flowers. In fact, it had been so long since Saskia stood alone on the stoop that the memories of those smells barely competed with the mossy damp from the pond down the street. It was all so wrong. The perfectly crafted memories were shattering against reality, and Saskia hated it. Wiping her hand across her cheeks, the tears came through even more, refusing to be forgotten or erased.

"Hey, Saskia. It's going to be okay, I promise you! They'll find them, they have to find them." Johanna wrapped her arms around her sister, gently blotting Saskia's tears away with her thumb. She then put her chin on Saskia's head, a gesture she had only accomplished last year.

"Wait, isn't this supposed to be the other way around? I'm the big sister." Saskia laughed and hugged Johanna closer, holding her a little sister tighter than usual. If their parents had stayed in Haiti, would they be doing this right now? Their family back there survived so much already, things they would never have to experience firsthand. But now this?

"Does that really matter right now?" Johanna laughed into Saskia's curls, her warm breath infusing the crown of her hair like their mother used to do when they were little.

Her voice always had a twinkling quality to it that always brought Saskia out of her head and back into the world of the living.

"No." Saskia sighed. "I guess not."

They stood there like that for a while, holding each other against the cooling night. Saskia's mind wandered to the memory fragments of the various characters of their Haitian life. Mami, Jean Bernard, Tatie Alice, Annaliese, Alex. In that moment, in that need to feel connected to them despite the incredible distance, time away from them smoothed their distinct features. How would she remember them if their features were already disappearing? If they were already turning into ghosts of her memories? The next time she'd see them, she would etch every wrinkle, every freckle, to memory.

"Saskia," Johanna timidly asked, "What's going to happen if they don't find Mon Oncle Jean and Mami?" Her voice was tension-filled.

Saskia stiffened and released a slow sigh. "I really, really don't know. All we can do is wait. Ok?"

Johanna squeezed Saskia in return.

A gust pushed the girls closer as they giggled uncomfortably against the cold. Then they could hear muffled yells and screams on the other side of the door. "They found them! They found Jean-Bernard et Mami! Merci bon Dieu! They are safe. They found them!"

A sigh of relief escaped both women. Looking to each other, wordlessly debating ongoing back in to celebrate with the family. But the toll of the day made it impossible to go anywhere but home.

After sending off a text to her parents, Saskia and Johanna scurried to the car before anyone could notice. Quietly opening the car door, the girls slid onto the fabric seats and carefully closed the doors. When they clicked shut, Johanna pushed the button to lock them.

Silence.

Neither Saskia nor Johanna reached for the radio. Neither Saskia nor Johanna said a word. All day they had been listening, and talking, and strategizing, and comforting, and to have one more piece of sound? They couldn't do it. To have this now, to have these moments just to breathe. And sit. And think. Neither of them wanted it to end.

When the front door opened, the voices of two aunties known for long conversations broke through the night. The sisters glanced at each other and nodded.

Saskia turned the key in the ignition and, as if it could read the situation, the Civic came to life without a fuss. Pulling away from the curb, they waved at the aunties with borrowed smiles to lighten the heavy mood. Rolling from one streetlight to the next, they miraculously reached the highway without getting lost among the sameness of the streets. There, the sounds of traffic replaced the silence of the deep recess of the neighborhood. They were back in the real world.

Within minutes, Johanna fell asleep against the window, eliminating the possibility of conversation, leaving Saskia free to think. In less than ten hours, she had swallowed her pride and started a job that brought her all the way back to the bottom of her career with a boss who hated her. She saw Paul, a man she had wondered about for years, and there seemed to be a remote chance he had been thinking about her, too. The island that held her dreams, held the intricate web of her identity, that represented the resilience, strength, and beauty of her family line, had cracked open. For one of these things to happen would be world shifting. To have all three? In one day?

Saskia felt exposed. Unmoored. No, more like she sat on the edge between one version of herself and the next. Each step toward this moment required that she peel away the stories she told herself, one tendril at a time. In this moment, the thick, unbreakable stories of her foundational beliefs, the deeply rooted vines of her life, had been hacked into pieces by the outside world. What if she started over? Who could she be if she threw off the expectations, the safe, certain path, and chose adventure?

Too much. The questions caused too much uncertainty. She had made a plan, and she was sticking to it: get a job, save up money, settle down. Everyone around her had done it, and she would too.

Sitting at a red light, Saskia took the bracelet out of the cup holder and slipped it onto her wrist. Then she grabbed her BlackBerry to sift through her text messages until she found the one she had ignored earlier from Liam.

> Hey, so our team is starting to plan
> our trip, and we could use someone
> who knows the language.
> Text me if you want to go.

She turned the phone over as if Liam had sent her something scandalous. Drumming her fingers against the steering wheel, she waited for the light to turn green. Should she go? Would she miss anything here if she did? Would she forever regret it if she didn't? As much as she hated her life in Florida, leaving felt like defeat or abandoning the friends and family who had shaped her. Going to Haiti also meant facing the reality that the dream crumbled with the fallen buildings. It could feel like an alien country.

Then the memories of neglected roads leading to stacked-up houses, children playing in the street, and a simpler life came forward. Haiti was so much more to her and her family than a place where they all lived, but the heart of a culture they all fought to protect. If she didn't go, was she abandoning something that had given her so much? The skin under the bracelet itched, bringing her back to the car.

Sliding a finger under the rectangular part, she looked into her rearview mirror. A pair of headlights sped toward her and, with seconds to spare, jumped into the lane next to her. A yellow Lamborghini roared past them just as the light turned green. Saskia waited a second to catch her breath, spinning the bracelet's beads to settle her nerves. Regaining her breath, she slowly advanced through the light, grateful, again, that life turned out the way it did.

Pulling into the driveway of their parents' home, Saskia gently nudged her sister, trying and failing to rouse her. The only light came from the street, which cast shadows on the house and left very dark corners untouched. In this light, Saskia noticed all the little details that made the house special, and that had made their lives special. A bay window looking out to a water fountain encircled by pink and purple flowers. The pair of rocking chairs her parents used after dinner to watch the sun's descent. Johanna's light snoring stopped, as Saskia nudged her awake.

The pair quietly moved through the routines of getting out of the car, entering the house, and getting ready for bed. Their movements slow, their bodies holding the weight of the day.

Settled into her bed, Saskia's mind flipped into warp speed. She watched the shadows war with each other across her bedroom ceiling. The questions flew.

Stay?

Go?

Who's alive?

Who do we mourn?

Who is at fault?

Will they recover?

Should I panic?

Is it even worth going to work tomorrow?

Yes, student loans, remember? Right.

But they could really use me down there.

But it's not safe.

But life isn't safe.
This could be the big adventure I am looking for.
But it isn't safe.
I can't go.
I should stay.
But what if?

The shadows stopped moving, as did her thoughts. In the stillness, she finally settled. Exhausted by the questions, the worries, and the managing, her mind stilled, her breath followed a slow, and regular rhythm. Each burden slowly released her and let her drift off to sleep.

Twelve. Douze. Douz.

Paul could not remember a time in his life when he stayed outside long enough to watch the skies go from vibrant pinks and oranges to midnight blue dotted with stars and a crescent moon. He could also not remember a time when he had to fight for his life against an actual dinosaur. But here he was swinging a knobby tree branch at an alligator under the velveteen skies of Winter Park.

They had been at this for about twenty minutes, and the alligator finally plopped down into the sand, gaze fixed on Paul. Standing completely still, Paul maintained his stance but relaxed his shoulders, accepting that he wouldn't be able to spend the night on this island. Assessing the surrounding houses again, he looked for any new squares of light. They all looked unchanged except for one. A navy blue one with white shutters had a little red boat pulled up on the lawn just out of the lake's reach and a long dock into the lake. The first-floor lights were on. If he could swim for an hour, he could make it and finally get help. Paul looked over the moonlit waters as the soft peaks grew and flattened as they settled for the night. From the other side of the lake, this would have been beautiful.

In the middle of a growing ripple, a pair of curious eyes looked back at him. Another alligator. A territorial snap and hiss from the island brought Paul back to the task at hand: dealing with a very pissed-off alligator.

"Whoa, is that what I think it is?" a hushed male voice rose above the gentle putter of an approaching boat.

"Yeah, yikes. Should we help him?" said another voice.

"Oh, I don't know. I have never seen one of those this close except at Gatorland. What if he wants to be there with the gator? This is Florida after all."

"You've never been this close to a guy like that, or the gator?"

"Haha, both!"

Both male voices chuckled while the alligator and Paul stood frozen on the sand. Assessing his position, Paul guessed that from afar, the situation didn't appear to be dire. That he could be some guy hanging out on an island with an alligator. Is that what Florida really was about? In Haiti, they used animals for food or ceremony, not to just hang out.

"You're bad," said the first male voice. "Honestly, I don't know how to handle a gator."

"Or a man like that," said the other voice.

"Um, a little help here, please," Paul cried out. From where he was standing, he could hear the voices but couldn't see a boat. They were his only hope.

"Right. Alligators. Liam?" the voice hushed as if Paul couldn't hear them.

"I seriously don't know what to do with an alligator, Ryan. What should I do? Pull up a YouTube video and wrestle it with a tow rope?" said Liam, using an exaggerated Southern accent for effect.

"You have lived here for how long, Liam?"

"Back off. It's not like all Floridians know what to do with an alligator. You just leave them alone, unlike that guy."

Paul seethed and yelled back, "I can hear you, you know. Please help me! All I need is a ride off this island and a way home."

Paul's voice roused the alligator, and with a snap of the alligator's jaws Paul went stumbling back. He tripped over a buried root and fell onto the sand. The alligator stalked closer to Paul.

"Jeez-us. Oh, Liam, we really have to help him now. I'm pulling the boat over there, and you pull him in."

"Right, after we save this guy's life, we are going to have a little talk about how this went and how it needs to go in the future."

"Liam, how often do you expect us to be saving people from alligators?"

Though the voices paused, Paul could hear the boat getting closer. Moon-dotted waves grew from gentle laps to aggressive slaps against the sand. The sound startled the alligator, and it turned around, looking for the source. As the boat got closer to the island, the alligator started hissing and snapping toward the approaching boat.

"Ok, hey dude, run to the other side of the island. There's a little dock, and you can jump on from there," Liam said over the roar of the motor.

"Yeah, I saw that. Good idea!" Paul ran for the dock, careful to avoid the buried twigs as he left a trail of flying sand.

Liam moved the boat back and forth while yelling at the alligator to keep it distracted. Rounding the final corner, Paul's legs burned from fighting with the sand to stay upright.

"Ok, I'm here!" Paul yelled from the edge of the dock while catching his breath, grateful for the smaller size of the island.

Liam nodded and turned the boat around just in time for the alligator to turn around and see Paul at the end of the dock. Liam and the alligator began racing to the dock, sand flying in all directions as the waves surged onto the island.

The wake rattled the dock, and Paul fought to keep his footing until Liam swung in front of the dock. Paul looked back and saw the alligator only a couple of feet away from the dock.

"Hey, dude! Ready, jump!" Liam called out, pulling closer to help Paul make it into the boat.

Paul turned back toward them, took a deep breath, and got ready.

Running toward the edge of the dock, he jumped toward the boat just as Liam glided in front of him. In the air, Paul felt a moment of relief that, after all of this, he might be okay. But Liam hadn't gotten close enough, and Paul plunged into the now icy lake. Seconds later, so did the alligator.

"Liam! How could you miss?!" Ryan screamed. "Turn around and get him!"

Liam rolled his eyes and flared his nostrils in frustration. "Do you want to drive, then?"

Ryan shrank back and grabbed onto the side of the boat as Liam turned it around so tightly that lake water filled the back.

"Careful! I just got this a month ago."

"You don't say? Is that why you don't know how to drive it?" Liam yelled back.

He cut the motor and let Ryan drop a ladder off the side of the boat. Paul struggled against the wake as he swam toward the boat.

"Hey, dude, watch out! It's gaining on you!" said Liam, fear wrapping around each syllable until it turned into a shout.

Paul looked back and saw the alligator gaining on him. He was exhausted, starving, and very much over this Florida experience. He kicked as hard as he could until his fingers felt the cool metal of the ladder's rungs.

"Oh no, there's a couple more heading this way," Ryan said, his voice dropping in volume as he watched four scaled tails cut through the water.

With the last of his energy, he pulled himself over the side of the boat, and Ryan and Liam pulled him the rest of the way over.

"Whew! That was close," Ryan said as a deep thud came from the side of the boat.

Liam looked over the side and spotted an alligator's tail disappear into the water. He looked over at Ryan and Paul, wild-eyed.

"Dude! That was close! He totally could have ripped off your arm or something. You're so lucky to have us! Oh! Look at that, Liam. We did it! Isn't he so lucky!"

Ryan hopped up and down, rocking the boat as small amounts of lake water flowed in.

Paul could almost hear Liam rolling his eyes again as he looked over the craft he had landed in. He had been on many boats growing up, but this one was newer than anything he had seen in a while. The pristine chrome finishes and the blue and white striped seating at the back had never cracked from the sun.

"Seriously, Ryan? Stop with the jumping. Whoa—Ryan! He's bleeding!"

Ryan didn't hesitate and disappeared into a small alcove under the wheel of the boat. Moments later, after a lot of rustling through layers of blankets and other items, he came back up with a first-aid kit. Kneeling down next to Paul, he carefully assessed the wound.

"Man, this is a pretty serious cut. What happened?"

Paul stayed quiet for a moment. He didn't know these guys. There was a real risk here that these strangers knew Marcello and could be helping him. What if they were eventually going to kill him? They could also be the kind of people who are too quick, too eager to work with law enforcement and bring him to the police. He needed a story until he could trust them. Looking back at the seats along the back of the boat reminded him that this area was used for boat tours. He and Marcello almost did one to ride out a bad night.

He finally said, "I was, ugh, on a boat tour and accidentally fell out. I must have hit my face on the side of the boat." Paul looked at Ryan's face, then at Liam's, to see if they bought it. Ryan stopped dressing the wound on his cheek and looked at Paul, his face unchanging. The stillness made Paul nervous.

"Yeah, I can see how that can happen," Liam finally said with a nod to Ryan.

He nodded back and dabbed some peroxide on Paul's cheek as he winced in pain. Liam leaned against the back of the boat, assessing Paul. Something about his face looked familiar, and he couldn't figure it out.

"So, you're visiting? Your accent is Brazilian?" Ryan asked gently.

Paul sat quietly, thinking through his options. If he told them he was from Haiti, and they knew Marcello, then the alligator would have been the safer choice. For now, he'd have to keep things as vague as possible. Then he said, "Um, the Caribbean."

Ryan brightened as he gently placed the butterfly bandages over the cut.

"My family's been to the Bahamas. Is it like the Bahamas?" Ryan asked.

Paul chuckled and shook his head.

"Nah, it's a small, little place. You probably never heard of it."

"Oh, okay," Ryan replied and shot a skeptical glance at Liam.

"Well, then let's get to work on that hand of yours." Ryan fished back into the kit for tweezers and alcohol.

Paul managed a small nod of his head. The rocking of the boat made it almost impossible for him to stop knocking his hand against the side of the boat. With each hit, Paul would suck on his teeth as the pain rippled from his hand to his head, threatening to knock him out… again.

Ready with tweezers, Ryan smiled quickly and pulled the twig out of Paul's hand.

Paul howled as his hand noted the absence of the twig. On the other side of the lake, someone yelled at them to keep it down.

"*Now* the neighbors are home. Where were they an hour ago?" Paul said, squeezing his wrist as if the pressure would slow the pain.

"Honey, this is Winter Park. Someone is always home unless it's New Year's or summer." Ryan quickly wrapped the bandage tightly around Paul's hand.

Paul stretched out his hand, testing the bandage.

"Wow, impressive. Thank you," Paul said as he opened and then closed his fist as the pain in his head and hand subsided.

"Yup. Just take some painkillers and then swing by the hospital down the road if it starts to swell." Ryan smiled and admired his work.

Paul shifted his weight in time with the waves, wondering if he should voice his next question. He didn't know these men. They were kind and obviously willing to help him, but what if they were connected to Marcello, or whoever had kidnapped him? Looking around the lake and the blanket of stars above, Paul decided to take a chance.

"Let me guess, you need a ride?" Liam asked from the back of the boat before Paul could say a word.

"Ha, yeah, how did you guess?"

"Well, it's not like you are gonna swim back to shore," Liam said, chuckling as he walked back to the center of the boat.

"Ry—"

"Of course!" Ryan replied from within the cabin. "You know I'm off tomorrow."

"Right, well, let's head back to Ryan's place then. And I guess we can call you a cab?" Liam turned the key still in the ignition, and the gurgle of the twin engines interrupted the lake's midnight silence.

"Wait, before we go anywhere. What's your name?" Ryan said from his seat at the side of the boat.

Paul looked from Ryan to Liam and back again, hoping to see some glimmer, some twitch of the face that could tell him if these guys could be trusted. Even if these guys were looking for him and going to kill him, they might as well get it over with now instead of dragging it out. But in the off chance these guys could help him, if these guys could get him to Saskia, then maybe it was worth the risk. Looking beyond the boat, the tentatively churning black waters turned the trust in these men from a necessity to a luxury.

"Oh, right! My name is Paul. Paul Lancelin," he finally said while bracing for their response.

Liam whipped around to face Paul at such a speed that the boat rocked back and forth again as lake water jumped on board.

"Liam! Are you crazy?"

"Sorry, I just wanted to be sure. Did you say your name is Paul? Are you from Haiti?"

Paul froze. *Shit, he knows and is going to kill me.*

"Ugh, no. Like I said, somewhere else in the Caribbean. It's a tiny island you've never heard of," Paul said with false confidence.

Suspicious, Liam turned fully to face Paul as Ryan carefully crossed from his seat toward Paul and said, "Well, Paul of the Caribbean, nice to formally meet you. I am Dr. Ryan Green."

"And my name is Liam," he said, smiling with a familiarity that put Paul at ease. He continued before Ryan could interrupt. "And my best friend, Saskia Roy, can't stop talking about a Haitian guy with your same name. Who knew there were multiple Lancelins in the Caribbean?"

"Wait, what? You know Saskia? And she talks about me? A lot?" Paul stood up too fast and brought more water into the boat.

"Okay, you two need to sit, and I'll drive. Otherwise, we'll end up at the bottom of Lake Virginia," Ryan said as he moved toward the helm and bumped Liam out of the way, inviting more water into the boat.

Liam rolled his eyes and took a seat next to Paul.

Within moments, the boat groaned from a gurgle to a whining roar. Ryan circled the island to get the boat back in position toward his house. Liam and Paul relaxed into their seats.

"I can't believe you're Paul Lancelin," Liam said, yelling over the sound of the motors.

"I can't believe you know her. I think she might be the only one I can trust at the moment. Maybe you can find her on Facebook? She's on there a lot," Paul yelled back.

Liam laughed. "She'll probably be up in a couple of hours. You can crash at my place for the rest of the night, and I can bring you to her in the morning?" he offered, envisioning the version of Saskia when she found out about the whole night.

"Um, yeah, that works for me," Paul said, worry threading every syllable.

"Don't worry, man, Saskia would invent the most painful death for me if something happened to you. You're safe," Liam said while he watched Ryan's lithe body navigate through the night.

"But she will want the full story about how you ended up on an island in the middle of Lake Virginia. And when we tell her that story, we'll leave that part about Ryan out of it."

"Why?"

"This is still new, and I don't want her to make this a bigger deal than it is," Liam said.

Paul nodded and relaxed into the gently vibrating seats, wondering how in the world his night would unfold like this.

Thirteen. Treize. Trèz.

"Mom, seriously. I don't need your permission." Saskia stood in the middle of the kitchen while her mother rushed around getting her coffee ready.

"Saskia. You have been on the job for less than one day, and you are already calling out sick? Be serious! You are threatening your future!" Jacqueline threw a spoon into the sink, causing a loud metallic clang that made Saskia jump.

Undeterred, she dug in. "What future? My 'amazing' future as a branch manager in a town so small I still see people I knew from high school at the grocery store? You've got to be kidding me," Saskia practically screamed.

Jacqueline stopped moving and slowly turned toward her daughter. In a tone reserved only for when her children stepped so far out of line, she contemplated violence. "Saskia, if you want to play around and continue building a bad work reputation, *ou grand mouns* enough to make that choice. But I promise you, I promise you, if you lose this job, you will have to find a new place to live." Then she raised her voice, "*Mwen paka gen ti moun* living in my house until I die. You are an adult, and if you are going to keep making these stupid, childish mistakes, then I will stop bailing you out. Because I am an adult too, and constantly bailing you out is a childish mistake."

Jacqueline grabbed her coffee mug from the counter and yelled out, "I'll see you all here at seven for dinner. I expect to see *all* of you." She glared at Saskia and then slammed the front door behind her. The glasses in a nearby china cabinet rang in her wake.

Stewing in the residual tension, Saskia seethed. Her mother wouldn't actually kick her out if she lost her job, would she?

"Whoa. How did you do that? I have never seen her that mad before, and I actually broke things."

Saskia turned to see her brother, Robert, leaning against the archway.

"I—I told her I was…" Saskia stammered and frantically looked for her words.

Once she found them, she took a deep breath and blurted out, "I don't think we should be going to work. We should be taking a sick day. After what we watched for hours last night? We should all be at home and talking about this. We should maybe grieve or something."

"What for?"

Her father entered the kitchen with his briefcase, ready to head to the office, but not before grabbing the coffee Jacqueline had prepared for him. Leaning against the counter, he faced Saskia and took a long, contemplative sip from his travel mug.

"Dad, we spent hours waiting to find out if our family members were still alive. Not only that, but everyone also had to bury a dream or an aspiration or, or, or an expectation."

That last word pooled tears along her lash lines, but she pushed through, standing her ground.

"We shouldn't pretend that we are okay because we're not. At work, we have to pretend that our lives depend on it every single day. Don't we deserve a break for something like this?"

Emile's back pressed into the counter as he took another long sip from his travel mug. She watched her father's face twitch in different places as he thought through what to say next. Throughout her life, he had been the parent who gave her space to talk, to think, and let her expand to her fullest self. If anyone in her family were going to agree with her, it would be him.

"Saskia, you have to learn that not a single person on this planet cares about what happens to Haiti unless it benefits them in some way. The sooner you can learn, the sooner you can move on to the beautiful things waiting for you in this life. We've all been through this a hundred times before. Family and friends who built towers of wealth just to lose it all a decade later because of a coup or a hurricane. That place is cursed. The sooner you let it go, the sooner you can move on to what God has waiting for you."

Her father analyzed his children's faces, making sure the message landed. Finally, he said, "I have to go to work, and I hope you all are on your way too."

He pulled away from the counter with his briefcase in one hand and his coffee in the other. Walking through the kitchen to the foyer, he clumsily opened the front door just as the tumbler slipped and splashed all over him before hitting the floor.

"Goddammit!" he bellowed. The glasses rang again.

"I don't have time for this. Saskia, I need you to help me and clean this up while I change. Robert, help your sister." He disappeared into the house and reappeared before they had found the cleaning supplies. He paused in the foyer and watched them for a moment, huffed, and then closed the door behind him. The glasses did not ring.

Her father failed her. He was supposed to be on her side, and instead, he told her to put it aside and pretend. But she couldn't do it. She'd spent the last six months pretending to be the ray of sunshine everyone needed her to be, and at night she sobbed in silence. With each performance, she felt like she was losing a bit of herself until she felt so hollow, so disconnected that food stopped tasting like anything at all. Worst of all, the performance wasn't working.

It had to stop.

Maybe that was what Paul meant when he said he didn't like her this way. Maybe he saw how much she had become a shell of herself. She could never tell him that he was right. The anger she'd been nursing for weeks was really meant for herself.

"What in the world was that? 'Saskia, clean that up. Robert, help your sister.' What a stupid thing to say," Robert mocked his father, hoping to bring his sister back to the kitchen and out of her head.

"See! They shouldn't be going out into the world like that. They are going to ruin someone's day," she replied as she opened the closet door to get the mop and bucket.

They worked in silence. Robert sprayed down the obvious coffee splatter and wiped it down while Saskia prepared the water to clean the splash zone and the surrounding area.

When Robert started cleaning under the entry table, he said, "It's like we lost a family member, but worse. Losing a city like that is so much worse than losing someone. When a person dies, we have a funeral, put memories of them in a box, and bury them in the ground, and that is that. It's normal to have moments when you miss them, you know? But a city? I guess we're not allowed to feel that way about a city because it never really dies."

Saskia nodded while the mop moved across the tiles covered in sprayed cleaner, sopping up the drops of coffee Robert missed. While annoyed with the chore, the meditative swish helped her think through what her brother had said.

After clearing the tiles by the wall, she moved inward and replied, "I wonder if it's because people still live there, like they continue to feed the spirit of their broken city. When the people leave, they carry that memory of its former glory everywhere they go. They enshrine it in books, and art, and stories, and movies so that generations of people can know what that city once was, so when it's not that, it hurts a whole new generation of people who didn't even live in that version of the city."

Robert nodded and leaned against the doorjamb to the kitchen and offered, "Maybe because it can never be forgotten, the wound stays open indefinitely? The scars are a permanent reminder of what was?" His eyes went wide, and he continued, "Sask, will we never move on from this?"

Saskia paused. Something in her younger brother's tone reminded her of when they were kids, and he'd sneak into her room to hide from his nightmares. She leaned the mop handle against the wall and crossed the foyer to meet him. Back then, she could hug him close and hide him in the crook of her arm like a living doll to chase away the fears. Now, she hugged the only part of her brother she could reach, his waist.

"Oh, Robert. It just takes a little bit of time, you know?" She could feel his arms wrap around her head and shoulders as a response. He held onto her for longer than usual until she wasn't sure who was supporting whom. Her bracelet started itching just as Saskia's phone vibrated on her backside. She freed one hand to get it from her jeans pocket. Pulling the screen closer to her squished face, the text she read didn't make sense. She pushed off her brother's arms to read the details of the message again.

"Shit," she whispered. Saskia walked away from Robert and read Liam's incoming text for the third time, trying to make sense of what it said. "I'm sorry, Robert, but I gotta go help a friend once we finish up here. Are you going to be okay today?"

Robert straightened, and the little boy Saskia had loved so much disappeared into the young man who stood before her now. In a voice a touch lower than before, "Nah, I'm fine. I'll finish taking care of this. You go ahead."

Saskia squeezed his arm, then grabbed her purse from the table. As she passed him on her way to the front door, she paused and gave him another hug with a kiss on the cheek.

"See you tonight, okay?"

Robert didn't respond and just hugged her back, a little softer this time, before opening the door for her. Once she had made it through, he quietly closed the door so the glasses wouldn't ring.

...

"What do you mean you were kidnapped?" Saskia shot up out of her chair and started pacing. The slapping of her sandals against Liam's tiled floor only sharpened the tension in the room. Since her arrival, Paul had only grown more frustrated with her. She hadn't sat down for more than a couple of minutes at a time, and everything that came out of her mouth was laced with condescension, as if it were his fault that he was in this situation in the first place.

"So, that's the only thing you got from what I said?" Paul said, scowling at Saskia. While Liam's couch was surprisingly comfortable, Paul had hardly slept, and his patience was thin.

To keep his anger in check, he looked around Liam's living room. Unlike his apartment in Port-au-Prince, Liam's apartment had defined sections. A doorway to his left led to a small hallway for the bedroom and bathroom, and the doorway to his right led to the kitchen and a small breakfast nook. Paul had expected an unkempt space with little piles everywhere. Liam's pile-free apartment could have been featured in a magazine, giving him the space to think.

For hours, he searched every corner of his memory, looking for evidence that Marcello was behind this. In Haiti, during the time of the kidnappings, they were almost always done for financial reasons. The whole experience was generally transactional. Unless, of course, the drugged-up kids were involved. High on power and desperation, those situations almost always took a tragic turn. Paul and his dad had survived that time without even a threat to their lives. When his dad bought the helicopter, he was convinced it was only a matter of time. But the time never came, and Paul began to believe they were immune. So why did it take coming to this random city in Florida for it to happen?

"This is Orlando! Stuff like that doesn't happen here. And on top of that, you don't know who did it, you don't know where your stuff is. Paul! What do you mean?!" Saskia said, her voice increasingly shrill.

"Well, there was that one time over by Winter Park High School…" Liam said, his voice trailing when his eyes met Saskia's.

"Right, I'll stop helping," Liam said as he uncrossed and then crossed his legs again.

Saskia moved closer to tower over Liam and Paul. Now that her sandals had stopped slapping against the tile floor, the simmering tensions became kinetic. One wisecrack and the whole thing would boil over.

"Sask—don't you think you are overreacting? Paul told you his story. I'm not sure it's his fault," Liam said, trying to ease the situation. Then he saw Saskia's face again and immediately regretted every word. If it were possible, steam would have blown from her ears. Liam had only seen that look once before in college, and the person on the receiving end had never been heard from again. Before she could respond, he said, "You know what? I'm going to make some coffee. I'll be right back." Sliding from the couch, he scurried toward the kitchen.

"Stop right there. How did you find Paul on Dog Island?"

Liam stopped and slowly turned in the doorway to the kitchen, buying himself some time to come up with a response.

"So, I am going to choose honesty. Remember that guy I see when I am in town? The one with the boat? We were on our way to a cruising spot on the other side of the lake when we ran into Paul."

A flash of recognition crossed Saskia face as she remembered the details of Liam's situationship. On any other day she'd remind him of how this story played out. On any other day she would have tried to convince him to make better choices. But this wasn't that kind of day, she would have to pick her battles and Liam's ill-advised romance would have to be let go.

"Gotcha. Well, I am glad it worked out of the best, and thank you for saving Paul. I think coffee would be nice about now."

Liam nodded in response and continued his journey into the kitchen as Saskia took a deep breath before returning to the bigger battle at hand.

Without Liam, Saskia finally looked at Paul. She could actually see a man who had been through hell, and she wasn't sure if she even knew the worst of it. The bandage on his cheek and on his hand stole her breath, and all the reasons she hated him, away. She walked toward the couch and settled down next to him. Holding his uninjured hand, she said, "Look, obviously it has been a long night for everyone, and…"

"Everyone?" Paul whispered and shot up from the couch, stung by how Saskia believed she had been through anything nearly as difficult. He rubbed his head as if that would help bring what he needed to say next to mind. Not finding the right words, he went with the closest ones he had.

"Everyone!? Saskia, what are you talking about?! You didn't have to fight off an alligator. You didn't spend all night wondering if you were going to die. You're not living with the terror that those guys are going to come back and finish the job. You didn't get a stupid twig through your palm to then get emergency stitches on some stranger's boat in the middle of a lake that you have never been in."

"Not a stranger, just a friend waiting to be made," Liam said while handing out the mugs. Paul took a sip of his coffee and made a face.

"Yeah, for some reason, he likes weak American coffee. Just add some milk and sugar, and it will be fine. Liam?" Saskia said in the sticky-sweet voice she used when she needed him to tread lightly. "You didn't tell him, did you?"

"Tell him what?" Liam leaned against the doorframe, genuinely confused and not reading her tone.

Saskia furrowed her brow and looked at Paul, and then again at Liam. How was this not the most important thing to him? On the way over, she had checked her phone every five minutes, hoping to catch updates on the others that were still missing. With her phone in her bag for the last sixteen minutes, her anxious fingernails had broken free a couple of fibers from the couch, itching for her phone. The fear of knowing too many names on the death list was eating her alive. Didn't Liam understand that? To be here, now, in his apartment in such a normal scenario, only fed the fear—no one cared about what happened to Haiti, not even the people who should.

"Tell me what?" Paul asked.

Saskia looked at him intensely. He could still see the world as safe and relatively uncomplicated. He could still nurture the belief that Haiti was finally, finally turning a corner. He could still live connected to the idea that a safe home waited for him. To take that from him, to pull him down into the inky depths of Saskia's fear-infused grief, just felt wrong. To do that in front of someone who obviously wasn't feeling what she was feeling felt abusive.

Saskia bit her top lip as she searched his face, looking for inspiration on how to handle this delicately.

"Um, you know what? How about I tell you in the car on the way to the hotel? It's a pretty big story." Leaving the couch, Saskia collected her purse and handed over her mug, staring intently at Liam, praying he would continue to forget about Haiti.

Confused, Paul placed his mug on the coffee table and went to Liam. He hugged Liam and thanked him for the help, then joined Saskia at the door.

With Paul in tow, she rehearsed various ways to deliver the news. Each version sounded shallow or cold. How does one break the news that their hometown is unrecognizable and will never recover? Saskia opened the door as Liam's phone chirped from the living room.

"Sask, wait." Liam rushed toward the door with his phone. "Ohhhhhhhh. Wow! These pictures my buddy just sent from Haiti are awful. Sask, you've gotta see these. That earthquake obliterated Port-au-Prince."

"Liam, seriously?" Saskia whispered and turned just in time to see the panic creep across Paul's face before it took root.

"What do you mean an earthquake?"

Fourteen. Quatorze. Katòz.

"I know it's a lot to take in. But your people may be okay. We need to find out," Saskia said as the car stopped, artificially cooling. Sheltered by the layers of cement in the parking garage, she assessed the situation.

Paul had been silent the whole ride, absorbing every detail, numb to every slow turn or gradual stop of the car. Parked on the first floor of the hotel garage now, Saskia watched Paul sit and stare at the cement wall. It was like he had turned into a zombie, a lifeless shell.

She felt this pull to touch him or hold his hand, but she wasn't entirely sure how Paul would receive it. Would he pull away? Would he hold her hand in return? They were in such a strange place. Not exactly friends, and not yet lovers. They were just floating in their individual lakes of grief, hoping the other would join theirs. The questions swirled and stirred and fed every thought of her and Paul together in ways that would embarrass her mother. Ways she'd dreamed of every time she visited Haiti, but the time was never right. There was always a long list of family obligations and not a moment to escape somewhere with anyone, but especially him. When they were in college, neither had access to a car for long enough to cross their terrain of friendship.

She knew this wasn't even close to the right time, but he was one of the few people who understood how personal everything felt. The only person who could chase away the weight of the earthquake. She needed to be touched, to be held, so she could stop feeling hard and breakable. He could help her feel human again. But they were still on shaky ground, and she shouldn't expect that from him. Not after last night, not without knowing how much he had lost.

Desperate for something, anything, to end the internal torture, she said, "Paul? What do you want to do?" Searching his face for an answer. Nothing; all he did was stare at the cement wall. It made her nervous. He couldn't be like this forever, could he? She continued, "We're here at the hotel. We can see if your stuff is upstairs."

Paul shuddered. Stuff. His stuff. Did he even have stuff? The question brought him back to the car. In less than twenty-four hours, he went from the gentle warmth of a Haitian morning to being kidnapped and the likely victim of a historic earthquake.

Wait. No. Not a victim. Haitians were never victims. Being a victim meant the fight was over, and for Haitians, the fight never ended; it only evolved. In that moment, they were… *impactees*.

Yes, he was an *impactee* of a historic earthquake. He didn't know who was alive or dead. Did he even have a home to go back to? Paul was a take-charge kind of guy. In his ideal world, he'd be enjoying an ice-cold *Prestige* beer with Saskia to celebrate solving these bizarre mysteries. They would cross over from their strained friendship into something more intimate. But he couldn't even get the gears in his mind to work. Blank, that was all he had up there. A mental blank.

The muffled scream of a toddler broke through the layers of metal and glass into the car, and both looked for the source. To their right was a pair of under-caffeinated parents wearing mouse ears. Three kids under eight ran around them in circles. Like hurricanes, the family slowly moved along the walkway from the garage to the hotel awning. Once they crossed the street, the older two took off, darting between the sea of cabs and cars offloading tourists of every variety.

Helplessly, the parents watched the kids as if watching alone would keep them safe from harm. On the mother's side, a toddler screamed and kicked and pawed at her button-down blouse until it popped open. She looked down, sighed, and used her free hand to button up her shirt.

"Did you see that?" Paul said, letting out a huff of disbelief.

"Yeah, that was wild! She just buttoned up her shirt and kept going. If she can do that, then I guess maybe we can go into the hotel and figure this out?" Saskia hoped the logic would break him out of whatever stupor he was in and bring him back to her.

Paul gave her a sidelong glance. "Fine. Let's go upstairs."

Saskia analyzed the tone of his voice. Practical, focused, cold. Whatever feelings or warmth she was hoping to find didn't exist there. Their relationship was just that: a friendship. A practical, focused friendship. She stuffed down her disappointment and said, "Yeah, let's see if we can find it. If not, you can always use mine."

Paul nodded in reply. When he opened the door and stepped out, her heart went with him, leaving her empty.

Saskia opened her door, and a cool breeze chased away the wet cement smell of the garage and brought with it hints of traffic, water, and trees. Saskia smiled briefly at how that smell always made her feel at home, made her relax no matter the circumstances. When she'd change trains in New York, she'd catch a hint of it, and homesickness would make the deep slate gray of winter so much worse. Then, she'd scour every restaurant to find a key lime pie. All winter long, it was her mission until she had to give up or settle for key lime pie-flavored yogurt at the grocery store.

When she got to Orlando, everything was too quiet. Too friendly. Too bright. It was January, and she'd sweat if she walked too fast or if she stood for more than five minutes in the sun. That was when she'd miss the unique feeling of being cold and warm at the same time. That was when the pain of leaving New York became particularly sharp.

The need to experience something that made her feel so present, like nothing else mattered, hummed through her. What she would give to feel Paul's hands slide into hers like they did during her summer trip. Walking behind everyone else on their way to the beach party, his thumb had caressed the gentle valley he found there.

She searched Paul's face again for any sign that he might feel the same way. But his face hadn't changed since they had left Liam's, focus and concern. She let out a quick sigh and matched his silent pace as they walked from the car to the pedestrian exit from the garage. There, the cement awning let them wait for logo-covered shuttles and taxis to crowd the driveway. Under it, the hotel could have easily fit at least twenty cars, something even New York City hadn't pulled off.

Once the passengers popped out, Paul and Saskia wove their way through the crowded drive to the front of the hotel.

"Paul, I knew this place was big, but this is next level," Saskia said, finally catching him. Paul smirked as he looked back at the driveway to watch the chaos of luggage and limbs as they tried to rush out of their respective cars. Disney characters, people in Spiderman costumes, and stuffed killer whales of all kinds clashed with business suits and leather briefcases. Kids helped or stressed their parents with missing toys or poorly timed needs. Frazzled by the chaos, the suits efficiently pressed on to whatever meeting they had next as if the world around them was irrelevant.

"Yeah, I don't know how you have the space for all of this," Paul finally said as a family of ten made it out of a taxi van.

Saskia giggled and kept walking toward the hotel lobby until she noticed Paul had stopped. Looking back at him, she found him standing still, frozen.

"Whoa, what's the deal?" She said, running back to him.

"Over there." Paul pointed to another awning that connected a different cement building to the parking garage. "I was getting out of the conference center to come here, and that's where it… happened."

Following his gaze, she could see a similar driveway crowded with taxis and rental cars. But instead of dodging balloons and mouse ears, guests juggled enormous trunks and oddly shaped suitcases while wearing wool blazers and pants. It wasn't as lively as their driveway and seemed a little off the path of the main activity of this complex. Out of the way of most of the activity. To Saskia, it looked like the perfect place to kidnap a person. She shuddered and patted his arm to bring his attention back to the present. If they stayed there too much longer, she was worried they'd get stopped by security.

"Ah, well, let's go find your phone, get you a new key, and see if we can figure out what is going on," Saskia said while carefully wrapping her hand around his arm to gently tug him toward the door. Expecting resistance, she was surprised that he let her pull him as he stared at the other driveway until the revolving doors blocked it from view.

Fifteen. Quinze. Kenz.

When the elevator doors opened onto the twelfth-floor, Saskia and Paul stepped into a small lobby with a side table and artificial flowers, each lost in their thoughts. Silently, they turned left from the elevator, the industrial carpet absorbing their steps. The muffled silence put Saskia on edge, and she flicked her fingers in time with her footfalls.

"Everyone must be at the parks," Paul said, hoping to break the eerie silence.

Saskia nodded in reply. They continued, following the numbers down the hall. Once they turned left, a horrific odor invaded every corner of their noses.

"God, what is that smell?" Saskia said between gasps.

"It's awful. It's gotta be *viande pourrie*, or rotten meat? Is that how you say it?" Paul said in a voice high in his nose, trying not to breathe an inch of the vile smell.

Saskia nodded and covered her face with her shirt. Matching her approach, he also covered his nose and led them down the hall. The closer they got to his room, the stronger the smell became until Paul stopped at a door on the left. Saskia handed him the new key card, and he slid it into the thin slot on the door handle until the light turned green. When the door opened, the smell flooded the hallway, and they coughed until their eyes watered.

Through each cough, Paul remembered running through the butcher area of his neighborhood street market. Back when they were safe enough for him to walk through, that section always turned his stomach. The vacant eyes of cows, pigs, and chickens kept him from eating meat for months. However, this smell had nowhere to go and concentrated until it seared itself into Paul's memory. With the door open, it only took a couple of minutes for breathing to become easier. Now that they could breathe without gagging, they entered the room.

"Paul, what the hell? Is this how you normally live? What did you bring from Haiti?"

Paul ignored the comment and carefully stepped into the room after her.

Yesterday, when he entered the room to drop off his suitcase, the view took his breath away. From the doorway of his twelfth-floor perch, Paul could see the rollercoasters launching tourists through never-ending loops and the nearly complete towers of Hogwarts. The room had been recently renovated, and every aspect was in a range of neutrals with turquoise accents, like a kind of modern beach house. Crossing the threshold, he could see a small couch in front of a television, a bed, and then a little side door to the bathroom. It was pristine and even had a little welcome note on the bed.

Standing with Saskia now, the room was completely trashed. His suitcase lay empty and tossed against the sliding doors. The papers and flyers he planned to hand out at his session covered every inch of the beige carpet. Careful not to crease any of the sheets, they turned the corner toward the bed. From there, they could see that everything that should have been in the suitcase had been scattered across the room.

"To answer your question, no, I don't normally live like this," Paul said, trying to keep the irritation out of his voice. "Someone's been here."

"Should we call the police?" Saskia asked without noticing the shift in tone.

"What are the police going to do? Come and collect a little money to find out who did it? I think we're okay." After he said it, Paul winced a little, knowing it was a bit harsh. He knew it was a simple question, but all he could think about was the neighbors who used to call the police for help, only to become victims of a break-in days later. It had been years since Haiti worked like that, but the habits endured. He could tell her all of that, but what if it scared her off from coming back to Haiti? She didn't deserve to have her memories of it ruined by justifying his tone. Scooping up the pages, hoping to salvage a few for his upcoming session, he didn't dare look over at Saskia. He'd already been through so much he couldn't go home empty handed. As if losing his portion of the company wasn't enough pressure, now the country would need every dollar they could find to rebuild. He had to come away from this trip with real connections to get mango sugar on the market. If it worked, everything would change and he'd have the resources to make it up to her.

...

"You know, things actually work here," Saskia said, while shaking her head at a pile of clothes by the window. "The police don't take bribes." She settled into the armchair closest to the pile. She folded each item of clothing, placing them on the wooden coffee table. It was nice to have a mindless task to let her brain run through everything that had happened.

Who is still alive?

Is everyone okay?

What will the city look like when the dust finally settles?

Why am I folding the clothes of a man who isn't family?

Looking over at Paul, her heart twisted at the flecks of bark and sand on his shirt. How had he survived so much? Even before all of this, she had heard whispers of how Paul had lost his mother and how, years later, his father never really recovered. There were even whispers of how

Paul's father may have ventured off the legal path to keep their lifestyle afloat. But as a community, they did what they did with many things: they ignored it until it couldn't be denied. And if it was true, how much did Paul know? Did it have anything to do with his kidnapping?

Folding a pair of jeans, she felt the hard edges of a card in the back pocket. Fishing in the pocket, her fingers clamped down on a plasticized business card. Saskia pulled it out, noticing the embellished borders and an address on the front. The detailed finishings reminded her of something from the Middle Ages or some fancy fairy tale book. Looking closer at the address, she only recognized *Rue St. Pierre*.

"Paul? Where is *Rue St. Pierre* in Haiti? I feel like there is a park there. Or like a plaza?"

...

Paul sifted through the last pile of papers by the closet. "Yes, there's a big church there, and it's been there for ages. Why?"

"I found this weird business card covered in plastic."

He looked up from the stack. Seeing the card, he set aside his session's flyers on a glass end table and joined Saskia by the window.

"You won't believe this, but some random nun gave it to me before I came to Orlando. Check out what's on the back. It's even weirder."

Paul flipped the card over and pointed to the inscription. Running his fingers over the raised lettering again, he could almost feel the gentle breeze from the day before, almost taste the air infused with land and sea. He could also feel the low simmering anger for his father. The condescending tone, his arrogant swagger, everything the man used to come off as some big deal. But what if he never saw his dad again? What if he were buried alive somewhere without anyone to help? The anger changed into something heavier. Something like a stone wrapped in hundreds of thin strings that dared to excavate long-ignored emotions.

But he wasn't at home. He was in just another hotel room in a sea of hotels that didn't protect him from what happened yesterday.

He ignored the stone of grief and said to Saskia, "*Tend to the Guardian Within.* What a weird phrase, right? It's not even French."

"You know what's crazy? The same phrase is on a bracelet my aunt gave me over the holidays. I can show you when we get back to the car," she said as she looked up to meet Paul's eyes. Paul's amber eyes, which turned almost gold in the late-morning sunlight. Along the back of her neck, she could feel the light hairs rise up, begging to be touched. Watching Paul's face darken, her breath came short. They were in a hotel room. No one else was around. Maybe they could enjoy the time together for once? Paul took a step toward her, and Saskia shot up out of the chair.

"Also, this place was a mess when we walked in, I don't see where the smell is coming from," Saskia said, placing the last of the clothes on the stack. They were so close, she could have had what she had been wanting for years, and she just bolted? Shaking off the need, Saskia walked away from Paul toward the bathroom.

...

"Huh, yeah, that is weird," he said, looking down at the chair she was just in. Did he misread the signs? Or did he move too fast? Maybe she just wasn't ready or interested. She probably just saw him as a friend. Letting the realization sink in, Paul suddenly felt very, very tired and very, very lost. Everything he understood about the people who shaped his world was wrong. His father was likely a criminal, Marcello was likely a criminal, and Saskia was likely just a friend. He needed all of this to end.

"Do you want to check the bathroom while I keep looking for my phone or wallet? I'd even be happy with my passport," Paul said as he let out a sigh. Exhausted from the defeats, he slid the card into his jeans pocket before collapsing into the chair. It was still warm. Leaning into it, he watched Saskia walk toward the bathroom. It was weird how they slipped into a rhythm reserved for family members or lovers. She had touched all his clothes, seen his hotel room, and was now going into *his* bathroom. He couldn't remember when someone had been this close to his things, especially someone he wanted this badly and clearly didn't feel the same way. Suddenly, it felt as if she were everywhere, and the walls of the room moved closer, shrinking in size. Why was she even here?

"Paul, you should come look at this," Saskia said from inside the bathroom. Her hollow whispered tone spiked the hairs on his neck. Her voice pushed the walls back to where they belonged, and he put down the bag of airplane snacks onto the T.V. console. Something in that voice made him nervous, and each step he took toward the bathroom only made it worse.

When Saskia came out and shut the door behind her, she had changed. Her face had closed up, her mouth set into a serious frown, eyes wide and glassy. When she risked a glance at Paul, he went on full alert.

"Didn't you just ask me to come and see what is going on in the bathroom?" Paul said, trying to hide his irritation and mask his fear.

Saskia scowled. "Are you kidding? You have me come up here to this crime scene of a hotel room. I fold your clothes and help you get this room right, while you play up this wild, unbelievable story about getting kidnapped. I felt sorry for you; I was worried that someone was actually after you. Only to have me open the bathroom door so you could get my fingerprints all over everything. So, I could be your accomplice to murder? I knew your dad was a criminal, but I had no idea that you were too. I trusted you, I almost let you kiss me, and you leave a body in your bathroom. Screw you." Her gaze locked onto his, making sure those last words landed exactly how she had planned.

Paul glared at her and said, "What are you talking about? How could there be a body in there? Also, all you cared about today has been your experience, your feelings. *I* am the one who has been through hell. *I* have been the one who has been so close to death, not you. No, you have been sitting here in your perfect little house, in your perfect little community. Safe. No one wants you dead; no one wants you involved in anything but parties and household chores."

Saskia returned the glare. "Screw you, Paul. You are only in this mess because you refuse to move any faster than a snail on anything. Why are you attacking me when it's your dad that got you in this mess in the first place?"

"You don't know that."

...

"For as long as I could remember, your dad's reputation has been that he is bad news. Why do you think I won't let you get too close to me? I didn't know how much you were like him until now."

Now she was pacing from the front door of the room with her hands folded on her head back toward the bathroom door, not even caring about the tears that fell. She almost trusted him; she almost let herself cross the line from close friends to being forever connected to a criminal. She couldn't risk going to prison for him.

"You don't know what you're talking about. He isn't a criminal."

"Then why is there a dead body of an old man in your tub, Paul?" she said through gritted teeth.

They stared at each other, Saskia terrified, and Paul unable to process the accusation.

...

"You're insane. You're seeing things. Why are you even here? It's weird, it's too much. You're too much. You should go," Paul finally said so quietly that he wasn't sure she heard him. He was too tired for this, too tired to deal with one more possibly traumatic situation. Back home, distressed women were known to hallucinate. Obviously, Saskia had worked herself up into enough of a hysteria to be hallucinating.

...

Saskia leaned against the bathroom door as if he had punched her in the gut. He didn't believe her. He was one of those idiot men who'd dismiss a woman for saying water was wet. Drawing on every ounce of strength she had left, she set aside her rage to regain her composure.

She had sacrificed her second day of work for this guy. Sure, he wasn't her boyfriend, but he needed help, so she went to help him. Did a part of her hope that would bring them closer and that he'd see she could be a good partner in a time of crisis? Yes. Did she now feel as disposable as a tissue from the box next to his bed? Also, yes. She had overextended herself for a man who was probably a murderer. How could she have been so wrong about him? Mortified tears threatened to break loose, but she wouldn't give him the satisfaction of seeing her cry. That would destroy her. She had to leave.

"You're right, I should go because from where I'm standing, you are in a whole lot of trouble, and I don't want to get wrapped up in your mess. I am going back to my life instead of getting sucked into whatever illegal shit you are into."

...

Paul didn't respond and only glared at Saskia. Memories of the last twenty-four hours flickered across his mind. His father. The kidnapping. The earthquake. Each one is a bubble in a rolling boil of impatience. This woman felt she could show up, help him, and then accuse him of doing something illegal? He didn't need this. He didn't need her. He needed his phone, his wallet, and to somehow figure out what the hell was going on. He had worked too hard to have an acquaintance accuse him of being a criminal. Back home, that was enough to get someone blacklisted or killed, and he had no intention of being either.

"Good, and so we're clear. All of this was *your* choice. *You* offered to come up here, *you* chose to come into this room, and *you* chose to open the bathroom door. You are just as involved in this mess as I am. So, if you want to go all psycho, then leave."

...

"I chose? I *chose*?!" Saskia screeched, then paused to find her next words. Each statement had cut Saskia deep and pushed the building dam of tears so close to the surface. She was too close to losing. She had to shut down. Stilling every emotion until it felt like ice coursed through her veins, she went cold. He was just like every other man she had the misfortune of developing feelings for—happy to have her around until they weren't. Happy to use her until they could discard her. She wasn't going to stay here and argue with him. It was very much time to leave.

Saskia peeled herself off the bathroom door and stomped her way to the front door. "*Gèt marenne'ou* and good luck. You selfish prick." When she tried to slam the door shut, it resisted. The automatic closer slowed the door, and Saskia just screamed at it and stormed off.

...

When the door clicked shut, Paul could hear muffled footsteps disappear down the hall. Then silence. The silence sucked the warmth from the room. He was now completely alone. Had he gone too far?

Rubbing his arms, he started to worry. What was supposed to be his safe space had become a room someone knew how to get into. This person also knew where all of his stuff used to be and might have things like his passport, phone, or wallet. His mind raced, looking for possible threats that lay waiting for him until he finally heard the muffled plink of dripping liquid in the bathroom. He'd almost forgotten about it.

Paul approached the bathroom door, took a deep breath, and slowly opened it. What he saw turned his stomach. Along the tiles, blood. The walls, blood. The mirror, blood.

Blood, there's so much blood.

In the bathtub, a man slumped under the weight of a bloodied hog's head. The body was covered in blood, which Paul couldn't tell if it came from the pig or the person. Approaching the body, careful not to slip, he noticed the man's subtle chest rise and fall. Paul exhaled a breath he didn't know he was holding. He wasn't dead yet. Looking closer at the blood-spattered name tag lying on the man's chest:

Dr. Thomas Oakley

"Dr. Oakley!" Paul rushed to his side and gingerly lifted the hog's head. Whenever his head would catch, Oakley would feebly moan and rattle his feet in the muck of the tub. With one last gentle pull, Oakley's face broke free, and he gulped in the fresh air. Tossing the head into the tub next to Dr. Oakley, Paul clutched the blood-stained fingertips of his favorite professor.

"Are you okay?"

Still gasping and wheezing, all Dr. Oakley could manage was a shake of the head and placing his hands on his chest. Paul nodded and squeezed the fingertips again before saying, "Let me call for help."

Dr. Oakley nodded and coughed so violently that Paul could almost hear his ribs rattle. Digging into whatever scraps of bravery he had left, Paul stood up from his place next to the tub. Unable to look away from Dr. Oakley, he watched him, inspecting every cough and every wheeze. Terrified, it was his last.

Walking backward into the hotel room, he sat on his bed and blindly reached for the phone. When his fingers found the smooth plastic, he lifted the phone receiver and darted his eyes to the keypad to find the front desk button. With shaking hands, he pushed the button next to the cartoon image of a desk. The digital rattle of a connected line soothed him at first. Help was on the way. When the pleasant female voice of the concierge came through, the only words that came out were, "I'm really sorry, but I need help. We need help. There's a body in my bathroom."

Sixteen. Seize. Sèz.

Unsure of where to go, Saskia paced back and forth in front of the large hotel windows, cheeks slick with anger-fueled tears. She wanted to leave and find somewhere to think about her really terrible luck. But if she left, what would happen to Paul? Was he really responsible for the crime scene in the bathroom? Or was this yet another example of her overthinking things, and she should trust him? Back and forth, back and forth, Saskia walked the cement sidewalk with her worry and flip-flops until something in the breakfast room caught her eye.

Beyond the tall windows sprawled a room filled with light wood tables for two and four. Along the back wall, a table covered in bagels and fruit waited patiently for the diners. In the far corner of the room, Saskia could see CNN continuing its coverage of the ash-covered ruins of downtown Port-au-Prince. The concerned news anchors listened to tearful interviews with people on the street. A couple more tears escaped her eyes as she watched the lips silently talk about what happened. Everything that had been lost, how their lives were forever changed, pulled the tears into a gentle stream. Thinking back to how long it took New Orleans to recover from Hurricane Katrina, she began to doubt if Haiti could ever really recover or even repair what was lost.

A dense thud against the window made Saskia jump. Looking down, she saw the familiar face of a small boy planting his forehead into the hurricane-proof glass. She watched him as he dragged his little tongue up and down like an abstract painter. Locking eyes with Saskia, he smiled with pride and dragged his little pink tongue further down the window. Finally catching up, his mother snatched him up, wrapped a protective arm around him, and then glared at Saskia. Unbelievable. Squinting her eyes in response, Saskia watched the pair return to a table with two other small kids wearing Disney T-shirts. The parents continued struggling to manage their kids, this time wrestling each one to get at least some eggs in their mouths before what promised to be a long day at the parks.

Looking around the room, she spotted a couple wearing Mickey ears while a slightly older couple at a nearby table took a picture for them on their neon pink digital camera. The woman proudly held up her hand, flashing the sparkling diamond ring, while her fiancé smiled. At another table, a group of men in suits fiddled with their conference lanyards while laughing at what was probably a very bad joke. Everyone on the other side of the window was living a perfectly normal, undisturbed life. None of them needed to question what life would bring them next, because everything was so certain, so normal. Not a single diner noticed the horror movie of the news playing on the T.V. They just went on living their painfully normal lives.

"It's so unfair, so horribly unfair," she whispered to the window.

Saskia turned her back to the breakfast room and leaned against a neighboring cement pillar separating the large windowpanes. She stood there breathing, seething, and thinking: *How horribly unfair.* A couple of strangers gave her worried looks as they passed her, but she didn't care. Her life had been rooted in her parents' homeland. When things were tough, Port-au-Prince was the solid backup plan if they needed it. Now, it was only a memory that swirled in the ashes of its legacy. Where would they go in case things went wrong here? Her BlackBerry rattled against the pillar behind her, vibrating from an incoming call. Without looking at it, she pressed the accept button and answered.

"Saskia Anaïs Roy. Why are you answering my call? Why are you not at work?" Her mother's voice filled her head with concern.

Saskia sighed and couldn't find the energy to lie.

"Mom, you aren't going to believe this, but this is what happened." When she was younger, she would leave out details that would send her mother into rants that always left her in tears. But Paul had already made her cry, so why not add more to the pile? Saskia shared every detail of the morning with her mother, unafraid of her reaction.

"And I left him up there," she concluded. "He's such a *salope*, how could he ever treat someone like that?"

"*Saskia, c'est toi qui est la salope*. How could you treat him like that? Didn't I teach you better?"

Saskia sucked in a lungful of air instead of responding.

"He was kidnapped yesterday. He hasn't talked to his family, so he has no idea if anyone he cares about at home is alive, and you left him alone at a possible crime scene, where they will deport him as soon as the airport in Haiti is open. They'll do it even if he isn't guilty. You have to go up there right now and help him figure this out. Does he even speak English?"

In the smallest voice she had, Saskia replied, "He speaks English well enough."

On her end of the line, her mother sighed and said, "Cherie, I thought by now you would have grown out of this child made of glass phase and into the living, breathing human adult that I know you can be."

"Well, of course you would take his side."

"I am not taking his side, *ti cœur*. But you missed your second day of work for a man you barely know. Then, he hurt your feelings over something so small, something he didn't even know he was doing, and you just ran out like a toddler? What do you think you are doing?"

"He's a Lancelin. It's Paul Lancelin," Saskia said softly as she could hear her mother suck in a big breath. Her mother thought for a moment and said, "*Bon*, that changes things."

Saskia made a face. "What do you mean that changes things?"

"Even though we've known them a long time, Saskia, I still think you are focusing on the wrong things. Right now, your job is the most important thing, not some guy you are getting to know. Especially one that might be connected to the gangs," her mother said gently.

Looking across the road, Saskia could see her car peeking through from the parking garage. She could leave now, catch the rest of her shift, and beg Sherri for forgiveness.

"Think about it, *ti cœur*. You can always leave your number with the hotel, and he can call you when you are out of work if he needs help. But right now, you need to make sure you are taken care of, not someone else. We have no idea what is in your future, but I am pretty sure he is not in it." In the background, muffled voices came through as if someone had walked into the room where Jacqueline was taking her call.

"*Cherie*, I'm sorry, but I have to go. Please make the right choice and go to work. Love you." A click, then silence on the other end, gave Saskia the chance to breathe.

Was her mother right? She was already outside the hotel, her car was so close, she could just get into it and make it to the end of her shift. Her hand vibrated again, and she answered it again without looking.

"How are things going? Want to meet up for lunch or something? You know you aren't too far from that new Cuban spot? Or we could be cliché and go to one of the parks?" Liam's voice rattled the speaker, and Saskia squirmed in the silence.

Maybe this was what she should do instead. This solid third option would give her space from Paul and avoid dealing with Sherri, while she felt like a hollowed-out meat suit going through the motions of living.

"Saskia? You there?"

After letting out a long sigh, she said, "Yeah, I am here. We could do something for lunch."

"Sask—what's going on?"

She hated that Liam knew her well enough to push when she went quiet.

Again, a long pause, but she finally said, "So, when I went up with Paul to his room, something happened."

"Oh, my god! You hooked up? I knew it! It was only a matter of time. How was it?"

"No, no, we didn't hook up. Um, someone had been through his room and destroyed it. I mean, literally everything was on the floor or dumped on the bed. And oh god, the bathroom, and he was being such a jerk. And we got into this weird fight, and there was so much blood in the bathroom. I just gave up and left."

"Blood in the bathroom? And you just left him there?!"

Saskia squirmed again while holding her silent BlackBerry.

"Yes?" she responded in a voice so small she could hear Liam gasp on the other end.

A police car and an ambulance roared into the covered driveway of the hotel. The sirens echoed in the cavernous awning, amplifying into an ear-splitting whine. Once parked, the first responders gathered their gear and passed Saskia on their way to the elevators. Through the window, she watched as they disappeared behind the closed doors of the elevator. When the lights above the elevator stopped at Paul's floor, her heart sank.

"Saskia? Are the cops there?"

"Yes," she said with a brittle voice, "I think I need to go up there."

"Ugh, duh! Get up there! I'll get dressed and be down there in a bit."

She didn't respond.

"Sask!"

"Okay, okay, fine. I'm going." She ended the call, took a deep breath, and went back through the lobby. With every step, she felt a new set of eyes lock onto her, watching her. Without pressing a button, the elevator doors opened, and she stepped inside, safe. The quiet rush of the elevator on its climb to the twelfth floor soothed her, and for the first time in the last twenty-four hours, she could breathe.

...

"Do you have anyone who can vouch for your story?" asked in a southern-tinted voice. Paul froze. Who could he ask? Saskia? After she ran out after seeing the bathroom instead of staying to help him figure this out? He'd rather eat grass.

This experience was a nightmare; his life was a nightmare. When he opened the door to the first responders, they flooded the room with their forensic kits and suspicions. Then, for the next thirty minutes, he just stood in the corner with his arms folded across his chest, watching as everything he had got put into a zip-top bag and converted into a piece of evidence as they did on T.V. Maybe he did need her.

He couldn't clear the memory of watching Dr. Oakley howl in pain as they lifted him from the tub onto the stretcher. The tight quarters made it almost impossible not to hit him against a wall or a corner.

When they managed to get Oakley onto a stretcher, he gasped out on repeat, "Marcello... Your father, he owes Marcello."

His mind kept trying to put the pieces together, but he just couldn't. How could his father be involved in any of this? They run a sugar and mango export business. He was going to revolutionize the sugar industry with a better alternative to factory-made sugar. His father knew this. What could he possibly be doing that he would owe Marcello, probably a small-time dealer, anything?

"Hello? Do you even understand English?" a police officer asked.

Paul stiffened. If this guy only knew how many languages he had mastered by the age of ten. Miracle of miracles, he kept his cool and calmly responded.

"I heard you, but I am visiting and trying to remember who I can call. I got hit on the head, remember?"

The officer bristled and scowled before saying, "If you ain't got anyone, you're gonna have to come with me."

"Not necessary. I got someone. But I need my phone so I can call her," Paul said as he rubbed his hand over his head, realizing he didn't have his phone. Between the headache from yesterday and the lack of sleep, all Paul wanted was for this day to end already.

"Do you know where your phone is?"

"No, sir, it was taken from me after I got punched in the face and dragged to some island not far from here."

The officer shook his head and spoke into the walkie-talkie on his vest, "Dispatch, this is Officer Brandt. Requesting a unit for a field sobriety and drug screening before transport. Subject's statements are inconsistent."

Paul curled up his hands into fists before saying, "What part of that makes you think that I am on drugs? I am the victim here. Someone attacked *me*. And did this to *me*."

"Ok, now cool it, son. We are just trying to figure out what happened. So, bring down your tone and relax those hands. Otherwise, I am gonna start taking this as a threat."

Before he could respond, a calming hand landed on Paul's arm, and his fists relaxed in response. When her melodic voice said, "Hi, officer." Relief flooded every cell of his body. Even if she didn't solve this mystery, at least he wouldn't have to figure it out alone.

Seventeen. Dix-sept. Disèt.

"Can you go over this again? Why is *that* man in *my* house?" Jacqueline hissed at her oldest daughter while pointing toward the living room.

"*Our* house," her husband, Emile, corrected.

Jacqueline responded with a glare. When Jacqueline and her husband first moved to Florida, their lives started in a too-small apartment that no amount of bleach could get clean. They fought for every cent that bought the house, and it had served as a safe haven for family members throughout the years. From relatives to wayward friends, the Roys always made space for those who needed a safe place to sleep. If they could be trusted, but could the Roys trust this one? Jacqueline had her doubts.

For as small as the Haitian community was, they didn't know everyone, and they loved to make stories bigger than they needed to be. Therefore, Jacqueline couldn't blindly trust him. As her inherited European high street manners dictated, she had to receive him as formally as possible. If he met her standards, then Jacqueline knew he wouldn't be trouble if he stayed.

Hidden in the shadows of the picture-covered hallway, she watched Paul perched on the edge of their overstuffed leather couch in the formal living room. She assessed the way he handled his water glass. If he went snooping around or just sat on the couch. Disappointingly, he hadn't given her a reason to turn him away. From what Saskia shared, bad luck hung around him like a persistent fog. The sooner he could get out of her house and out of her daughter's life, the better off they would be. Saskia and the family had been through enough already and needed to get back on track. A young man fighting to overcome his fortunes will only make her difficult situation harder.

"The police let him leave with whatever didn't go into evidence, but they kept his passport until they can clear his name. If it were just the hog's head, they would have let him go. But with Dr. Oakley barely alive, they decided to treat this as attempted murder. Paul is their only logical suspect." Saskia paused and watched Paul carefully sip from the water glass and return it to the coaster.

The station hadn't found his phone or wallet. They did let him go with just enough clothes for the week and a folder full of fliers on mango sugar. When Paul came out to the car, and she saw how little he had, the red-hot anger finally disappeared. Watching him now anxiously twisting the handles of his bag, her heart melted all over again for him. He had almost nothing.

"So, how did he end up here? Can't he afford a hotel?" Jacqueline said.

Saskia winced at the frustration in her mother's voice.

"The police recommend that he not stay alone in case his kidnappers return, and…" Saskia paused to brace for her parents' reaction. "And, the police have me listed as responsible for him until this gets sorted out."

"What?" Jacqueline and Emile yelled in unison, catching Paul's attention from the couch.

He lifted his glass toward them and went back to staring at the glass coffee table in front of him.

Both Jacqueline and Emile forced a smile at him and turned to face their daughter again.

"Saskia Anaïs Roy. You can't be serious right now."

"I almost wished you had just gotten a tattoo or come home too drunk when you were a teenager. I could survive that, but this? What if he actually killed that guy?" Emile said as Jacqueline slapped his arm.

"*Vraiment?* Are you honestly wishing for that now?" Jacqueline hissed again at her husband. She took a deep sigh and continued. "We really don't need this right now, Saskia. There are still family members missing, and we are still waiting to see if your cousins are going to come here until things get better down there. We might need the space, so why are we giving the room to someone we barely even know?" Jacqueline hoped this would change her thinking.

"Mom, he hasn't spoken to anyone in his family. We might be all he has," Saskia said, feeling the weight of that reality. To lose everyone he cared for in just a matter of minutes, only to be caught up in some bizarre prank. Or… threat? Nervous energy got her fingers flicking rapidly.

Jacqueline noticed her daughter's fingers and softened. She really had something for this guy. Over the years, her daughter had roped her siblings and friends into all sorts of rescue missions for injured birds, frogs, cats, and, in high school, other friends. It drove Jacqueline crazy having to constantly clean up after her daughter's rescue projects. Why was she surprised that when her daughter found a man who needed help, she'd want to save him too?

"Fine, we'll set him up on an air mattress in the family room. But if anyone in the family needs the space, he's out. With school back in full swing, we can't give up the bedrooms for him. And if either of you thinks about doing anything that will piss me off…" Jacqueline stared intently at Saskia, ensuring she couldn't miss the point.

"Let's just hope that your bet pays off, *ti cœur*," Emile said as he patted Saskia's shoulder before leaving the hallway to join Paul on the couch.

"Exactly. I hope you know what you are doing, Saskia," Jacqueline echoed and followed her husband.

"We should have named her Rita, the patron saint of lost causes," Jacqueline said to Emile, hopeful that Saskia couldn't hear her.

He chuckled quietly in response. She hoped her daughter could walk the complicated tightrope of her own making.

...

With the family settled for the night, Paul rolled across the air mattress, crinkling and crackling under his weight. The noise brought on a sense of grief at missing out on the hotel bed. The layers of cold plastic wrapped around cold air only sharpened that grief. From here, he could see most of the first floor: a formal dining room, a kitchen, and even a bit of the front door entryway. A hallway led to a couple of bedrooms and a staircase to a couple more above.

When he first arrived, he found the house much cozier than the one he grew up in. Back home, his father's house had sweeping staircases and floor-to-ceiling views of the city below. Reginald had every material imported and even had a custom fragrance for the staff to spritz in the air twice a day. Nothing stayed out of place for long. Here, the house was significantly smaller, crowded with memorabilia of the family's highlights, and seemed to take the whole family to maintain. While at his own apartment, he didn't have help, he expected that a family of this size would have one.

Before the awkward dinner with all the Roys, Saskia pulled him aside and gave him her phone. When the purple BlackBerry landed in his hand, he felt a tremble. He had been setting aside his feelings about everything at home to focus on the mountain of issues here. To receive that phone, the connection to the murky unknown of what home he had left scared him. What if everything truly were gone?

Meeting her eyes, he nodded at Saskia and walked through a pair of French doors to a screened-in patio to make the call. Punching in the numbers with trepidation, he lifted the phone to his ear to listen to the ringing. No answer. He tried Stanley. No answer there either. Which wasn't too surprising since they didn't know her number, but still disappointing. When he poked his head back in to share the update,

Saskia already had her laptop in hand for him to borrow.

Sitting down on the cushioned patio couch, all he could hear was the wind disturbing the leaves. No insects, no frogs like at home, just leaves rustling and the occasional mechanical groan of a street racing car. It was eerie, as if the surrounding environment were keeping a secret. Opening the laptop, he went straight to Facebook. His feed was filled with grief-laden posts, overwhelming relief, and the depressingly mundane. For at least an hour, he went through the profiles of friends, extended family, and colleagues to see what had happened. While most were lucky, too many were still missing. Too many presumed dead, and too much property was damaged. Before closing the laptop, he updated his Facebook status in case anyone was looking for him.

I'm alive and not in PAP.
I can't get a hold of *Papa'm*. Does anyone *gen nouvèl li*?

Within moments, likes, hearts, and heartfelt comments flooded his notifications. To stop the near-constant pinging, he closed the computer and lay down on the couch. The eerie silence returned, but this time it came as a comfort. Everything he saw on Facebook was impossible to wrap his mind around. Where would they even start their recovery? Could they even recover?

Those were questions for whenever he returned home. While he camped out on the floor of a woman who didn't exactly want him there, he could only focus on making it through minute by minute. When Saskia waved him in for dinner, it was the needed reprieve from trying to think through problems with no solution.

Hours after dinner, he just lay there in the shadows. Wondering and stewing. Staring at the silent ceiling fan above him, the blades hypnotized him as he thought through the highlight reel of the last couple of days. Each memory added to the weight on his chest. Heavier and heavier the grief felt, threatening to suffocate him with it. What if he survived all this, just to have to bury his father? What would happen to everything? The weight increased as he remembered the far-off warehouse that Didier had convinced his dad to purchase, the one they had gone to before he left for Orlando.

Didier.

According to Facebook, he was unjustly still alive. The disappointment at Didier's survival surprised Paul. They had started as childhood best friends. Didier had been the only boy in his class willing to talk to him after his mother had died. Over time, they became professional rivals. Didier believed rules didn't exist. Paul couldn't function without them. That difference in perspective created such a deep divide. Paul doubted they'd ever mend it.

On top of that, something wasn't right about the relationship between Didier and his father. It wasn't just jealousy. How could his father be missing, but Didier was fine? Without his father present and Paul out of the country, what if Didier was positioning himself to become the de facto owner? Paul pushed away the thought.

Then the *other* memories began to surface, long-buried and almost forgotten. It had been over ten years since it happened, but Paul could still smell the burning house and the people within it, paired with freshly turned earth around the mango trees. Every hair on Paul's body stood to attention; his listening sharpened, eager to rewrite the past, eager to be ready this time for anything instead of being caught off guard. His fists clenched tighter, and his breathing came shallow and quick. The screams got louder until they choked out with the smoke. His mother reached for him through the window until he couldn't see her anymore. Tree bark dug deeply into his hands, leaving scars that would never disappear, even if they were no longer visible.

The creak of footsteps on wood flooring, then the metallic strain of a doorknob turning, brought him back to the family room. Looking around at the moonlit room, all he could see were more family photos and the stuff of an American family life, not his Haitian plantation home. According to the movies and the stories his aunts and uncles told him, this was supposed to be the safe place. No threats existed here like they did in Haiti. Here he could relax. Could he?

Since he'd arrived, he'd been assaulted, kidnapped, robbed, and he started to suspect, set up for attempted murder. Not a single one of those things had happened to him in Haiti. Not one. Was the U.S. not as safe as it seemed?

Paul froze when the metal patio door clicked shut. He forced his ears to find another auditory clue. Did someone come through the front door to find him? Or is someone hiding out back in the garden? The sound of footsteps crushing dried leaves grew fainter as they led away from the house.

Curious, Paul rolled off the mattress to investigate. Careful with the wooden flooring, he tiptoed his way to the doors in the living room. Thankful they were French doors and not noisy sliding doors, he opened them and stepped down onto a patio bathed in moonlight. Mrs. Roy had applied the same level of care to this space as to all the others. Patio furniture with pillows that encouraged long-term lounging, surrounded by decorative lanterns and plants. From the patio, he could hear the wind rustling through the trees, but not a single car. Winter night sounds in Florida were much quieter than what he had at home, but they soothed him. He wondered about taking a moment to soak it all in, to indulge in the cool night breeze, and to finally relax. But if there was even a remote chance that Marcello, or someone else, was in the house, he had to find out. Hearing the concern from Jacqueline and Emile about having him here, he needed to make sure the family would stay safe.

Leaving the safety of the patio, Paul stepped onto the stone path that stretched into the garden, out into the night. The backyard was much bigger than he imagined. From where he stood, the path wound past a small pond filled with orange fish and then onto a vegetable garden. It ended at a small gazebo within a small gathering of trees swollen with oranges, tangerines, and grapefruit. In the gazebo, he could see a young woman wrapped in a long, thin black sweater sitting on a bench, sipping from a clear glass bottle. Her hair had been let loose, and it draped past her shoulders in a curtain of loose curls. While he hoped it was Saskia, it could also be her sister, Johanna. Moving closer, Paul walked around the pond where the fish floated peacefully. He looked up at the gazebo, and the young woman didn't move. Continuing down the path, he almost made it past the vegetable garden unnoticed until he stubbed his toe on a raised stone.

"Gah," he whispered as he grabbed his foot, checking for blood or a lost toenail. Putting it down, his vision was still a bit blurry from the pain. Then the woman looked straight at him and smiled. Saskia. Even from this distance, he could feel the pull toward her, this need to be in her orbit.

"You okay over there?" she said.

Embarrassed, Paul responded, "Yeah, just… stubbed my toe, but I'll be alright."

He could see her smile and wave him over to the bench. Straightening, he limped his way forward and finally noticed the details of the gazebo. Laced through the trellises were a couple of bougainvillea in fuchsia pink and soft white, brightening the gazebo's white wood. Through the spaces in the trellis, he could see the other houses with their yards veiled in silvery moonlight. After the last couple of days he had, the view felt serene and free of predators. He felt a little silly for starting this walk, thinking he was tracking down Marcello.

When he stepped over the threshold, he noticed benches attached to the latticed walls that wrapped around the small space. Saskia looked up at him expectantly with both feet up on her part of the bench, leaning against the supporting wall. He watched as the moon dusted her features. She almost glittered, like those vampires in that movie everyone talked about. Her hair unleashed, her eyes sparkling, her smile warm and inviting. She was stunning, and his body felt electric with want. He needed her.

What if he sat down next to her? His fingers twitched, yearning to twirl into her curls, to wrap his arms around her and be reminded that everything would be okay. But what would happen if he did, and she pulled away? At no point in today's chaos did she signal to him that they were anything more than friends. There was no flirting, no looks of longing. She just went through the day getting things done. Also, she held the key to his safety. What if he offended her by getting too close? She'd push him away and make this nightmare so much worse. No, he'd give her space, respect her, and avoid giving her the wrong idea.

His feet took him to a bench opposite Saskia. Sitting down, Paul leaned his back against his wall to face her. Did she deflate a little, like she was disappointed that he chose to sit farther away? Paul shook the thought away and instead tried to think of something to say. He had nothing except words and thoughts that made him blush, and that he couldn't say out loud.

"Couldn't sleep?" she finally said, teeth clinking against the glass rim of her bottle with a false breeziness that made Paul wonder if he had made the wrong choice.

"Yeah, can't seem to get my head around everything. I'm not entirely sure where to go from here either." He was unsure how to communicate, as if he were standing in the midst of a dust storm.

"What do you mean?" Saskia turned toward him and crossed her legs onto the bench to face him.

He had her full attention now, and it only fed his need.

"I guess, who is setting me up and why? Is my dad okay? Is there anything to go back to? Before I gave you the computer back, I looked, and there aren't any flights for the next two weeks. Do you think your parents will let me stay that long?"

Paul immediately felt uncomfortable. He met every crisis in the past with fortitude and steadfast confidence, and easily overcame every obstacle before him. But this crisis, really these crises, attacked him from all sides, and he was defenseless, leaving him uncertain and paranoid. Saskia would never willingly choose a man like him.

Instead of responding to any of his questions, Saskia pulled out another bottle, opened it, and held it out to him. White liquid sloshed around the red label. Carefully wrapping his fingers around the bottle, he brought it to his lips and took a couple of sips. The cool liquid soothed his throat while the alcohol calmed the frayed edges of his nerves.

"Smirnoff Ice, really?" Paul laughed.

"Funny story. My parents don't really know what it is, so it lives undisturbed in the fridge. Well, except for when Johanna or Robert takes one. It's our little secret, and we hope our parents don't get curious. If they figured it out, it would be a nightly debate on why it was there and whether anyone *really* needed alcohol." She giggled as she took another sip from her bottle.

Then she said, "Yeah, that's a lot for you to figure out. But all you can do is take it one step at a time. I'll be here to help as much as I can."

The way she said it brought on a fierce guilt. She was hopeful, kind, and completely lacked an agenda. He felt so undeserving of her generosity, even though she had her own challenges.

"But why? I mean, I know we've been dancing around our feelings for years, but after everything that has happened today…" Paul's voice trailed off only to start again. "Obviously, I'm cursed or something, and if you stick around, you might get burned. You might become cursed, too. Why would you help me?"

"Do you have that card from earlier?"

"Yeah." Paul planted his feet on the ground to fish for it in his jeans pocket. When he found it, he twirled it between his fingers as it caught glints of light from the moon. In his fingers, it felt a little warmer than it should for having just put on his jeans. Saskia's fingers grazed his as she went to touch the card. Paul held his breath, unsure what she would do and hoping she would come closer. She maintained her distance. The gap deepened his yearning for her. What would she do if he put his hands on the small of her back and brought her closer?

"Oh, it's warm." Saskia pulled her hand away from the card, and stepped away from him to return to her drink.

Paul let out a long, frustrated sigh.

...

"So, when my aunt gave me the matching bracelet, I thought it was so freaking corny. They have all been pushing religion on me in all these sneaky ways. But since she gave it to me, it's like I have this inner knowing or inner guidance. And for some crazy reason, that guardian keeps telling me to keep an eye on you. Whether you want me to or not." Saskia brought her wrist to her other hand to twirl the beads before lifting the bottle from her seat in the gazebo.

With her drink in hand, she turned around to face Paul and smiled, noticing that his expression had changed. Before, he seemed anxious and a little nervous. Now, he just watched her, noticing her every move, making her feel... exposed. Her breath caught, her palms grew slick with nervous sweat. Tightening her grip on the bottle, she could feel a need radiating within her, a need she had pretended for too long that didn't exist. Having Paul be the one to meet that need made her shudder. They were too close, too intertwined. If things went poorly between them, trips to Haiti would become even more difficult to plan and maneuver. Besides, they were outside of her parents' house. Nothing could happen here. Again, they would have to wait.

Regaining her composure, she continued, "Being here, being in the safe place, I feel some responsibility to help anyone we know from Haiti. You know? Things are hard here, but over there, you all are fighting these insane battles that would break me, yet you keep going. You keep living. I can't change what is happening in Haiti, but I can do what I can to be kind and make things a little easier for you."

Tears pooled in her eyes, surprising her. She blinked them away.

"When I'd ask my grandmother how she survived the almost constant instability, the violent riots, and stuff. You know what she said? *'Je demande à Dieu de me protéger et en retour, je mets de la joie dans tous les rues.'* I sat there, shocked. She had every right to be angry and bitter, but every day she chose kindness to others and shared joy with anyone she could find.

Oh god, what if she… she…" Saskia gasped. The reality of what could have happened stole her breath and cracked open the walls of protection that had kept those feelings at bay.

"Oh, thank God she survived. I don't…" The choked-down sobs kept her from saying another word and shook her until the sobs echoed across the neighboring yards. It was as if her heart, like the land, had broken apart, demanding she mourn for every thought, every feeling she'd held onto until it burst forth and out. When Paul's arms encircled her and pulled her to him, the tears came faster and fatter.

Finally catching her breath, she felt him pull away and noticed his wet shoulder. It was completely soaked, and he didn't seem to care. Meeting Paul's eyes, her pulse quickened. His thumb rubbed her cheek as he whispered, "We're going to get through this, *kenbe la, nàp suviv sa tou.*"

Saskia nodded, unable to break away from his gaze. His eyes absorbed all the terror, all the baggage of returning to her hometown. All the confusion about where they stood until she felt lighter. Slowly, he brought his face closer to hers, and the closer he got, the more the tracts of grief filled with a need for his hands, his lips, to take her over the terrain of their friendship into something new. When his lips met hers, her body filled with a feeling, a feeling she knew would cultivate until the end of her days: the relief of being seen.

Eighteen. Dix-huit. Dizwit.

Up before the rest of the house, Jacqueline quietly entered the kitchen. Normally, she'd rush into coffee-making and preparing breakfast. Normally, she'd fixate on all the details and logistics of the day while she mindlessly packed lunch for her and Emile. Today, she did something different. She paused and wiggled her toes on the tile floor, feeling the cool ceramic devour the warmth from her feet. Suppose her mother caught her doing this. She smiled. Thank God her mother was still very much alive and couldn't see her doing this.

For the past two days, worry scraped against every corner of her mind, interrupting her thoughts and her moods. Grief stole her voice and tossed back a broken one. It plunged its talons so deep into her psyche that she couldn't tell the difference between them. She barely spoke, and when she did, it was loud and wrong. Creole words replaced English ones, and her accent bled out at the worst moments. She could still feel the searing hot humiliation on her skin from yesterday's panel interview when she said "fishes" instead of fish. The condescending smirks that flashed across their faces confirmed it: she wasn't good enough for a promotion. At least not in the land with streets of gold. Even if she wanted to go back to Haiti, where would she go? Port-au-Prince didn't have the resources needed to recover. Haiti was going to be her retirement plan. What was she going to do now?

Today needed to be different. Obviously, there was nothing she could do for the buildings that framed her youth. There was nothing she could do for the countless families who didn't know if it was time to grieve or time for gratitude for surviving. She couldn't do much but let in new air. Crossing the kitchen to her newly installed windows, she took a moment and watched the birds and squirrels run across the fence line. She and Emile really had built something wonderful.

Slowly, her nose found the gentle fragrances of dewy grass, her jasmine bushes, and the bougainvillea vines, infusing the cooped-up musk of the house. The smells evoked her memories, bringing on an intense wave of nostalgia. Alone, she relaxed her shoulders and let go of the tears she'd been holding in. Wave after wave of grief left her cheeks completely soaked.

"I know love, it reminds me of the home we left behind, too." Emile's voice surrounded her and accompanied his gentle arms as they wrapped her like a porcelain doll. Placing his chin on top of her head, he began to slowly rock them from side to side, the stream slowing to a trickle.

"We haven't done this in a long time," Jacqueline finally said in a watery voice.

"We didn't need to. We seem only to do this when we are both a little off balance. I'm sure there's some psychology about it," Emile chuckled.

"Ha, we can ask Thierry," Jacqueline said while laughing, then gasped as large tears began to flow. "Oh, can you imagine if we lost him? Mariel would never recover."

"Aye, Jacqueline, but we didn't. We must count our blessings. We have been very, very lucky."

Jacqueline replied with a scowl and then pulled him closer.

"What do we do about the boy?" she said, pulling away from Emile. She turned to face him.

Emile shook his head. "The boy has a name. *Paul* is a young man who seems to have a good head on his shoulders. Maybe he's worth giving a chance?"

Jacqueline bristled. That soft, begging approval usually worked, but not this time.

"She has to get back on track. We… I mean, she has worked too hard to have everything crumble in her hands, all because of a boy who, if we're going to be honest, will be gone by tomorrow. If she had just focused on her work and hadn't gotten involved with that *salopri* coworker of hers, she'd still be there. He encouraged her to go to the press with what he told her and got her in trouble, and who still has a job? He does. You'd think she'd learn by now to focus on her career, and that will save her. Not some boy." Jacqueline slapped the back of her hand against Emile's chest.

Emile sighed as he reached for Jacqueline and laced his fingers through hers, as he always did when trying to bring her back to Earth.

"She can have both, *ti cœur*. She can have love and a big career. You did it, didn't you? Besides, Paul could be a good match for our *tête dúre*, our stubborn little girl. Might soften her edges?"

Jacqueline scoffed.

At the sound of a kitchen chair scraping against the tiles, the pair turned back toward the kitchen.

"*Bonjour,*" Paul said sheepishly, waving as he placed the stack of fliers on the table. Wearing some borrowed work clothes from Emile's closet, he looked so much younger than a man who ran his father's company.

"Ah Paul! Good morning! Want some coffee?" Emile said, breaking away from Jacqueline to greet Paul.

"Yes, please. And do you know the number for a taxi? I was hoping to catch whatever was left of the conference and maybe deliver my presentation. I also have some errands to run, like maybe going to the hospital. So, a taxi would allow me to get around without disturbing your routines." Paul cast Jacqueline a look and watched her raise an eyebrow in response.

"You're at the convention center?" Emile said as he prepared the travel mugs for all three of them. "It's close to my work. I can take you."

Emile responded over the sharp hiss of the coffeemaker while he put the finishing touches on his breakfast toast.

"Great! Thank you! I really appreciate it," Paul said, relieved, easing the weight of what lay ahead. He knew returning to the conference was risky, but if he could do what he came to do, then maybe he could go home with something more than fighting off an alligator.

"Good, will you be ready to leave in ten?"

Paul nodded and double-checked the contents of the messenger bag he was allowed to keep. The click of plastic hitting the lacquered wooden kitchen table caught his attention. In front of him was a slightly beaten silver flip phone with the name Nextel across the front.

"This is an old phone of Emile's. We keep the number for times like these. You should have enough credit for a couple of days. Don't get this one stolen, too," Jacqueline said, face neutral. While she still didn't like him, she couldn't let him go back out there without a phone.

"Thank you," Paul said quietly, and he slowly took the phone and slid it into the bag.

Jacqueline nodded and patted his shoulder as she passed him on her way to the kitchen. He shouldn't feel comfortable, but she wasn't heartless. Besides, she couldn't let Emile be the only kind person in the household. Emile smiled at her as she rolled her eyes.

"Ok, let's go." Emile waved his travel coffee mug to direct Paul. After saying goodbye to Jacqueline, he followed Emile with his messenger bag.

As the door clicked shut, Saskia sauntered into the kitchen. Wearing the clothes she'd wear on a Saturday morning, she gave her mother a distracted kiss on the cheek on her way to the coffeemaker. Looking around for Paul, she knit her eyebrows together. Her mother noticed.

Jacqueline sighed. "Saskia Anais Roy. He's already left for the conference because he is focused and committed to his work. Maybe you should do the same?" She watched as the jab landed where she hoped.

Her mother's truth-laden response stung. After last night, Saskia thought their daytime interactions might be different so that they could have the kind of intimacy of wishing each other good morning. Instead, she felt dumb. She almost abandoned everything for what? A kiss?

"Right. Would you mind making me a coffee while I get ready?"

"Absolutely," Jacqueline said, nodding in satisfaction as she watched Saskia turn back toward the hallway.

When Saskia was far enough, she returned to the open windows and faintly said, "I'm proud of you for making the right decision." With that, the windows slid shut.

...

"Um, hello? Anyone home?"

Lost in the haze of an unfocused stare, Saskia jolted when a pair of fingers snapped close to her face. The branch had been quiet all morning, hardly ten customers had come in. With so few phone calls and emails, she struggled to focus. Her mind chose to analyze every corner of her life. What to do about Paul? What to do about her cousins who were only sending back one-word responses? Everything that was certain and sure became a pile of ashen puzzle fragments overnight. Clearly, she'd been at it for so long that the others had noticed.

"Oh, sorry! Hi Bob, how's your morning going?"

Bob towered over the piles of paper, assessing Saskia like a scientist observing a strange bird in the wild. He looked her up and down, continuing the assessment until he was satisfied. Slowly, a mug with the bank logo on the front, with steam gently billowing out, landed on the only small bare square of desk space.

"We figured today would be tough, so we thought a cup of tea might help," Bob said and then smiled at Saskia.

"Aw, thanks, this is so kind." Nervous, Saskia lifted the mug and inhaled the fragrant steam of chamomile.

You don't know what's in that. What if they are trying to poison you?

Don't you remember? Never take food or drink from anyone. We never know what's in it.

She could almost see the great-aunts and uncles who taught her these things throughout her childhood. But they were from a different time and a different place. She was in America. No one was interested in hurting her, let alone killing her in such a public way. She let the rim of the ceramic mug touch her lips. Taking in that first sip of the flower-infused water warmed her and carefully relaxed her muscles.

"This is nice, thank you!" she said, letting the warmth infuse her hands.

Bob simply nodded and walked away.

After watching him return to his desk, she looked around the bank floor. A short line of patrons jutted out from the teller's window, and Bob shuffled manila folders around his desk. Sherri could be heard clacking away at her keyboard in her office. It was a very normal day at Walnut Bank.

Saskia leaned back in her desk chair and continued sipping from her mug. It was only yesterday that she and Paul sorted through his scattered mess, looking for anything he needed to survive. Flashes of the bathroom scene created a disjointed highlight reel that belonged in some haunted house, not in the back of her mind. The weight of the losses, the Haitians still unaccounted for, Paul's favorite professor, the belief that Haiti could always be a backup plan, knotted her stomach and countered the tea's help in relaxing.

But as she thought through everything she saw yesterday, something wasn't right. How could one person hurt Paul and Mr. Oakley, carry an enormous hog, and arrange it all without drawing any attention to a hotel so close to the happiest place on Earth? Could one person really be responsible for all of that?

Then she remembered Marcello and his familiarity with Sherri. At the time, she did not like how close the two had been. Not only because of the age gap, but because they seemed to be bound by something sinister. The way Sherri gushed over Marcello and kept seeking eye contact with him had made her so uncomfortable. But how do they know

Dr. Oakley?

Thinking back on the state of the hotel room, whoever did it had just opened and emptied things as if they were looking for something. No threatening notes, no compromising pictures like there would be in CSI or Law and Order. It wasn't until she opened the door to the bathroom that the mess felt intentional and threatening. But even there, at least two or more people had to pull something like that off. Paul also had a *"Tend to the Guardian"* thing, like hers. Why? Was Paul actively in danger, or was that just a warning? Did it have anything to do with the Guardians? Were they coming for her next?

"Hello! I am looking for some assistance with shuffling papers. Do you happen to know of anyone who can help?" said a voice with a horrible English accent.

She looked up to find the source, and there was her favorite goofy grin and shiny bald head.

Deciding to play along, Saskia replied in an equally terrible accent to sound like a drunk Marilyn Monroe. "Mr. Liam, please sit down, and I can begin working on that for you right away."

Liam chuckled. Dropping the accent, he said, "I figured you could use a drop-in, and I wanted to hear what in the world is happening with Paul? Did he stay the night?"

Looking around to make sure no one was listening to them, Saskia finally said, "Yes? But not in the way you're thinking."

Saskia glanced at the clock and figured 11:30 a.m. was reasonable enough for a break.

"Let's go around the corner, and I'll tell you everything on the way. Meet me out front?"

Liam nodded and sauntered toward the door. Before leaving the lobby, he remembered Saskia's story about how Bob had treated her when she was younger. It had started over a debate on whether or not to use bleach when cleaning the kitchen. As she went over every detail, he remembered the posters. They haunted him for a long time and had kept him from coming out to his family. What would his politically motivated father do if he ever found out Liam wasn't the kind of man his brothers would become? What would his mother do without a church wedding to plan for him? That fear had nearly torn him away from them.

He looked back to make eye contact with Bob. It took a little bit for Bob to feel the intensity of his glare. Looking up, their gazes locked in. Liam glared so intensely that Bob pushed back a bit from his desk, as if ready to engage in a conflict with Liam.

That'll teach him.

Nineteen. Dix-neuf. Diznèf.

The gentle whir of life-saving machines and the soft squeeze of his wife's hand woke Dr. Oakley. Fluttering his eyelids, he slowly adapted to his surroundings. Bright fluorescent lights blinded him while thick plastic tubes stretched out from his arms. He had survived the attack. Looking at his wife, he noticed a few new wrinkles had etched themselves between her eyes. This wasn't a dream; he was alive and flooded with relief.

"Oh, oh, Thomas, you're awake!"

Dr. Oakley nodded slowly and snickered as she lunged toward him. She kissed him long and hard, squeezing him into a hug as if that would keep him safe.

"Don't ever do that again. You are submitting your resignation on Monday, and those kids can learn on their own. All of them are terrible. And the minute you are out of here, we are driving to Maine to spend time with my sister at the lake. We can't stay here a minute longer, or we'll die. Because you aren't leaving me."

He laughed. "Oh, but it's not that—"

A coughing fit interrupted him, each one making his body shudder. Gasping for air, he desperately gestured for water.

His wife rushed to get him a cup and let him sip from it. But the coughing continued.

"Oh! I have to tell a nurse. Hang on, my love, no dying on me today. I'll be right back," she said, desperation threading every word. Pushing herself from his bedside, she went to find a nurse.

The fire in his throat soothed, and he could gather his breath. Slowly, he relaxed. In the quiet, memories at the conference hall came flooding back. After speaking with Paul, he went for a glass of wine with some old colleagues. Feeling the urge, he walked to a nearby restroom. When he came out of the stall, Marcello stood there waiting for him. Without preamble or explanatory speech, Oakley could feel the unnatural piercing of cold metal entering and exiting his body. He couldn't tolerate the pain and was knocked out in minutes. Then, waking up inside the bloody ribcage of an animal brought on levels of terror he had never experienced. Feeble and barely able to breathe, panic coursed through his body as he flailed his arms and legs to get out. The animal's weight and the slippery liquid he sat in made escape impossible.

"Hello, old man," said the same chilling voice Dr. Oakley heard right before the stabbing.

Dr. Oakley turned and saw Marcello standing in the doorway.

"Marcello, please, I haven't told the cops anything. Please, leave me alone."

But Marcello just prowled closer to the bed, savoring every second of Oakley's terror. This was a side of Marcello that Oakley feared. He'd seen shades of it when he was a student, but never anything like this. If he had known that his former student would one day hunt him down like this, he would have said something to Paul sooner.

"But you told Paul, and that was my job." In his left hand, he scraped his hunting knife along the metal railing of the hospital bed. The sound echoed in the hollows of the bed frame like the ominous warning Marcello wanted it to be.

"Look, I was just looking out for him. He needs someone he can trust. I can be that someone. I can tell you everything he tells me. Please, whatever it takes. Please," Oakley begged.

Marcello locked his eyes on Oakley as he dragged the knife from the bed frame to the beeping oxygen machine. Lying the edge against his breathing tube, he dragged the knife along the length of the plastic tubing repeatedly, weakening the tube wall.

"My lungs haven't recovered yet, please," Oakley said, desperate for Marcello to quit turning his breathing tube into ribbons of plastic.

"Too late for apologies, Oakley," Marcello replied, moving the knife even faster, excited to hear the inevitable hiss from a punctured tube. A wooden handle from a golf umbrella hit him in the eye, and he dropped the knife. Yelling in pain, he brought his hands to his face to assess the damage.

Oxygen broke through the compromised tube and squealed out as Dr. Oakley choked out a raspy, "Help!"

Stumbling away from the bed, Marcello could hear footsteps approaching from down the hall as Oakley's monitors sounded the alarm. It was his cue to leave. Looking back at the suffocating Oakley, he was certain the man would not survive much longer. Running out of the room, he found a set of double doors just across from Dr. Oakley's room. Pushing through, he disappeared down the hall until he found an exit.

When the nurses arrived, Dr. Oakley took a few labored gasps in time with the sound of his heart monitor as another nurse ran out to find a replacement tube. Dr. Oakley frantically looked for his wife until she appeared at his bedside. Feeling her hands wrap around his, he could only mouth, "I'm sorry," over and over until the monitor flatlined.

Twenty. Vingt. Ven.

Saskia took a sip of her mango and strawberry smoothie, then chomped into her tuna pita sandwich while Liam picked at his pile of *Power Up* chips. The *Power Up Cafe* had been their place to debrief after a night out in college. It was off campus, and it felt safe enough to share their secrets without the nosy classmate in the wings. While the dining room held only about ten tables, the floor-to-ceiling windows and the hand-painted mountain scene on the back wall made the space feel much bigger. It connected to the restaurant entrance through a small opening, framed with pictures of famous patrons and positive reviews from the local newspaper, and sat a bright orange counter where solo diners could watch their sandwiches being made. At that hour, Sam, the owner, called out names and took orders from newcomers while his wife, Mariam, settled checks.

Saskia had just finished giving Liam the gist of what she believed was going on with Paul.

"So, that is what I think is happening: Marcello and Sherri are somehow involved, and Paul only thinks of me as a friend he likes to kiss," Saskia said. With a defeated finality, she hoped to get a reaction from Liam.

"Sask, are you sure? That is a wild story, and you don't really have any evidence," Liam said carefully.

She scowled. "Of course, this story is wild, but think about it. Who would have known where Paul was? Marcello. Who could help Marcello find ways to get a hog's head and kidnap an old professor? He couldn't pull any of that alone and go undetected. He needed someone to help him."

"He probably knows a whole bunch of other people. The rest of it fine. But, Sherri? I know you don't like her, but I'm not sure…"

"Fine, but something is not right, and I think this has something to do with Paul's dad. You know he hasn't talked to him, and he seems totally fine. Everything about this is so weird."

"Well, my company says we'll go out in about two weeks when the commercial flights are on again. Apparently, the airport is barely usable."

Liam paused, cautious to continue. "And another thing, I know you hate your job with the bank. Would you want to come down with me to do recovery work? With your skill set, you can make sure we stay on budget and identify any weird stuff. Apparently, they've raised a million dollars so far. Managing that amount of money can be a nightmare."

Saskia didn't reply. This could be her ticket out of her Orlando life. She wouldn't have to watch Bob ooze over clients and could try something new in a town she knew well. She could actually give back and make a real difference to a place that had given her so much. But her family had just gotten used to having her here, and convincing her parents to travel there now? Could she do it?

"Can I think about it? I want to help, but it's gonna be different for you than it is for me. And depending on what Paul ends up doing."

"What Paul ends up doing? Saskia, are you dating him?"

"No," she said in a voice so small that Liam barely heard her response.

"Babes, just because you had a moonlight kiss doesn't mean he has the kind of feelings you can make plans on. I say this as your friend who cares about you. Focus on yourself and just put those little sparks away for now. You've been through enough."

They sat in silence as Saskia thought through Liam's perspective. Maybe he was right. Between watching her favorite place in the world crumble to dust on national television and working at a place that made her question her sanity, Saskia was fried. Maybe, just maybe, she should just let everything go. She could stop trying to analyze everything in her life, so it fit neatly into little boxes.

Over the din of silver metal chairs scraping against the terracotta floors, she recognized the dull click of heels crossing the floor. Slowly, she turned to her right and spotted Sherri, followed by a rough-looking Marcello.

"Oh my god, Liam!" she whispered loudly. "It's them! Sherri and Marcello."

Liam turned toward the entrance and watched the pair settle into a table in the darkest corner of the dining room. Marcello tried hiding his swollen left eye, red and pulsing. Sherri carefully touched it like a mother checking a child. After they finished the pleasantries, both looked serious and focused. They huddled close to one another, and Liam swore he saw an exchange of something under the table.

"Should I apologize to you now or later? Because, Saskia, you might be right. Something funny is going on between them. But maybe he's her dealer?"

Saskia shook her head. "No, they are too cozy for a dealer relationship. But why? Why are they working together?"

"Sask, what if the answer to that question is worse than not knowing?"

The weight of Liam's question silenced them both as they watched Marcello and Sherri lace their fingers.

"If you're right, we'll have a hell of a time proving it to the local police. Do you really want to go down that road?"

Before she could answer, her BlackBerry rattled against the tabletop. Glancing at the readout, she didn't recognize the number and answered it.

"Hello, Miss Roy. This is Officer Brandt, in charge of the investigation into Paul Lancelin. We need him down at the station today to ask him a couple of follow-up questions. How soon can you get down here?"

Saskia glanced at Liam and then glanced in Sherri's direction. She knew she should ask Liam to bring Paul in. She knew she didn't need to be at that interrogation and could let Liam do it, so she could go back to the bank and finish her shift. But she didn't want to. The hours spent at that wooden desk under the strange pressure of being too much and not enough isn't what she wanted now, or maybe ever.

"We'll have to pick him up at the convention center. He has his session today for the *Food Science of Tomorrow Conference*, but we could be there after that."

"The convention center downtown?"

"Yup, that's the one."

"Ok, that's not too far from the station. I leave at 5:30 this afternoon. So, any time before that," said the officer.

After the phone went silent, Saskia quietly placed her phone on the table and said, "Liam. I want to learn more about Haiti. I am leaving this bank job, and we are going to find out what is actually going on with Paul. He is my friend. We have known each other for a very long time. If he's in trouble, I'm going to help him."

She looked at Liam to examine his reaction.

"Okay, Nancy Drew. I'm in. I'll let my team leader know you're interested and I'll have them send over the paperwork."

Saskia nodded, still in shock that she had said yes. Why wait for retirement to chase adventure in life? If she didn't go now, she'd forever be one of those people mourning the paths they wished they'd taken. Pushing back from the table to pay, she could feel a familiar hum course through her. She was onto something big. Glancing over at Marcello and Sherri's corner, she thought of the ways she could settle the score with her coworkers. Then the bracelet itched against her skin.

Tend to the Guardian Within, it seemed to whisper. Saskia clenched her hands into fists and then spread them wide. She was going to help the cops find their way to Sherri. Paul's freedom depended on it.

Twenty-One. Vingt-et-un. Ventyonn.

"What do you mean she isn't here?" Jacqueline clipped the end of every word. It had been a light morning at the office, and she felt guilty for discouraging Saskia from going to work. Surprising her at the bank and taking her to lunch would give her a chance to explain her position. It would also be a treat for doing the right thing: committing to a job to build her own ladder out of the mess she found herself in. But she wasn't there.

"I'm sorry, ma'am, but that's what is going on. Saskia was here this morning, and then a friend showed up, and they went out. Her stuff is still here. She should be back after lunch," Bob said, as he relaxed in his desk chair, appraising Jacqueline.

Jacqueline took a moment to keep her anger in check. To say or do anything now would not end well for either of them. After all, this was still Florida, not Haiti where she actually had leverage. Not only was her daughter missing, but she had to deal with the man who introduced her to her bleach allergy. All of this was because she tried to be a good mother and keep her daughter on the right track. If she couldn't do it with Saskia, what would happen to the other two? Were all of them going to become wayward adults committed to never reaching their potential?

Aware of Bob's unwanted attention, she said, "Well, if she returns, tell her that her Mom is looking for her."

Turning around, she stomped back through the lobby, leaving the echo of her clicking heels in her wake. After pushing open the glass doors, she grabbed her cell phone from her purse and called Emile as she crossed the parking lot.

"Hey, *ti cœur*! What's going on? You never call me this early."

"Don't '*ti cœur*' me. Your daughter has skipped out on work. *Again.* I am going to find her and drag her back here if it is the last thing I do," she said as she opened and slammed the car door shut. Throwing her purse onto the passenger seat, she let out a frustrated scream.

Emile paused, then said, "Are you sure you want to track her down? She's an adult, *cherie*. You don't need to save her from her bad decisions. And you might want to stop letting her get you so upset. It's her life, not yours."

Jacqueline glared at the phone and counted to three. Ignoring him, she said, "Emile, where did you bring Paul the other day?"

Emile hesitated. "*Ti cœur*, you need to let this go."

"Emile, if you don't tell me where you dropped him off, I won't tell you when I am going to Haiti next. You'll come home one day, and I'll just be gone."

Silence filled the space between them until Emile sighed.

"Fine. I dropped him off at the convention center. His hotel is attached to the building. Just park in the garage across the little street. It's free."

"Perfect. Thank you."

"Of course, you're not going to just go down without me, are you?" Emile asked, seeking reassurance that they were back on the same team.

Jacqueline ignored him. "I am going to be late for dinner. Don't wait up. I have to have a long chat with your daughter."

She clicked the phone off before he could respond, then threw it at her purse. Ramming the keys into the ignition, Jacqueline turned on the engine, mapping out the fastest route in her head. She'd bring her daughter back to work, whether she liked it or not. There was no other choice. This is what Caribbean mothers do: protect their kids, make them successful, and enjoy the inevitable grandkids. Jacqueline only hoped that she'd find Saskia fast enough to salvage her workday.

...

Checking his watch again, Paul saw there were only thirty minutes left in his ninety-minute session. Sitting back on the cloth and metal conference chair, he looked out at the small windowless room. Placed by the main atrium, the room received sunlight from the sprawling glass skylight. From the front of the room, he could see that the tables closest to the door benefited from the sunlight, giving them a celestial glow. On each table sat a handful of flyers in case participants walked in late and couldn't find a seat. The same fliers that almost went into evidence for the investigation into what happened to Dr. Oakley.

Having the smallest room at the conference stung at first. Mango sugar, he thought, would be the most interesting session of the conference. Something fresh from the same old conversations about supply chains and how cell phones could help track the weather. But with twenty-eight minutes to spare, no one darkened the doorway. He suddenly felt silly for having any nerves at all about presenting his research and finding creative ways to use the smaller space.

Refusing to sink into sour feelings, he went to his laptop and started to read through his presentation. When the title image reloaded on the projector, he said to the empty room, "Hello, my name is Paul Lancelin, and I am the COO and lead researcher at Lancelin Exports, the number one exporter of mangoes and sugar in Haiti. With a footprint in every state and active harvests of all one hundred and fifty varieties of mangoes, we are in the unique position to find a low-glucose sugar derived from mangoes. Because in Haiti, it's always mango season."

Clicking to the next slide, a picture of him and his father at the country house in the mango orchards loaded. His father's voice rang in his ears:

How did you think this was a good idea?

Nobody cares about new sugars, focus on selling better mangoes.

This was a waste of time. You are useless.

Looking around the room, he suddenly felt very small. Maybe his father was right. Reginald had been vehemently against this at every step of Paul's journey because he probably knew he would fail. He should have just listened to him.

Papa.

Paul hadn't heard from him, even after texting him and Stanley on the temporary phone. What if something happened to him? He didn't have close family who lived there anymore, not after what they went through after losing his mother. He and Reginald would occasionally drop in at his uncle's place downtown.

At that house, a wide veranda faced a pool surrounded by mango, cherry, and passion fruit trees. His uncle would bring out the cigars and a couple of tumblers for ice and American whisky. They'd reminisce about the days of working in the factories where they helped to produce some of the world's most expensive luxury products. Then his father would bring up the reason they thought everything had gone to hell. Seconds later, the family time ended in a shouting match with no survivors. Over time, the visits became fewer and fewer until his uncle was practically a stranger he'd wave to while passing on the street. Even his grandmother became a stranger.

Sifting through his memories, he struggled to find enough happy ones to make him feel something, anything, about his father. The more he tried to feel something, the more frustrated he became because everything his father did only brought on heartache and distance for everyone around them. Paul had excused the behavior for years. After everything his father had gone through, of course, he had sharp edges that cut deep whenever anyone got too close. But Reginald was all he had. Even if he couldn't feel something like grief or sadness for himself, who else would he spend holidays with? Who else would take the time to get to know him?

He glanced down at his watch, fifteen minutes and his session was over. Paul sighed and went to collect the flyers from the tables and push the chairs back to their place. When he made it to a table in the corner, he noticed a flyer in the middle of the stack had a bright red circle with some lines within it. Looking closer, he realized that the swirling lines were actually a thumbprint—a thumbprint that might be what he needed to prove his innocence. Quickly, he folded the page and put it in his pocket.

"Paul Lancelin?" The familiar voice made Paul straighten as he searched the conference room entryway for its owner. Seeing the uniformed officer from the day before made his blood run cold with concern.

"Officer Brandt, I'm surprised to see you here," Paul said as politely as possible.

"Yes, well I am sorry to have to track you down like this, but I wanted to see you myself. You are no longer a person of interest. Here is your passport." He lifted a plastic bag holding the passport and offered it to Paul.

Confused, Paul crossed the room, took the bag and opened it to take out the navy-blue booklet. Running his fingers over the seal, he could feel the grief surge.

"Why did you bring this to me? Do you know who did this to us? Dr. Oakley and I?"

Paul searched Officer Brandt's face for clues.

"Well, your DNA couldn't be found on Dr. Oakley or the hog, and someone paid a visit to Dr. Oakley who didn't match your description. I reviewed the security footage myself and saw it wasn't a match."

Relief flooded Paul, he was off the hook. Maybe his luck was finally turning around.

"But before you get too excited, I'm sorry kid, but the person who visited Dr. Oakley came to finish what he had started and he didn't make it."

The words landed like cement bricks on his already suppressed grief. First his missing father, then the earthquake, now this?

"What do you mean? He died?"

"I'm afraid so. We are still looking for whoever did it, so if you have any information, please share it with us."

Paul's hands dove into his pocket looking for the folded sheet.

"Here, it came from the hotel room, and it might help you find who was involved?"

Officer Brandt took the sheet and analyzed the page.

"I'm choosing to ignore that you took this away from the crime scene, but this could be very helpful. I'll reach back out with any updates."

After pocketing the folded sheet, he shook Paul's hand and made his way to the conference room entryway. Before leaving, he turned back to meet Paul's eyes.

"I'm sorry for your loss kid, well, losses really. Hang in there."

Paul nodded and waved goodbye as the officer disappeared.

Dr. Oakley was gone. He still hadn't heard back from his father, or Stanley. His hands searched his back pocket for the borrowed cellphone, pulling it free with shaking hands. Slowly he clicked through the contact list hoping to find Saskia's number.

"Wow, what a turnout." Paul froze. The melodic accent he had been so jealous of through college sounded much more sinister now. He turned and faced Marcello, leaning against the door frame, sipping out of the long green straw in his smoothie cup. Could Marcello be behind this?

"Thanks, I'm sorry you missed it," Paul said cautiously. "I'm surprised to see you. I thought you only came to this conference for the happy hour?"

Marcello smirked and pushed himself away from the door frame to walk toward Paul. "I came to see your presentation and to reconnect with old friends. Is that a crime?"

Passing a table that still had flyers, Marcello picked one up and casually read over the text, making faces at certain points. Paul noticed a scattering of cuts across Marcello's hands that made him wonder if his feelings were actually intuition.

Finally, he put the flyer down and said, "You know there is a rumor going around that you killed Oakley."

"That's your only feedback? Besides you were never one to get sucked into rumors." Paul retorted, careful to hide what he knew. If Marcello was behind this, he could be in real danger.

Marcello smirked as he sat on the table, legs dangling and ready to run if needed. Paul could tell he had a secret, but he wasn't interested in hearing it.

"Oh, and the science behind this seems shaky. No wonder no one showed up for your session."

"What do you even know, or care about the science?" Paul said, frustration weaving into every syllable.

"You shouldn't have come back. This makes things a lot more complicated," Marcello said, ignoring his response.

Paul made a face and widened his stance, making sure he kept two whole tables between them. He hadn't contacted Marcello since he had declined going out with him the night before. Judging Marcello's reaction, Paul had all the evidence he needed.

Marcello is behind this.

"Look, you are a pawn in a much bigger game, *wajon.* You were supposed to stay put until someone came to get you. When you left that island, you really fucked us all over."

Paul continued staring at Marcello as he looked for what to say next.

"I'm sorry I inconvenienced you all with my survival skills. So, you admit it, this is your fault? Oakley, my kidnapping, all of it?"

Marcello gave him a sad look and shook his head. He got up from the table and left his smoothie cup on the table while crumpling the flyer. As he made his way toward the door, he shoved the flyers off every table that confronted him.

"Look, no hard feelings, dude, but the sooner you get out of here, the better for everyone, especially your dad." He turned to face Paul and tossed the crumpled flyer at him. He missed.

"My dad? What does this have to do with my dad?" For Paul, this was the missing piece. At the heart of this mess stood a very absent Reginald. The rage from sitting in the car returned.

Marcello raised his eyebrows at that. "You don't know?" Sucking his teeth, Marcello pinched his nose as if this information made his complicated life more complicated.

"*Wajon*, you are in the biggest pile of shit, and you don't even know it. Man, I feel sorry for you."

"What the hell are you talking about?" Paul was furious now and yelling. He didn't care if anyone hear him. Marcello did this? Marcello could have killed Oakley, put him under police surveillance, and basically killed the only thing he cared about for years. He could feel his fingers close into fists and his body pushing up from the table.

"Whoa, *marica*. Look, I have to run another errand this afternoon, but I'll find you, and I'll explain everything. Your dad is bad news, and it's time you knew what is going on."

Their eyes locked, and Marcello tipped his head to the right before he disappeared into the passing crowd. Without Marcello, he could only feel the icy bite from the industrial air conditioner.

His father? Bad news?

Obviously, Paul struggled with his feelings for his father, but that was because their relationship had become rooted in obligation. Without his mother, he and his father had fallen into a kind of transactional relationship. Their only focus: helping the other survive. He figured his dad was only this way with him. Wasn't it normal for there to be conflict? Normal for his dad to maybe hate him to a certain degree? But what if that hate and anger weren't only reserved for him? What was his father capable of?

"Hey!! Sorry, we missed it! We got a little lost on the way here. This place is huge. I haven't been inside since they renovated it."

Her voice alone was like a bucket of cool water over his roiling anger. It smoothed all the sharp edges of his mood. At least he could count on this, if nothing else.

"Hey! Oh, don't worry about it. No one came, so I was cleaning up the flyers." Paul kissed her on the cheek and then hugged Liam.

As he pulled away, he could see Marcello watching them in the distance, leaning against a giant pot with a decorative palm tree. Ignoring the shiver that came from knowing Marcello was watching him, he brought the others into the room.

"Mango sugar. Huh, you can really turn mango skins into sugar?" Saskia asked.

"Well, a kind of sugar. I'd like someone here to fund further research and discuss possible go-to-market strategies, but it sounds like rumors are flying about what happened. I might have just to let that go," he said, letting out a small sigh of resignation.

Paul watched as Saskia and Liam looked around the bare room. Saskia examined every detail from the ceiling, then back down to the podium where his computer was still plugged in.

"Sask? Is this your first time in a convention center?"

She paused, then blushed, making Paul ache with need.

"I'm embarrassed to say, for a conference, yes, it is. Obviously, I've been here for high school proms and stuff, but a real grown-up conference? This one is my first."

Paul smirked and walked over to her to show her his planned presentation. Saskia's hand rested against his, making it almost impossible for him to concentrate.

"And this is where I was going to, to… *les etapes*?"

"Show the steps?" she offered.

"Yes, exactly," Paul chuckled. He could feel Saskia move a little closer to him.

Toward the entrance of the room, Liam shouted, "Ok, lovebirds, we gotta go. A new session is coming, and we've got some errands to run."

Paul pulled away first and quickly packed away his materials, feeling the chill from the A/C again. Zipping his messenger bag closed, he watched as Saskia serpentined through the tables back to the room entrance. She was light, fun, and seemed to be ignorant of life's challenges. Her family still had members missing, and he could sense that hope was fading. But here she was dancing to the ambient music from the atrium through the tables. How could he possibly be in her world? His dad was missing, and as each day passed, he gained more and more evidence that he was up to something bad, probably criminal. And that was all he had.

"Are you coming?" Saskia asked.

The way Liam and Saskia looked standing in the doorway, cloaked in filtered sunlight, pulled at Paul. In that moment, he had no way of knowing what Marcello had planned for him. He didn't know how to resolve any of the other worries that swirled in his mind. For now, he'd choose to enjoy this moment when things are simple, joyous, and light. He'd deal with Marcello later.

Twenty-Two. Vingt-deux. Vennde.

"So that's it. We think Marcello is Sherri's dealer, and they are definitely hooking up, which is so gross and so weird because she is terrible. No one like her should be allowed to be in a relationship," Saskia concluded as they walked from the convention center atrium to the parking garage.

"Even with her drug dealer?" said Liam, and all three laughed.

Saskia liked how they all flowed so easily together, as if they had been like this for years. Although Paul hadn't said or done anything about *the kiss,* she wondered what it would be like to be in a relationship with Paul. He fit so effortlessly into her life. It didn't take much to feel like he had been there all along and could be there in the future.

A cool January breeze picked up, nudging the trio as they crossed the street along the covered walkway. They were buoyant and light. The worries they had carried all week just fluttered away with the dead leaves of winter. Under the cool shade of the parking garage, they didn't have to go far to arrive at Saskia's beat-up Civic.

While she fished for her keys, Paul asked, "Hey, so where are we going? Are we thinking lunch? Drinks? Hanging out at Liam's?"

Saskia glanced at Liam over the hood of the car, hoping to get his help with what she was about to say.

"Well," Liam started, "I think Saskia was considering a run down to the police station? To answer some questions?"

Saskia watched as Paul froze in place. As much as she wanted to be mad at Liam, she wasn't sure if there was a better way to say it. The light, relaxed energy between them suddenly felt fragile and uncertain.

"Is this up for discussion, or are you trying to force me to go?" Paul's face darkened, masking away deeper feelings she couldn't read.

She gave Paul a weak smile in response. This was not how she wanted this to go. She had hoped that he would understand her position and be willing to help them all stay in the police's good graces with a quick conversation. Judging from Paul's reaction, she realized she had made a huge mistake. Didn't they survive a big fight where going to the police was the spark? How did she think that he'd be okay with this errand and not see it as yet another opportunity to get in trouble?

Looking to fix the dynamic, she said, "Well, it's kinda up for discussion. But it's also not really up for discussion."

Paul's face didn't change as he waited for her to finish her thought.

She hesitated. "If we don't meet there by the 5:30 p.m. deadline, I'm worried they will start looking for us and maybe arrest us once they do."

He screwed up his face in frustrated little lines, and she could feel the warmth of the moment before it extinguished in her hands. They finally had a moment where it felt like they were on the same team, working toward something beyond just being friends who might have feelings for each other. But did she go too far into the fantasy and forget that he deserved to have a say? If how he paced between her car and the next one was a signal, she definitely had.

Finally, he stopped and leaned against her car while he chewed the inside of his mouth. The move made Saskia uneasy about what would happen next.

After a couple of minutes of silence, he crossed his arms and said, "Got it. Well, I say we're not going. If we go, they are going to keep me for something I didn't do. I didn't get this far only to get locked up."

He began pacing, and Saskia worried he'd wear the concrete down before they could decide.

"You know, I think you're right. Marcello did it." Paul stopped pacing to check the vibrating phone in his pocket as he said it.

"That's great! Then, we go down to the station, and you can tell them that. Maybe they can help us find Marcello and put him away for good," Saskia said, desperate to get them back on the same team, to feel like they agreed.

"Then we should have talked about it instead of you manipulating this whole thing and forcing me to go to the police station," Paul said, letting his words slice as necessary. The phone in his pocket vibrated again.

"I'm going to take this," Paul said, holding up the phone at Saskia and Liam as he walked down the aisle of parked cars.

"Shit, I really messed that one up. What if he doesn't come back?"

Liam scoffed. "Where is he really going to go? It's not like he knows anyone here."

Saskia glared at him. "Liam, come on, this is serious."

"Saskia. Anaïs. Roy."

Her mother's voice interrupted them.

"Not as serious as her," Liam said under his breath.

Saskia heard him and threw him a look.

"Mom?" Turning around, Saskia could see her mother stomping down the parking-lot aisle toward her car. Flames of indignation could have exploded from her head. Saskia had never seen her so furious.

"I didn't believe it, I wouldn't believe it, but something told me that you would be here and *not* back at work. I have been searching this parking garage for thirty minutes, and when I found your car, I parked close by so I could see you when you got here." Jacqueline gestured toward the middle of the garage.

"The whole time I wondered, why would my beautiful daughter be here? She couldn't be chasing after a man when she could earn her way to freedom. But instead, you are chasing a dangerous man who doesn't seem to be interested in you at all and throwing away your best chance at rebuilding your career. Why are you so committed to ruining your life?" Jacqueline's heels stopped clicking when she reached Saskia's car, and her face flushed with frustration.

Unbound. That was the only way Saskia could describe her mother in that moment. And for what reason? Saskia had kept her anger in check until now, but this was too far.

"Ruining my life? What are you talking about?"

"Your job, Saskia! How are you ever going to recover from New York if you don't show up for your job!"

That was the last straw.

"Did you literally hunt me down like an animal, just to give me a strongly worded lecture? Come on, Mom. I didn't want that job; you wanted that job because you love being inside tight little companies with tight, stupid rules, and instead of living a real life."

Saskia pushed off the side of her car and approached her mother in a different tone, hoping to de-escalate the situation. "I needed more time to figure out what to do, to make sure the next step I took was the right one, not just the one you think I should take."

"And how long was that going to take? You know your cousin Didier did the same thing, and he spent years figuring it out, and now look where that has got him. Selling drugs, guns, and making the country worse. Do you want that to happen to you, too?"

Saskia paused, unsure of where to go from there. Finally, she said, "What are you talking about? We are two completely different people. I wouldn't even know how to find drugs if I wanted them."

"Um, guys," Liam interrupted.

"You are a very smart woman. I am sure you could find a way to get into selling drugs if you wanted to."

Saskia's nostrils flared. "But I don't want to. So why would *I* end up getting in the drug trade if *I* didn't go to work at a bank that *I* hate for a boss who I'm convinced is evil?"

"Guys!" Liam shouted.

"What?" they said in unison, turning to face Liam as their voices bounced around the cement.

"Paul is talking to some guy in a van."

All three looked over and saw Paul step into the open side door of a white Sprinter van. Annoyance raged within Saskia. After everything she had done for that stupid man, here he was getting into a strange car to be probably kidnapped again. The person who came back from that island was terrified and edgy, blunting her favorite parts about him. If he went through another experience like that, she could lose him again.

Before the doors could close, Saskia said, "Liam, you drive," as she tossed the keys over the hood of her car and into his hands.

"Mom, get in the car. We aren't finished, and we can't lose Paul again."

Jacqueline rolled her eyes and tried to open the front passenger door at the same time as Saskia. Narrowing their eyes, they fought for the door until Liam yelled through his window while checking the mirrors. "We don't have time for this, ladies!"

Jacqueline let go of the front passenger door and sternly opened the back door to slide in. Saskia sniffed at her mother as she slid into the front seat. Both crossed their arms after buckling their seatbelts.

After the van passed them, Liam backed out of the spot and started following them. Pulling out of the convention center complex and onto International Drive, both cars blended into the thick traffic.

"Yeesh, why are there so many cars?" she said, squinting her eyes to keep track of the van.

"I don't know, it's not even rush hour yet," Liam said.

Jacqueline let out a heavy sigh. "One of the parks is doing a Mardi Gras parade, so all these people are hoping to get there before it gets too crowded. Why anyone comes here for conferences or vacation amazes me."

Saskia and Liam shook their heads in agreement until Jacqueline said, "Wait a minute. Liam, what is your last name again?"

"Dougherty, why?"

"It looks like the van we are chasing has a Dougherty Pig Farms sticker on the window. How weird."

Saskia and Liam assessed the back of the van looking for what her mother was talking about and when they saw it, they couldn't believe they had missed it. On the right rear window, within a white circle was the sketch of the Arcadia farm with three pigs grazing out front. She had seen the logo on so many vans over the years, she stopped noticing it. The logo had blended into Orlando's landscape.

"Why is it weird, Mom?" Saskia said, displacing her anger.

"Well, my daughter, of all the families in all of Orlando, his family has to be involved in this mess?"

Saskia noticed Liam flush but remained silent as he maneuvered through traffic.

"Why, Mom? Why did you have to do that?"

"Do what?"

"Embarrass Liam!"

"I'm not embarrassing him. I'm just making an observation."

A tenuous silence filled the car as they all watched the white van continue to weave its way to the major highway, I-4. The closer they got to the van, the clearer the logo on the door became. It was undeniably Dougherty Pig Farms, Liam's family's company.

As the van merged onto the highway, his phone rattled in the cup holder, and the screen read "Dad."

Looking back up at the van, Liam noticed it had picked up speed and that if he didn't focus, he'd lose it. Liam gripped the steering wheel a little tighter, his face set into sharp, focused lines.

"You can call him back, no?" Jacqueline said from the backseat. Liam nodded into the rearview mirror as Saskia took stock of their situation.

While she did not expect the day to turn out this way, having her mother with her during the car chase brought an authoritative calm. No matter what came next, at least they were doing it with a parent.

Twenty-Three. Vingt-trois. Venntwa.

Inside the Sprinter van, what should have been shelves for slaughtered pigs had been converted into a mobile bachelor pad. Temporary leather benches replaced the lower shelving. Hooks now suspended a tray filled with bottles of whiskey, rum, vodka, and gin. If Paul's relationship with Marcello were on better footing, he'd push to have this van be a regular feature of their nights out.

When Paul stepped in, memories from the hotel bathroom immediately filled his head. He forced a smile and sat on the bench opposite Marcello. A man who slightly resembled Liam and a bulkier man who probably served as a bodyguard maneuvered the van through the tourist traffic.

Paul pushed aside a twinge of sadness for his college best friend. Back home, if a wealthy family drove around with a security guard, rumors would convict them of shady dealings. The man he knew in college had a low-stakes, violent side, possibly a small-time dealer, but Paul never considered that Marcello would end up here like this.

In the past, stepping into this van wouldn't have scared him. If Marcello wanted to kill him, he had so many opportunities to do so. Why keep him alive on the island, or even at the earlier conference? Besides,

Paul didn't believe Marcello had it in him actually to kill anyone. Hurt, yes, but kill? Nah. He was the type who would rather pay someone to do the dirty work. But there was something about how any figment of joy or warmth had been snuffed out. All that was left was something dark and uncomfortable.

"Thank you for joining me here," Marcello said as he pulled a pair of frosted whiskey tumblers from an ice chest bolted to the floor. He opened up a bottle from the rack above him and poured about a thumb-full into each glass as it cascaded over two large ice cubes.

"Now drink, *marica*. It's been a long day for both of us." Marcello took a large gulp, letting the amber fluid slosh around the glass.

Paul obliged and winced as the whiskey made its way down, leaving behind a fiery trail down his throat. Taking a look out the back window, he noticed they had left the convention center and were driving on the highway. For a moment, his heart ached for smaller roads and the lack of overpasses. Haiti's highways had their own risks, but it felt manageable compared to the high speeds in the States. Even if he wanted to escape this van, he couldn't survive the speed. Then he noticed, among the sea of gray and blue cars, one red car. As it changed lanes, he spotted Liam, Saskia, and someone else in the backseat. He could feel his shoulders relax a bit. Seeing her made it clear he wasn't alone on this bizarre adventure. If they were just seconds behind them, he had the support to do what he should have done back in college. It was time to confront Marcello.

"Marcello, what are we doing here?" Paul said.

Marcello only shook his head and made a couple of *tsks* before saying, "Paul, I wanted to kill you, or just have you killed, but you are proving to be more valuable alive than dead."

Paul was taken aback. "Kill me? Why? If you were the one in trouble, I would protect you."

A sinister cackle emanated from Marcello's twisted mouth, filling the space, while coaxing hollow cackles from the front of the van. The sudden change in dynamics brought back the nerves. Maybe he really was in trouble.

"I guess, maybe in college, I'd do that for you my brother, but *marica*, you are just so boring. And I had hoped that time would pull us apart, but then your dad, *wajon*, your dad!" Marcello brought the frozen tumbler up to the blue-and-red mess of his eye, then rolled it up to his forehead.

"Your dad is using his cement export business to hide things for my business."

"His cement business?" How did his father have a cement business? When did he have the time to run a whole other business that Paul didn't know about? Frustration sluiced into the fears he had set aside for his father. He had been the obedient, constant son, the one who kept everything in their lives on time and on budget. Didn't that count for something? Betrayed. The only way Paul could describe how he felt about his father was deep, humiliating betrayal. Reginald's only responsibility was to love and care for him. If his father couldn't do that, could anyone else? Paul's face contorted as he worked through the information.

"Oh wow! He didn't tell you about that either?" Marcello chuckled again. "*Wajon,* you literally have no idea what is going on at your own home. Now, I really wish we could have just killed you like an injured animal. It would be more kind."

Paul bristled at the comment as the world continued to break apart from underneath. If he were really honest, he always had his suspicions that his dad took advantage of Haiti's *flexible* market. He'd heard rumors of how legitimate businesses worked with illegitimate businesses that didn't believe in borders to fill in the revenue gaps.

When Stephen called back, he had told Paul they had found his father and that he was alive. He also said he had been down at the port sheltering with the cement exporters. At first, Paul thought nothing of it. His dad had connections all over the island. Some were reasonable and responsible. Others only ever knew the gray space between legal and illegal. If this whole time, his father had been building this illegal business, then why keep up with the mangoes or the sugar? Also, how much did Didier know?

"Well, my dad had been trying to get me into other parts of the business for a while, and I kept pushing him off. But…" Paul trailed off, thinking through his next words carefully as he felt the van slow and jerk, as if changing lanes among disoriented drivers.

"What do you want from me then? Why keep me alive?" he asked, and Marcello just smirked.

"*Marica*, your father owes me a lot of money. I'm talking over a million dollars. I was going to use your ransom to get that money back, but the damned earthquake has made that almost impossible. Haiti will be keeping all of its cement, and now we have lost one of our major transportation lanes. So, this is what we are going to do. Now that we've found your father, we are going to keep you at one of our warehouses until your father can wire what we are owed." As if closing the case, he added more whisky to his glass and splashed more into Paul's.

Paul took in Marcello's response and carefully sipped at his refreshed tumbler. He knew his father had been less than squeaky clean, but this? Illegal businesses, enormous debts to international organizations, one of which Paul probably brought to his father on a silver platter. Paul needed to find a way out. He shifted his weight as he launched into a different tactic.

"We can do that, but I've seen how my dad is about kidnappings, and he'd rather let me die than pay a ransom. So, let's do this. I can be your spy. I can help you find a new warehouse and new entryways. The country is in chaos and is about to be flooded by people from all over the world. There's no way Haiti can keep track of everything coming in and out. So, now is the perfect time to find a new way."

Paul watched as Marcello processed the offer, his face contorting as various factors came into consideration.

"Why should I trust you? Why not help your dad?" Slowing for traffic, Marcello grabbed the bottle and refreshed his glass, then topped off Paul's.

"*Wajon,* you're still full. Drink, bro, drink."

Paul glanced out the back window and could see Saskia's car still following them. Even if he got too drunk to function, they were close by and could maybe help him. The van turned off the highway and began the slow descent down the off-ramp. As the van inched along, cars on all sides boxed them in. Escaping would be tricky, but his chances at survival increased at these slower speeds.

He took a longer sip until the ice cubes sat on the bottom of the glass instead of floating at the top like icebergs. Immediately, he felt his blood vessels dilate, his muscles relax, and his vision soften. If he was going to negotiate this deal successfully and work out his escape, he had to finish this conversation before he could only slur.

"Remember that spring break trip to Tulum before it got big?" Paul said. "That would have been impossible with anyone else. We don't have to like each other to work together. Besides, screw my dad. He causes more problems than he solves."

Then he saw it, a twinkle flash in Marcello's eye. The twinkle that gave Marcello away in poker. The same twinkle Paul saw before they were about to do something memorable. He was going to agree, and Paul would officially cross the line into the gray waters he'd avoided his whole life. Is this how it started for his dad? Dipping into this space out of survival instead of some lack of integrity? Maybe one day he'd get a chance to ask him.

"Alright then, *wajon,* you've got a deal. And if I don't get a clear path in sixty days, then I get to kill you? Deal?" Marcello offered.

Paul smirked. This was a deal he could live with for the next sixty days. It would give him enough time to maybe figure another way out, another way that got him out of the gray.

The van slid into the right-turning lane. Peering out the window, he could see cars on one side and life-saving grass on the other. Paul nodded and said, "Deal."

Before they could shake hands, Paul opened the sliding door and threw himself out onto the grassy shoulder of the road. Watching the van stop in a panic, he looked up to see a sign for a theme park-driven shopping district. Rolling off the shoulder and down into the ditch, he paused to catch his breath.

It worked.

He was uninjured, and with a mouthful of dirt and grass, he could see the Sprinter van turning the corner. Standing up, Paul hurried up the other side of the ditch that held the promise of an empty parking lot. He didn't know how much time he had, but he needed to get to safety as soon as possible. With only ten steps to spare, he could hear the honk of Saskia's car waiting in the lot.

"Paul! Hurry! They're on their way back!" she screamed.

Looking to his left, he could see the van making the turn toward the lot. Using whatever strength he had left, he ran toward the open car door of the backseat. Sliding in next to Jacqueline, he slammed the door shut as Liam sped out of the lot. Turning around at the abandoned restaurant, they caught a glimpse of the Sprinter van turning into the lot behind them.

"Shit, hold on, guys, this is gonna get rough." Liam pushed the gas pedal to the floor and swerved back onto the main road, grateful for the healthy break in traffic.

"*Jesú, Marie, Joseph. Priyez pou nous!! Nous appel les quatre évangéliste, Saint Jean, Saint Luc, Saint Marc, et Saint Matthieu, protége votre petit enfans!*" screamed Jacqueline as Liam nearly missed hitting the car in front of him.

"Amen," said Saskia and Paul in sync.

...

"What's she saying, Sask?" Liam asked.

"Don't worry about it, just know she's calling on every saint and angel to protect us," she said, eyes fixed on the road ahead. Liam nodded, uncertain if the prayers made him feel better or worse.

"You've got this, Liam. Just get us to safety, and thank you," Paul said with his alcohol laden tongue.

He squeezed Liam's shoulder weakly, like he was using the dregs of his positivity. Liam sat up, straightening to accept the responsibility. Ahead of one of his more dangerous assignments, Liam had to take an evasive driving course. It was funny that he didn't need to use it then, but as he wove around a tourist-filled SUV, it made a huge difference now. Stretching his neck, Liam let out a breath and, with it, the normal way of driving.

Ignoring the red light in front of him, he bolted through the intersection, nearly avoiding a bus destined for the nearby theme park and a rented van full of tourists. The Sprinter van didn't hesitate and came in right behind him, avoiding a collision with a car proudly holding Canada plates.

Liam looked into the rearview mirror and spotted his brother Josh at the wheel. This time without the hog's blood and the ATV. Tightening his grip, he smirked as years of video game races came to mind. He knew his brother's tactics.

"Bring it on, Josh," Liam whispered, swerving into the expansive parking lot of the shopping district. Darting between columns of traffic and aisles of parked cars, the passengers slid from one end of the car to the other.

"Liam, I get we are racing, but you are going to make me sick. What if we get pulled over?" Jacqueline said.

"Mom! Let him drive!" Saskia yelled. "Liam! They're gaining on us."

Flicking his eyes to the rearview, he could see Josh closing the gap between them. Josh's meatball passenger looked a lot like the guy who gutted their hogs. Racking his brain to remember who he was, Saskia yelled, "He's got a gun, Liam!"

She was right. He could see the barrel catching shards of the fading afternoon sun. He knew none of them had a gun, nor had he received that kind of training. However, he knew how to avoid getting grazed.

"Saskia, how much do you want to keep this car?"

"What?"

"I'll make that decision for her. It is a *táco*, a piece of junk. Get us out of here alive, and we can replace it," Jacqueline said.

"Really, Mom?"

"Don't get excited. Your dad has an '86 diesel Mercedes in storage that I'm tired of paying for," Jacqueline replied flatly.

"Okay, well, here we go." Liam threw the gearshift into low, making the Honda crouch closer to the road, ready to jump with whatever it had. When the gear shift returned to drive, it jumped up and sped off along the parking lot. Ahead of them, a van unloaded a mechanical wheelchair, and Liam jumped the curb to avoid them. Speeding onto the sidewalk, he dodged panicked pedestrians until he found his opening through the car traffic. Making a sharp left, he launched through a clear aisle of cars. He went for the open space and could see that ten cars down was the end of the parking lot. Beyond the cement barrier lies another grassy ditch to keep the lot from flooding.

"Hold on, guys." Liam put all his weight on the gas pedal. Gathering speed, the engine roared in warning to anyone tempted to get in their way. Faster and faster, the parked cars blurred before the front wheels collided with the cement curb.

Flying into the air, screams from Jacqueline, Saskia, Liam, and Paul bounced off every surface. When they safely landed on the road beyond the ditch, they left behind a trail of dented metal and active sparks.

Jacqueline hollered, *"Ou wè, ou pa janm doute kat évangéliste yo! Amweh!"*

Liam's shoulders relaxed as the car puttered away from the parking lot, attempting to survive the abuse. Checking the rearview mirror again, he could see their family farm's van circling the aisles, deciding on their next move. They'd be long gone before Josh figured out what to do next.

"You know what, Mom, you were right. Don't doubt the four holiest angels."

He could hear Saskia say with a touch of sarcasm, and just shook his head.

"Exactly, if you *tend to the guardian within*, they will take care of you!" Jacqueline continued.

Saskia, Liam, and Paul all burst into nervous laughter.

After checking the rearview to double-check he had lost his brother, Liam said, "Okay, let me take you crazy Haitians home."

Twenty-Four. Vingt-quatre. Vennkat.

When they pulled into the driveway, nightfall draped over the Roy's neighborhood. Only the streetlights and gently illuminated outlines of the neighboring houses guided them home. Looking ahead, Jacqueline could see the house she had built and protected for years. With the tastefully applied floodlights and path lights, her house glowed like no other. Peering at Saskia in the front seat, her heart ached. Her little girl was long gone. In her place was a woman wrestling for complete control. The life she was living terrified Jacqueline. How many times had they come close to death today? All for a man who would only complicate her life further. Saskia should be running away; instead, through each experience, she seemed to gain more confidence. Her daughter kept rising through each test and evolving into a more complete version of herself. What will happen to her when Saskia becomes more than she could become?

"So, I guess we are getting you a new car?"

She heard Emile say. The car had shuddered to a stop. Jacqueline could hear the gentle patter of oil dripping from the engine, leaving a mess on the driveway. Behind Emile, she could see her younger two walking across the front yard. Jacqueline guessed the scraping of the bumper brought the rest of the family out to greet them. While Saskia, Paul, and Liam rushed to get out of the car, Jacqueline pretended to look for something in her purse to give herself a moment to observe her daughter. She examined her face, her movements, and couldn't find a single sign of the terror from the day.

Maybe Saskia has already evolved beyond what I can give her.

Maybe she has already evolved far beyond who I can be.

Jacqueline could feel the arrival of new worry lines at her temples. The car door opened, and Emile stretched out his hand to her.

"Come on out *ti cœur*… I want to hear what happened. If the front of that car and the oil dripping on our driveway tells me anything, it's that there's a story."

Jacqueline smiled. "*Amour,* you know this was a *táco* and we needed to get rid of it. We just made sure to have a little fun with it before we turn it in."

He laughed, and she just smiled. When Jacqueline finally got out of the car, she fell into her husband's arms. Squeezing Emile tighter than she ever had, she could let down her guard. Jacqueline was home, safe, and all her children were alive. What started as a tremble turned into a full-body shake. Letting out a deep moan with every convulsion, she released the fear she had held back that week.

"*Ah mon amour,* it's alright, *cocotte,* you're alive, you made it."

Lifting her face away from his shoulder, she wiped away the solitary tear she allowed herself to release. It was all she had left.

She turned to analyze his face, then said, "I never want to do that again, and we need to find a way to get him out of the house."

Emile chuckled and hugged her to his chest. "You have been in my arms for less than five minutes *et wap jere moun.* Always a mother hen managing her chicks. If you don't slow down, you know you'll have a heart attack."

Jacqueline scowled. "He brings too much chaos. *Cœur'm* can't handle it. If Saskia wants that much chaos in her life, that is her choice. But for me? Small doses of that one."

Emile laughed and squeezed Jacqueline again.

"Let's go inside for some *thè*, I got some *ti baume et sitwonèl* from the garden, so it'll be fresh. You know mint and lemongrass soothe the nerves?"

Jacqueline rolled her eyes playfully and hooked her arm into Emile's. Together, they walked up the drive, past the battered remains of Saskia's car, past the little lights along the path, and up and toward the house. When Emile pushed open the front door, she felt at peace that the worst of this journey could finally be put behind them.

...

"And you won't believe it, Liam drove the car up and over this grassy ditch. I totally thought we were going to die."

Saskia, her siblings, Liam, and Paul sat around the kitchen table with warm mugs of tea in front of them.

The verdant steam calmed the air, and evaporating away the conflicts from the day before. In its wake, the kitchen returned to feeling like the warm, inviting place it had been throughout her life. Thinking back to the friction with her father, Saskia let the tea smooth the edges of the pain that remained. They were all together. They were all safe, and they could relax in that knowledge. It felt a little unjust that not so far away, her extended family didn't have the same knowing or feeling. The guilt pulled at the edge of her relief, but Saskia pushed it away. Those would be feelings for another day.

"And *maman* was sending prayers to literally every corner of the universe," she continued, rolling her eyes for dramatic effect.

The siblings howled with laughter as Paul and Liam smirked as if they weren't ready to let go just yet.

"*Anr*, and did those prayers work? Aren't we still alive? *Kisa ou beswen di? Mesi Jesu!* Thank you, Jesus, for making sure we got home safe,"

Jacqueline said from her perch in the kitchen.

Emile chuckled and squeezed her.

The kitchen table paused, then exploded into laughter. Jacqueline scowled. When the doorbell rang, she didn't hesitate.

"I'll get it," Jacqueline said as she moved from the kitchen to open the front door. At first, she saw no one. Then she looked down the driveway and noticed an orange glow coming from the backseat of Saskia's car.

"Saskia! Your car is on fire!" Jacqueline yelled, jumping back from the door. The rest of the table jumped into action, but Saskia stayed rooted. Would they ever know peace? Not just for the moment, but the kind they could rely on. As everyone in the kitchen dashed for a tool to douse the fire, Saskia accepted the truth. Enduring peace would not find her.

...

Paul noticed Emile react first as he dove for the fire extinguisher under the kitchen sink. Following his lead, everyone at the table pushed back their chairs to find buckets and bowls to douse the flames. Jacqueline ran into the living room for her cellphone. One by one, they ran out the front door toward the car, prepared to tackle whatever they could. Flames quickly moved from where the Molotov cocktail had landed on the backseat, the intensifying heat breaking the windows one by one. Emile carefully approached the fire with the extinguisher, searching for the source of the flame. The cloud-like foam attached to the burnished remains reduced the flame until it became more controlled. When the fire trucks pulled up, Emile had almost completely put it out. Paul approached the car to see if anything survived when he felt the borrowed phone vibrate in his pocket. Flipping it open, he saw a text from an unknown number.

You can run, but I'll always find you: a deal's a deal.

Closing his phone, Paul's face turned stern as he fought off a shudder. All he seemed to bring to Saskia was chaos and risk. For years, he lived in peaceful harmony with the chaotic members of his life. He ignored what bothered him and held on to what he enjoyed. This dance kept his life interesting. It always felt as if something big was just around the corner, even if it came with a little bit of risk. However, looking over the wreckage of Saskia's car, the impact of his life couldn't be clearer. If all he ever wanted was her in his life beyond stolen moments, he'd have to change some things about his life.

A swell of sadness practically choked him. With Marcello getting ever bolder and closer to his promise of killing him, he knew what he had to do. If he was successful, if he could settle his father's mess, then he could be the man Saskia deserved. He looked around the front of the cooling car and spotted a couple she might want. He fished out a couple of pens, a couple of coins, and the wooden bracelet. All stacked on each other, all completely intact. Pocketing the bracelet, he grabbed a couple more things before moving away from the charred remains of Saskia's car.

To do what needed to be done, he'd need help from the only person more than happy to never see him again. Unsure of the outcome, he walked up to Jacqueline and asked, "Mrs. Roy, I think I need to head back to Port-au-Prince before this gets any more out of hand. Do you know of anyone who can help me?"

Jacqueline sighed with relief as tears finally pooled in her eyes. She smiled. "I know just the person. But you'll have to leave tonight."

Twenty-Five. Vingt-cinq. Vennsenk.

From the parking lot, the Roys, Liam and Paul, could see a small plane surrounded by adults wearing the same neon green t-shirt. Like beacons in the inky night of the small airport, they stood next to each other in two lines. Passing cases of plastic water bottles and bags of used clothing from one volunteer to the other, the words "From our bended knee to yours. Holy Redeemer Church," crunched and bent with each pass. The pilot circled the small plane to make sure it was ready to fly. He was middle-aged and wore a baseball hat, a tank top with an American flag, and sneakers that didn't deserve to be donated. Every moment or two, he'd call over to a man in overalls for tape or an oil can.

Jacqueline chuckled to herself as she watched him point and bark directions at the volunteers. They'd respond with faces laced with the terror of being caught breaking a rule. She shook her head as she thought back to the dozens of missionaries who were scattered around her home island. Their enthusiasm for giving back to the Haitian communities inspired and infuriated her. Constantly being associated with the extreme poverty of her home country dented her peers' ability to see her as human. The furtive looks, the kind-hearted offerings of food or clothing, felt less like generosity and more like a barrier to their community.

In the complex mix of gratitude and shame, she muttered under her breath to Emile, "So, American."

He nodded, knowing the internal conflict. "*Bien sûr*, but at least they are doing something kind for us, I mean them. You know as well as I do, they have to build from nothing again."

Solemnly, she nodded as flashes from the news came to mind. The gray-white dust of decay on every crevice of everything on the screen. Familiar buildings and features powdered into barely recognizable shapes. People turned into folkloric living zombies. Jacqueline reached for Emile's hand and squeezed it. He squeezed hers back.

"Wow, that's a lot of green shirts," Paul said, coming up next to the pair.

"Yes, there are a lot of them. So, what do you think, Paul? Ready to head back?" Emile turned toward him, breaking away from Jacqueline.

She assumed Emile was eager to head back home, but this business was behind him.

"I mean, it's better than staying here and wondering what is happening back home," Paul replied.

"True, that is not as enjoyable," said Emile.

Paul nodded, and Emile opened his arms wide to hug him.

Jacqueline could hear Emile say as he held Paul, "Safe travels, and give us a call if you ever find yourself here in Orlando again."

Watching the men, she noticed how natural it looked, even familiar. It amazed Jacqueline how close they'd become in such a short amount of time. Emile was going to miss him, and she just might.

Catching Jacqueline's gaze, Emile released the embrace, and Paul continued, "I just don't feel it's fair to keep putting your family at risk. Marcello has turned into a very dangerous person. I hope he'll focus on me, and he'll lose interest in your family. Hopefully, you can get back to your lives."

Jacqueline nodded in approval.

"Well, I'll miss the excitement. It's been nice having something other than house chores, or whatever is in the news, to talk about for once." Emile chuckled as he clasped Paul on the shoulder, holding him at arm's length.

"I certainly won't, but I'm glad we were able to help you out," Jacqueline said. Approaching Paul, she took a deep breath before giving him a quick hug. Freed from the interaction, she then said, "Try to stay out of trouble. There's a church you should go to when you get home. The nuns are a little funny, but it's a good place."

"Wait, is it on Place St. Pierre?"

"Yes! Saskia has a bracelet from there, but I doubt she'll ever see them. She has weird ideas about religion."

Paul nodded with a smirk and said, "Ah, yes, I've heard of it. I'll have to check it out when I get back."

A breeze kicked up the surrounding sand and dust, swirling around them like a sandy snow globe. Jacqueline reached for Paul and gave him a quick hug, breaking the embrace to seek refuge with Emile.

...

Paul smiled and put out his hand to shake Emile's one more time. The firm, yet kind handshake twisted his stomach. The firmness reminded him of his father's handshake, one where kindness was never found. Even in his handshake, he tried to dominate that simple greeting. He'd be seeing Reginald soon. Turning again, his stomach told him what he already knew: he'd have a very hard time pretending he didn't know anything. Leaving the Roys and the comfort of their lives here in Orlando scared him. Maybe he should stay. If he shook off his father, he could rebuild a life here, a safe, quiet life.

"Hey! Don't think you are leaving here without saying goodbye to me." Liam came up from behind and clapped him on the back, interrupting Paul's thoughts.

"No, never," Paul said in reply and pulled him in for a tight hug. Memories of Liam driving a motorboat as he fought against the alligator brought back the swell of sadness. He really wouldn't be here if it weren't for Liam. Without him, he'd still be on that island in the middle of a lake, or worse, plotting ways to escape Marcello. Neither option worked for him. Trying to convey all the gratitude he wished he could voice for Liam, he held him tighter.

"I know, man, I know," Liam said as he clapped at Paul's back again before pulling away.

"Oh! And I'll be in Port-au-Prince for a couple of months in the next few weeks. Maybe we can hang out when I get there? I'm kinda nervous," Liam said, his face scrunching as if the idea had a sour smell.

Paul squinted his eyes at Liam for a moment, deciding what to say next. He could then feel his hands shake a bit. Putting his hands in the pockets of his jeans, the knots in his stomach slowly tightened as the reality of what he was going back to fed the swelling sadness. Landing in Port-au-Prince and returning home were what he needed to do. But what home would be there when his feet touched the ground? What will rebuilding actually look like for him?

Then Paul said, "I have no idea what I am going back to, but I'll let you know once I get my bearings. There will be a lot for me to figure out, but we can absolutely hang. I'll show you around what's left."

Liam nodded and gave him one last shake of the hand as the sound of doors thunking shut echoed across the tarmac. The pilot waved over to the group, beckoning them toward the plane.

It was time.

...

"Well, that's it then. I guess it's time," Saskia said, leaning against the fence and letting the breeze tousle a handful of loose curls.

The move made Paul smile. Not the forced ones she'd seen him give colleagues and her parents, but one that didn't care where the lips landed. She didn't need to doubt his feelings for her. It was all in the smile.

"Walk with me?" Paul asked as the floodlights brightened the eyes she wouldn't be seeing for a while.

Saskia nodded and pulled away from the fence, committing to keep her emotions at bay. As much as she wanted him to stay, the last couple of days had almost burned all the goodwill she had with her parents. The minute his bags were packed in the car, her mother practically danced to the car door and floated into her seat. And while she didn't live for her mother's approval, she needed to account for what she was putting her through. It was one thing to take these risks herself; it was another to bring her whole family into it. What if something had happened to one of her siblings? She'd find a way to see Paul again, maybe.

Joining him on the winding sidewalk that connected the parking lot to the terminal, the pair walked in silence along the fence. Keeping to their sides of the sidewalk, an electric tension between them grew until they reached the terminal. Walking through the front doors, they made their way through the crowd of green-shirted volunteers until they finally made it onto the tarmac. The silence grew heavy as they both realized they really were going to be apart.

Pausing just beyond a gray awning from the terminal, Paul turned to look at Saskia. He stood there, staring at her face. If she were going to say anything, now was the time. But when she reached for something to say, her mind came back empty. What do you say to someone who felt impossible to reach, only to discover that he was exactly who she needed? His steadfast nature and his practicality challenged her dreamy perspectives on life. He could have been perfect.

Obviously, before all of this happened, he was only here for a conference. He was always going to leave. Still, she wasn't sure how to go back to being without him.

"I almost forgot to give you these," he said. His voice slowed down her thoughts enough for her to open her hands as he fished into his jeans pocket. Turning over his hands so they hovered over hers, he opened them and let the contents fall.

"Oh! My bracelet! Where did you find it?" She brought the bracelet close to inspect for fire damage, but didn't find any.

"I grabbed it out of the car before the fire department took over. It's crazy how it looks completely fine. And it's wood," Paul said with a smirk.

Looking up at Paul, she said, "Thank you for this. No one has dug around the ashes of my burnt car for me before."

He smiled in return. "It's the least I could do. Especially after everything I put you through. My life is not usually *this* chaotic. I am really, really sorry."

Saskia smiled. Protectively folding her arms across her chest, she said, "Oh, we both know that's not true. Besides, I was starting to get a little bored around here. And it was nice to get a break from the trauma porn on T.V."

The pair let the silence return, each searching for what to say next. Without a plan, they would continue this long-distance situationship, afraid to answer the question: Should we give it a try?

Paul finally said, "Come with me."

She looked up at him to see if he was joking. He wasn't. Cautiously, he put his hands on her shoulders and seemed relieved when she didn't shake them off. Her breath caught as it could be the last time his hands would be on her body.

"I don't know what I'm walking into, but it could be an adventure?" Paul said, trying to meet her eyes.

She tried to meet them, but a growing fear wanted her to let him go, to close this chapter. Her job at Walnut Bank is where she needed to be. It would provide safety, stability, and care for her in ways that going to Haiti would not. Even Paul didn't know what waited for him on the other end of this plane ride. And there was still so much she needed to learn about him. Was he a criminal? Were the feelings she had real or stress hormones pushing her to find comfort in the closest pair of arms? Pools of tears formed as she thought through what they would be missing. So many memories to make, so much left to say, but they were out of time. The questions would have to go unanswered; all she'd have to hold would be the what-ifs. She watched as Paul's eyes became glassy, already knowing the truth she had yet to say.

Saskia let out a heavy sigh. "I want to, but I think I need some time to figure out what I want out of life instead of just following whatever shiny object crosses my path." A sad smile grew at the painful realization. That was how she had been living her life, desperate to avoid sitting in discomfort for too long. Then she said, "I don't know when I'll see you next, but having you here has been a dream come true and—"

Before she could finish her sentence, Paul's lips gently touched hers. His arms wrapped around her body to bring her close. Touching her forehead to his, they held each other. Standing in the grief of a life they would not know, they tightened the embrace, hoping never to let the other go.

Saskia's arms ached from holding the position. She couldn't let him go just yet. Then she felt it, he let a little bit of air come between them. He was ready to pull away.

Cheeks soaked, she let the space grow until she could see his face again. Everything she saw there made her weak with want, made her dumb with a desire only he could fulfill. Paul moved toward her, grazing his pillowed lips against hers. Squeezing a handful of his shirt, Saskia yearned for more time, more of him. Responding to her unspoken need, he pressed his lips against hers with an intensity that tempted them to find a quiet corner.

"Paul, we've gotta go!" said the pilot, his voice carried only by the winter breeze.

Breaking away from Paul, she lay her cheek on his chest and could only say, "God, I'm gonna miss you."

Paul squeezed her tighter against his chest and said into her hair, "Me too."

They could have stood there forever. Safe in each other's arms, holding onto the quickly disintegrating future they could have had. If only Saskia could be brave enough to follow him. The grief of losing him swelled in her chest. Her mind scrambled for ways to keep them together that didn't require flying in a tiny plane to the embers of another city. She came up empty. She had no choice but to let him go. This was where she would have to leave him.

The loud whirring of the motorized propellers startled them apart as the pilot waved Paul over from the cockpit.

"*Au revoir*, Saskia."

Paul grabbed her hand to give it one last squeeze, and with it, the last time they would touch. His hand, leaving hers, pulled open the door to her grief. Tears fell, blurring her vision as she watched him jog across the tarmac. After tossing in his small bag, he closed the door to his side of the plane. As the plane turned around, she watched as Paul settled into the seat next to the pilot. Facing down the runway, the plane gracefully sped up to catch the wind and lifted into the air in a matter of seconds. The further the plane flew, the emptier she felt until the warmth of her mother's arms surrounded her. They stood there until the plane disappeared into the clouds as if it had never existed. He was gone.

Twenty-Six. Vingt-six. Venn sis.

With her head against the cool glass of the car window, Saskia watched dots of electric lights guide the family home. Chatter about how Haiti used to be, and what Liam could expect now, became the soundtrack to their drive on the highway.

"You should come Sask! It would be a lot of fun, and you could show me around, and you'd get a break from here," Liam said brightly.

Meeting his eyes, she could see how much he wanted her to go. How often had he taken one of these trips alone? He could finally have a friend to share the experience with. She could feel a warmth on the right side of her cheek. Glancing at the rearview mirror, she could see her father's stern face shake a subtle, "no."

"It could be a lot of fun, but I need a little more time to think about it." She could see his head dip in approval, and Liam deflated in disappointment. Hollowed. Saskia felt like the old blocks of ice she'd seen on the streets of Haiti. Vendors spent all day carving a deep groove to make the only snow on the island. Then they'd cover them in brightly colored syrups and chargrilled peanuts for *fresco* or shaved ice. The metal scraper grooved until it hit the cart's wood. Then the *frescos* were done, the ice left to turn back to water.

The adventure was over, and her best friend would continue without her. It was time to return to who she was before. Her car was gone. She probably didn't have a job, and she almost got the chance to build a romance with a man she had dreamed about for years. She could still feel his fingers graze hers when he handed her the bracelet. The calm she felt the first time she met him.

...

Closing her eyes, she could hear the ocean waves at her uncle's beach house. She was barely seventeen. That day, it was a full house. Everyone had spent the morning in the water. By afternoon, they needed a break from the salt and had gone over to the neighboring resort to use the pool. One by one, her family and the younger cousins just popped over the seawall until it was just her reclining on a lounger. With each minute that passed, the sun licked away one more droplet of ocean water off her skin.

At first, she hadn't noticed the careful evaporation until the sun's warmth descended past her skin. Simmering her blood, it begged her to return to the ocean. Carefully rousing from the lounger, Saskia lazily slipped her toes into her flip-flops. She stretched her body awake from the sun-kissed nap. Grabbing the sun-warmed towel from the edge of the lounger, she went down the stairs to the pebbled beach. Dropping it next to her now abandoned sandals, she luxuriously entered the clear, warm waters of the Caribbean. Eyes closed, she let herself sink, sink, sink to the powdered shells below.

Even then, she realized why people the world over lusted for a chance to feel these waters. Both cooling and warming, Saskia felt suspended somewhere between earth and heaven, somewhere between humanity and spirituality. Somewhere that felt like being cradled in the safety of her mother. Never in her whole life had she ever felt this relaxed, this safe, this warm. Rising to the surface, she lay on her back letting the sun bathe her in its light, while letting the ocean hold her at the surface. Blinded, she kept her eyes closed and let the sounds of the tides lull her into a delightful daze.

"*Alo, ça vas?*" came the water-warbled husk of a male voice from shore.

Saskia opened her eyes and turned her body to behold a man she didn't know, but pricked her curiosity. He must have been around her age, taller than her, and built like someone whose fingernails preferred a permanent line of dirt beneath them. His mahogany buzz cut turned him into an island rugged Justin Timberlake or Usher. As if this were a movie, he was waving her back to shore.

Curious, Saskia daintily shouted from her spot in the pulsing Caribbean, "*Oui, ça va!*"

"*Je. Didier. Où. il?*" he shouted, covering his eyes from the sun to see her better.

"*Quoi?*" Saskia shouted in return, unsure if the limits of her French had been met or if the lapping of the waves swallowed this man's voice.

"*Je. Didier. Ou est-il?*" the man said a little louder, irritation slipping in.

"*Attends, j'arrive,*" Saskia finally said, annoyed at the limits of her French. Swimming to her towel and sandals, she made a mental note to take French in the next semester.

Emerging from the water, Saskia immediately felt exposed in the bikini she had snuck into her luggage when her mother wasn't looking. It was fine when she was alone. It was fine when her parents weren't around to argue with her about the merits of modesty. But this man, this boy, really, fidgeted and paced while pretending not to look. She grabbed the towel first and quickly wrapped herself up, hoping to dampen the awkward tension between them. The boy held out his hand. She took it, grateful for the steadiness. Sliding her wet feet into the blue plastic sandals, she was careful not to slide out. Covered in all the right places, Saskia looked up at the boy and felt a little unsteady all over again. His amber eyes had flecks of gold and were set in a kind, sun-roasted face. The lines framing his eyes showed this boy had seen too much but still remained kind. His crooked smile softened the hard edges. Saskia's mind went blank.

"*L'eau est magnifique pas vrais?*" the boy had said with a smile, expecting Saskia to respond.

Her mind couldn't find the words in French. The longer she took to respond, the more panicked she became. What if he thought she was dumb or stupid? Or the worst possible option: completely uncool?

"*On peut parler Anglais, s'il te plaît?*" Saskia asked in her heavily American accent, hoping to save face. She tried to learn at home, but by sixteen her parents kept their lessons to simple conversation. When she was in Orlando, this wasn't a problem. But now that she was here, with this boy she wanted to get to know, she couldn't help but feel like more formal lessons would have been worth it.

The boy smiled and said in the same accent she'd heard since birth, "Oh! *Oui, bien sûr,* sorry, yes of course! Ah, I was asking if the water was, ah, nice?"

Saskia smiled at his English, fragmented yet coherent.

"Yes, yes, it was. My name is Saskia. Are you looking for Didier? He's my cousin, and this is his parents' house," she said, grateful to be speaking a language where she wouldn't miss a thing.

The boy smiled back. "*Ah, très bien.* Nice to meet you, Saskia, I'm Jean-Paul, but my friends call me JP, and my teachers call me Paul. My family is just down the beach, and they were hoping to see him today. *Écoute,* do you happen to know where he is?"

Something in the way he delivered the question told Saskia this wasn't the whole truth.

"Ah, yeah, he's coming later tonight. I can tell him you stopped by?" Saskia said, unsure if she wanted to keep him close or return to floating in the water. But before she could decide, another man interrupted them from the shoreline.

...

The next morning at the kitchen table, Johanna and Robert competed for the craziest Saturday night story. Eggs sizzled as coffee percolated into the top chamber of the moka pot. Everything in the Roy household hummed back to the normal Sunday morning routine. Jacqueline arranged the food on the plates for each family member, while Emile read the local paper.

"Huh, Saskia, did you see this?"

Since Paul had traveled home, Saskia had been in a daze. She'd spend hours just staring at walls, random spots on the table, or sitting in the gazebo watching the wind juggle the branches of the surrounding trees. Life felt vacant. She was vacant. This was all she was going to do with her life. The same boring motions repeating on autopilot until she died. She could be in Haiti right now. She could be doing something that mattered, something that actually helped people. Instead, she helped people with more than enough move money around until they felt important. Until they felt worthy. She wanted to scream but every time she tried, nothing came out.

"Sask, come on *ti cœur*. What's going on?" Emile had been worried. Every day, he'd try subtle ways to pull her out of it, hoping she'd find her spark again. Today, he chose to be direct.

Her siblings looked to each other, then silently sipped from their mugs.

"Oh, nothing. What did you want me to see?" she said, reaching for the paper. Emile handed her the relevant sheets while keeping a couple for himself. He pointed to a headline that read, *Central Florida Businesses Step Up for Haiti Victims*. Looking closer, she noticed a picture of Sherri standing next to a man in a suit, wearing a cowboy hat. Underneath, the caption read: *Walnut Capital and Dougherty Hog Farms come together to save Haiti's ruined capital.*

"There's no way," she said softly.

"Oh, I know. How wonderful of your boss to be willing to invest in Haiti. Maybe all of this activity will actually turn the country around instead of relying on the government to do it," Emile said as he flipped through his newspaper sheets.

The loss of what could have been left her vacant, empty. Now, a molten rage sluiced its way through the spaces the loss had made. Though she was lucky to still be Sherri's employee, her boss didn't deserve to be the hero of a country she knew nothing about. Sherri had been truly awful to her in the days that followed the earthquake. Between sneaking around with Marcello, the man who wanted to kill Paul, and then tearing her down until she was a manageable little morsel, Sherri solidified herself as Saskia's villain. There was no way she was going to let Sherri do more for the country that defined her very being than she did. In her anger, she let herself believe she could get to Haiti. But what would happen if she did? In that possibility, the fear of what could happen in a place so physically broken crept in. Not only that, but she'd also have to face the loss of her version of Haiti: the version she held so dear. But if random strangers who didn't even know what landing in *Maïs Gâté* smelled like cared more about Haiti than she did, what did that even mean?

Then, it clicked.

Grabbing her phone from the table, she texted Liam:

I'm in.

This would be her way back to the place that had clamped its claws into her heart from the day she first visited. Inhaling to fill every pore in her lungs and slowly exhaling what was left, she prepared to do what she should have done a long time ago.

"Mom. Dad. Sibs. I have decided. I know you're not gonna like it, but I don't care. I have to do this." Saskia looked from one grief-stricken parent to the other. Guilt for hurting them like this almost extinguished her nerve, but she couldn't keep pretending. Orlando wasn't working, and there was only one place that could.

"You don't need to say it. Fine," Jacqueline said, aware of her other children. "I won't support it or agree with it, but I'll make sure you are ready, and you are as safe as can be."

Emile solemnly nodded behind his newspaper sheets.

Stunned, Saskia flew from the table and hugged her mother. Arms filled with the body of her mother, she squeezed until Jacqueline begged for space. Bit by bit, feeling returned to her body. She had a purpose now, and she was going to meet it.

Twenty-Seven. Vingt-sept. Vennsèt.

Guided by the faint light of early morning, Paul inserted his key into the lock of his apartment. Muscles heavy from lack of sleep, he struggled but finally unlatched the door. Creaking every inch of the way, the door protested to being used and released dust-filled air with every centimeter it opened. Taking breaks to cough, he continued to push open the door slowly. After about ten centimeters, the door caught on something. Popping his head through the opening, Paul could see that his apartment was a complete wreck. Not a shred of clear floor space between broken dishes, glass, and dirt from his potted plants. Sliding his body through the opening, Paul carefully navigated across the terrain until he could see his bookshelf pushing against the front door. After returning the bookshelf to its proper position, he carved a path to the windows. Sliding them open in each room, dust escaped out into the day like an anxious animal left for too long in its cage. Once all the windows were open, the dewy smell of trees and fire, and a faintly sour smell, made him relax. He could breathe a little easier. He was home, and it was still standing compared to so many others not even a ten-minute drive away.

Too tired to really start cleaning, Paul managed to find just enough coffee beans in the unbroken jar on his kitchen floor. After grinding them, he filled the bottom chamber of his coffee pot with water from the fridge, grateful he hadn't ordered the next round of filtered water jugs. Careful not to flood the release valve, he dropped the basket into the bottom chamber. With the two items in place, he poured the grounds into the basket until the tiny mounds threatened to escape. Normally, the metal whine of the top chamber grinding against the bottom chamber would echo off the tiled floors. Now, every book, every artifact of his life, created a carpet of debris that killed every sound from the kitchen. Another reminder of how much had changed.

Waiting for the stove to boil the water in the coffee pot, Paul could feel the exhaustion pulling at him, his mind thinking back on his journey home.

...

They flew through the night until the plane bounced onto the grassy meadow of his mango farm. Upon landing outside the capital, he felt as if the hardest part were behind him. Of course, there were challenges ahead, but this was his home, his land passed down for generations. Here, he knew every blade of grass, every animal, and how to deal with them. No surprise attacks from modern dinosaurs or a legal system he didn't understand.

The pilot, Thomas, landed on their farm to avoid the chaos at the main airport. From the news reports alone, he knew it would be covered with U.S. military and U.N. personnel. His local contacts shared that getting out of the airport would take hours and bring on too many questions.

At Paul's, it didn't take long to get everything off the plane onto the front patio. When he opened his house, everything had mostly been intact. This far from the epicenter of the earthquake, only a couple of pictures lay face down instead of their prized place on the wall. From within the confines of the house, he watched as the volunteers loaded their vans with the bags and boxes of donations. Once everything was secured and accounted for, the volunteer vans scattered pebbles across the drive until the sound of tires evaporated into the morning dew.

Thomas sat on a rocking chair on the terrace watching the sun make its lazy ascent. Paul joined him with cups of coffee. From there, a thin fog veiled their view of the mango trees swaying in the breeze. Early mornings on the terrace always came with a chorus of birdsong, melodically threading through the bellowing of cows and the bleats of irritated goats. Today, only the cows and goats dared to make a sound. Even then, it was tentative, furtive, as if they were afraid to be too loud. Everything else seemed to hold its breath in fear that it could bring another wave of tremors, or worse, another earthquake.

"You know, I'm not sure your country will ever recover from this," Thomas said after sipping from his small espresso cup. "We've been coming here for decades, and every year it's something. It's like the island can't break from this cursed cycle."

Paul leaned back and took a couple of sips from his small cup. The nun's card warmed in his pocket, hoping to grab his attention.

"I used to agree with you," Paul said, careful to choose neutral-sounding words. "But never count Haiti out. Our rich, rebellious history is what got us here. Hell, we ran around the Americas freeing slaves and winning revolutions when everyone else did everything to make sure we failed. Haiti isn't cursed by anything other than jealousy and greed."

Thomas let out a brittle chuckle in response, then said, "Well, son, I think those two things curse the whole world."

Paul chuckled too and clinked his delicate espresso cup against Thomas' cup. Taking celebratory sips, the men were interrupted by the roar of an SUV coming up the long dirt driveway. Both looked up to see who could be coming this early. The fear ebbed when Paul recognized the car and driver. His heart swelled to see the person he trusted most on this island: Stephen. Pulling up in front of the house, Stephen jumped down from the driver's seat, his face stern. Paul handed him another small cup he had waiting for him. While Stephen introduced himself to Thomas and they exchanged pleasantries, he poured the coffee from the moka pot into the cup. Paul noticed the etchings of worry on his face and his stiff movements as he interacted with Thomas. Stephen had news he was afraid to share. When the last drops of coffee were gone, they packed up the house and clambered into the car.

Only twenty minutes from Paul's country house, Stephen pulled in front of a smaller house with a fence surrounding the property. It looked completely intact, not a crack in sight.

Maybe destruction was only in one part of the city? There's still something to work with.

Thomas opened his car door after thanking Stephen for the ride. Paul climbed out of the back seat to take Thomas' seat and properly say his goodbyes.

"If you need to get back into the States without getting noticed, let me know." Thomas clapped Paul's back.

Paul nodded, hoping he'd never need to call on that favor. But if the last week had shown him anything, it was never to assume. Paul extended his hand, and Thomas shook it. Swinging his small duffel over his shoulder, Thomas turned for the fence. His long, sneakered strides had him at the fence in moments, where a guard opened a door within the fence. As Thomas walked through, the guard dipped his head at him with a well-earned familiarity.

Paul waved at the closing door, and Stephen pulled back onto the main road, completely intact. Passing the homes scattered across the flat rice fields was completely fine. Once they passed the fields, Stephen took a surprising turn up the backside of a mountain.

"Wait, why are we going this way? It's going to take forever."

Stephen's face turned into chiseled stone before saying, "We can't take the beach road. It's blocked by things you shouldn't see."

Paul nodded solemnly. Then he noticed the crumbling ruins now bordering the road, tarps tessellating what should have been sturdy roofs. Winding through the streets to get back home, the road became difficult and choked with boulders of cement and shell-shocked people. Paul was never more grateful that he wasn't driving.

"Stephen, this is so much worse than I thought."

"And we didn't even go through downtown. *Chans pa ou.*"

Paul shuddered, unable to imagine what could possibly be worse than this. Weaving and dodging the now unrecognizable road, Paul prodded Stephen.

"What are you not telling me?"

"*Nap pale demain.* We can talk more about this when you've gotten some rest. A couple of hours won't make a difference."

...

The coffee pot hissed and gurgled on the stove for his second cup of the day. Paul poured the brown liquid into another set of fine espresso cups from his grandmother. Moving from the kitchen, he pushed off the books and dust from the sofa and sank into the soft leather. He could feel each sip melt the tension from the last two weeks and the worry about whatever lay ahead. Sip after sip, his muscles relaxed until all he could really think about was how much easier it was getting to breathe.

Tasting the grit in the dregs of the espresso, he wondered what wisdom the grit held for him. He flipped cup over onto the saucer, the way his grandmother used to. Carefully lifting the cup back up from the saucer, he analyzed the patterns left in the grounds. Swirls in one corner made him feel relaxed and hopeful. Sharp angles in another clenched his jaw with worry. But when he wondered about Saskia, he noticed a cluster of grounds that came together, making a flower like the one on the nun's card. Again, the card felt warm in his pocket.

Pulling out the card, he watched the sun's rays play across the golden details. What did Saskia and the weird nun have in common? What was the point of *Tend to the Guardian Within* when some people here could barely read French, let alone English?

The new phone Stephen gave him in the car rattled against the papers and books on his wooden coffee table. Lazily, he picked it up, and when he read the notification on the screen, all he could do was smile.

Book 2
Coming Soon

Author's Note

This story is a work of fiction. However, my family's experience of the devastating earthquake in Port-au-Prince on January 12, 2010, inspired this novel. When I took the leap to live there in 2013, the idea for this story began to take shape. In 2020, I typed out the first words. Years later, revisiting this time comes with the weight of grief.

Being connected to Haiti comes with a lot of heartache and near constant exposure to unspeakable trauma. That said, Haitian culture is so much more than those experiences. Therefore, it was important to me that Saskia and Paul not experience the earthquake, and that the book not spend a lot of time reliving it. Haitians deserve joyful, healing stories to help us fight for the day we dream of.

Growing up, my siblings and I were fortunate to be surrounded by a vibrant community of friends who knew my family back in Haiti. Each one helped me figure out how I wanted to shape my identity, and how I could embrace my Haitian-ness. Orlando in the '80s and '90s was tough as a Haitian American. How society viewed us changed dramatically in a short amount of time. Our survival tactics had to change rapidly in response. Without the village that surrounded our family, our lives would have turned out very differently.

When the earthquake happened, I was living in Orlando. I used that experience to craft those various scenes. To balance the heaviness, I wanted to feature the unique reality of living in an area shrouded by the constant presence of tourists.

I used real places to inspire some scenes. For example, the island where Paul fights the alligator is inspired by Dog Island on Lake Alabama, and the *Power House* inspired the Powered House in Winter Park, Florida. *Pounders* was an actual bar name in Orlando, which I borrowed to highlight my experience at Pulse nightclub before it became a prolific landmark. The peacock standoff did happen to me, but the alligator fight did not. You really have to go out of your way to find one in the wild. The next time I visit, I hope you do. They really are remarkable creatures who are misunderstood.

Acknowledgments

This book would not be possible without the incredible village of support I had throughout its development. First among them, my dear friends and first readers: J.D. Casto and Kimberly Stewart. They read so many drafts and calmed the doubts that inevitably surfaced along the way. Their inputs helped to develop the story into what it is now.

My beloved cousin, Lyska Richetti, also read multiple drafts, making sure I got the non-English dialogue right. Along the way, my author's voice became clearer, and she believed in it long before I did. Thank you for helping me tell the story that needed to be told.

To Deborah Balogun, my copy editor, who helped bring this work over the finish line and caught important things at the last hour. Linda Epstein, my developmental editor, helped steer the story in the early stages and helped me brave my inner critic. Ciara Butler, my book coach, guided me on how to get this book into your hands. I am eternally grateful to both.

To my dear step-brother, Andrew Baussan, for the artwork that graces the cover of this book.

My dear friends, Ryan Burdick and Eliot Thomas, read the earlier drafts and helped me find my way to this version. Without their sharp perspective, It's Always Mango Season would still be in draft.

Thank you to Carlos Saavedra, Angelica Serna, Ricardo Guisse, and Kevin Todd for helping me shape key characters.

It has been a very long road to getting this book done. The number of times I had to put this down to make space for a new job, or a move to a new city, made me think there was no way I'd ever finish. I wouldn't have finished if it weren't for my family and friends who encouraged me every time I wanted to quit. Thank you for delivering the encouraging words I needed to keep pushing forward, especially Caitlin Mitchell, Kavita Desai, Jaleesa Beavers, Aissata Traore, Sammi Conner, Lauren Fishburn, Megan Almasi, Kyndra DiCarlo, Stephanie Cardace, Abigail Nicolas, Aliyah Germain, Letycia Ory and the countless others who never let me give up.

I am also deeply grateful for my big Haitian family. Our respective journeys are the root system of this series. Without your generosity, love, and authenticity, there would not be a reason to write this book. As we all grow and leave parts of that life behind, I wanted to capture the essence of what you gave me. With so few books available on our experience, I hope the younger ones enjoy this journey and their parts in it. From my chosen family in Orlando to my biological one rooted in Port-au-Prince, I am grateful for your influence, your love, and your sacrifice. I'm especially grateful to Jean Elie, for lending me his parents' names for Saskia's parents. I miss them terribly and letting them live on in this book has been a gift.

I am also grateful to my parents, Bernie Baussan and Michel Germain as well as their spouses Daniel Baussan and Clare Germain. Everything you have done for me has brought me to this moment. Thank you for taking me to the local library almost weekly, wandering the stacks at Barnes & Noble and Books-a-Million. I'm sorry for hiding from chores and staying up way too late to read one last chapter. Thank you for instilling in me the belief that I am capable of doing anything if I really work at it. This journey really has been something.

About the Author

Marissa Germain is originally from Orlando, Florida, and now calls Arlington, Virginia home. She comes to writing after a career in humanitarian aid. She has a dog and plans to continue writing from her experiences of living in the District, her travels, and her upbringing.

Marissa was long-listed in CRAFT Literary's First Chapters Competition 2025 and self-published the short story collection *Complicated Cluster*.